In All Honour

In All Honour

Beth Elliott

ROBERT HALE · LONDON

ISBN 978-0-7090-8730-4

Robert Hale Limited
Clerkenwell House
Clerkenwell Green
London EC1R 0HT

www.halebooks.com

2 4 6 8 10 9 7 5 3 1

Typeset in 10¾/14pt Palatino
by Derek Doyle & Associates, Shaw Heath
Printed and bound in Great Britain
by the MPG Books Group

For Andrew

With grateful thanks to Dr Ian Kemp,
who patiently supplies advice on
suitable wounds and ailments.

CHAPTER ONE

From the doorway Sarah could see that he was a tall gentleman. His figure set off the dragoon's uniform to perfection: such broad shoulders in the blue jacket and such long, powerful legs in their white breeches and highly polished black boots. Sarah admired the back view and felt a stir of interest. She advanced a couple of steps into the drawing-room, her eyes fixed on this stranger. He moved his head and she saw the copper gleam of his hair. It was all very appealing – but, no doubt, when he turned round, he would be disappointingly plain. So why did she feel such a pull of attraction?

The gentleman had his right arm in a sling. He was talking to General Gardiner, her friend's uncle and guardian. Sarah moved forward into the room, looking round for Lizzie. As she advanced, the general spotted her and raised a hand in greeting. The tall gentleman stopped what he was saying and turned towards her. Sarah realized with a stab of pleasure that he was handsome. In fact, she could happily spend the rest of the day gazing at his face.

'Welcome, welcome. So you received Lizzie's letter from Portsmouth?' The general struggled to his feet and winced. 'Afraid my gout is bad again.' He took a hesitant step forward. 'Pleasure to see you, my dear.'

Sarah dragged her eyes away from the stranger's face and hastened towards the general. 'Please do not trouble to stand, sir. I can greet you well enough seated. It is fortunate I was still in Town when your letter arrived.' She smiled up at his weather-beaten face, 'But you are very grand! Full dress uniform! Do you have to attend a ceremony?'

He nodded and leaned forward to kiss her cheek. 'Off to Carlton House within the hour. Oh, but you are a sight for sore eyes, my dear girl. Pretty as a picture. Lizzie is impatient to have your company. She has been talking of you this age. Where is the girl?' He sat down again thankfully as Sarah urged him back into his chair. He settled his sore foot on the stool she placed in front of him and glanced up at the young man with a chuckle.

'See what happens when you let the females take charge? Oh, but I am forgetting – you have not met. This is Major Gregory Thatcham, my dear, just returned from Spain' – he waved a hand towards the sling – 'and, as you see, he is a hero of the battle of Salamanca last July. This is Miss Sarah Davenport, my little Lizzie's best friend.'

Sarah returned Mr Thatcham's bow and feasted her eyes once more. Yes, he was handsome. He had a striking face with high cheekbones and a wide, sensual mouth. His nose was straight and his jaw firm. The whole was set off by thick, copper-coloured hair, neatly brushed back from a wide forehead. His large amber eyes seemed almost to glow in his tanned face. There was a pleasant, open look about him, but there were lines round his mouth and a hint of sorrow in his expression. Then she noticed the black armband.

He was looking at her keenly, a smile twisting his lips. His eyes moved to linger on her fair hair. Sarah quelled the urge to put up a hand and smooth her curls. She turned her head towards General Gardiner. 'Did you have a good voyage, sir?'

'Tolerable I suppose, but I am no great sailor. Lizzie looked after me. Where *has* she disappeared to?'

Before he could add more, they were interrupted by an exclamation of delight from the doorway.

'Sarah, dear Sarah – at last.'

Sarah did not even have time to turn round when she was enfolded in a tight hug and Lizzie was laughing and exclaiming at her. 'So sorry I was not downstairs to greet you when you arrived. I was putting on my pelisse. We must go shopping at once – but let me look at you – yes, you are just as I remembered you. What a long time it has been. How I wish you could have come to Lisbon with me.' She danced across to her uncle and put a hand on his shoulder. 'Poor Uncle Charlie has an attack of gout and he has to go to Carlton House to deliver Lord Wellington's dispatches. But our kind friend Greg is here to help him.'

Sarah felt a pang. Lizzie was on first name terms with this gentleman. That meant she must suppress her own interest in him. In amazement she realized that it would be difficult – and they had only exchanged a murmured word of greeting so far. How could she be so fascinated on such a short acquaintance? She glanced at him again. She saw his lips twitch as Lizzie explained to her uncle that she could not wait another moment for new clothes.

'You must have noticed, Uncle Charlie, that I do not have a stitch to my back.'

'I have noticed no such thing! And I seem to recall you said much the same when we were in Lisbon,' grumbled her uncle. His attempt at severity was ruined by the twinkle in his eye. Lizzie adjusted the lace at his cuffs and tweaked his sash into place.

'Yes, but the fashions are quite different in London. Would you have me a laughing stock, Uncle? And you so fine with all this gold braid.'

'Well, I suppose you know what you need, miss. Off with you then to get your falderals – and do not ruin me.'

Lizzie laughed and kissed him.

Sarah noticed that Major Thatcham watched with an indulgent smile. He was obviously familiar with their joking ways. The two girls exchanged a bow with him and then they hurried out of the house and set off in the direction of Bond Street.

'Now, then,' said Lizzie, tucking a hand in Sarah's arm, 'we can have a comfortable chat and catch up with our news.'

'Two whole years,' said Sarah thoughtfully. 'Have you been in Lisbon all that time? What an adventure.'

'No, not really,' said Lizzie with a laugh, 'Life is very restricted in Portugal you know. Ladies are strictly supervised at all times.'

'What, even you?' exclaimed Sarah. 'The madcap of the school. . . ?'

Lizzie sighed. 'I had a very strict duenna. And Uncle Charlie wanted to be sure I could be put on a ship if the French Army should break through our defences.'

'Well, that was exciting!' Sarah looked at her, round-eyed. 'Were you scared?'

Lizzie stopped to examine a bonnet in a milliner's shop window. 'No. . . .' she said at last. 'I fear the brim is too wide for my face— What were you saying, Sarah? No, we never doubted that Wellington would keep the French out.'

'We have heard of many battles in the last two years,' said Sarah, lengthening her step to keep up as they headed for the next milliner's display. 'Are your brothers both well?'

'Yes, thank heavens!' said Lizzie fervently. Then she gave Sarah's arm a sympathetic squeeze. 'I was so sorry to learn of your father's death.'

Sarah just nodded. Impossible to say what changes that had brought about in her life.

'Oh!' Lizzie jumped excitedly, 'I do believe I can see the very thing. Come on.' And she led the way inside the shop.

Ten minutes later they emerged again, Lizzie triumphantly carrying a bandbox.

Sarah shook her head and smiled. 'The bonnet you have on is very smart.'

'Thank you, but this one' – she gestured at the box – 'is just what I have been looking for. I look best in a small brim. Now you, Sarah, can wear anything and still look lovely – it is not fair.'

'You are not exactly ugly yourself,' retorted Sarah. 'You are fashionably dark-haired and I, alas, am a blonde. And my clothes are not in the latest fashion.' She could not help a tiny sigh.

Lizzie looked at her closely. 'You did write and tell me that there were problems with the estate. Things have not improved then?'

'Alas, they are far worse now that James has inherited.' An embarrassed look flitted across Sarah's lovely features. She fixed her green eyes on her friend and continued awkwardly, 'That is why I am in Town. My sister is trying to find me a husband before the family is quite ruined. But, let us leave such details for the moment. It is such a pleasure to escape for a few hours and enjoy

10

your company.' Sarah gave a bright smile. 'Where next?'

'Gowns,' said Lizzie. They both laughed and hastened on their way.

'Well,' exclaimed Sarah when they had finally selected two new day dresses and an evening gown, 'I do not think you can now say to your uncle that you no longer have a rag to your back. That sky-blue silk will set off your dark hair marvellously. How fortunate they had a dress made up in your size.'

'Yes, and I mean to wear it tonight. Will your sister chaperon me? Uncle Charlie will no doubt want to stay at home and nurse his gouty foot.'

'Of course she will.' Sarah devoutly hoped her older sister would not make too much fuss about the extra journey to collect and return Lizzie to Green Street. 'Do you think your friend, Major Thatcham, will want to join us as well?'

'I expect he will make his own way, if he attends the function. Perhaps you noticed that he is in mourning?'

Sarah nodded. 'He looked so sad.'

'Yes, he has lost his older brother. A shocking accident, I believe. And naturally he is desperate to go home and see his father, but he had to deliver Lord Wellington's dispatches to the Prince Regent first – together with Uncle Charlie of course.'

Sarah did not reply to this. It seemed that Lizzie and Major Thatcham were very close. She hid a sigh. The first man for whom she felt a real attraction was already attached – and to her best friend. How ironic!

CHAPTER TWO

The orchestra struck up for the next dance. From the side of the room Sarah watched the couples take their place in the line. Thankful for a respite, she walked towards her sister who was seated by the wall. Lady Tarrant raised her beaky nose and fixed a stern glare on her younger sister.

'Why are you not taking your place on the floor?'

Sarah stifled a sigh. It was humiliating to be treated as a piece of merchandise. She sat down beside Alice, carefully smoothing her pink muslin gown as she did so. Alice had bought it for her and expected it to remain like new. Sarah opened her fan and wondered if anyone could see that it had been mended more than once.

'Well?'

Sarah smiled ironically. 'Nobody asked me. Perhaps they prefer fresher meat.'

Alice glared even harder. 'Nonsense! You are but one and twenty.' She looked her sister up and down. 'And even if it turns your head, I must say that you are as pretty as any girl here this evening. Particularly,' she added, her sharp eyes flashing, 'with that emerald clip I have lent you in your hair.'

'Yes, thank you, Alice, you are most kind. But, no matter how you trick me out, you know as well as I do that what matters is not appearance but money.' She paused a minute and sighed. 'And they are aware I have none of that.'

For a moment, Alice slumped.

'It is common knowledge that our brother is running through

the Davenport fortune as fast as he can,' continued Sarah. 'You were lucky to be married while our parents were still alive, but I am dependent on James's luck – or lack of it.' In spite of herself, her voice was bitter. How she hated being so helpless in this matter.

For the past year, since her father's death, she had had to watch the new Lord Davenport squander his inheritance. He was a weak character and had fallen under the influence of wild friends. The estate simply could not support his expensive lifestyle and more-over, he showed no interest in managing his affairs. He was wholly given over to a life of dissipation. Even the money that should provide Sarah with a dowry had been gambled away.

When her married sister became aware of how serious the problem was, she had summoned Sarah to London. Sarah, strug-gling to hold the family estate together, had accepted with reluc-tance.

'I can only spare one month,' she told her sister.

'A month should be enough,' Alice replied decisively. 'In any case,' she warned Sarah, almost as soon as she arrived at the rather narrow house in Benton Street, 'I am in an interesting condition again. In another month, I shall be disinclined to be gadding about to balls and routs.'

Sarah knew that Alice was doing her best according to her own notions. She already had four young children and the arrival of yet another infant was an expense that would set Alice scrimping and saving even more than usual. Sir Walter Tarrant, her husband, was comfortably off but Alice carefully counted every penny. Her current efforts to find Sarah a husband were no doubt motivated by fear of having the expense of her unmarried sister living with her permanently.

It soon became obvious that Alice determined that in four short weeks she would find a husband for her younger sister. Sarah closed her eyes briefly at the memory of the hectic routine. She was heartily sick of meeting the same, empty-headed young ladies and their eagle-eyed, haughty mamas. To her dismay, many of the young gentlemen were as empty-headed as their sisters. The conversation generally was mere gossip about the latest scandal

13

or the next entertainment.

In short, there was nobody who caused the slightest flutter in her heart. Used to her own father's scholarly mind and his keen wit, Sarah knew she could only marry a man with intelligence and a conscience – as well as being agreeable to look at. Someone like the magnificent Major Thatcham. He had made her heart flutter! In fact, it was fluttering now as she recalled his face. And he was unavailable, especially because his attachment was to her dearest friend.

But who else was there? Sarah looked along the line of dancers and pictured the men as they would be in another ten years. A depressing number of them looked as if they would be like Sir Walter, given over to drinking and dining. Alice's husband had quickly lost his youthful figure and looks.

A few seemed to be more dynamic and would be conscientious landowners and politicians. Then there were some very hand-some young bucks and several of those looked dissolute. Her sister had warned her about them. Most were fortune-hunters, said Alice, and their attentions could only give a girl a bad repu-tation. They should be avoided at all costs if Sarah wished to make a respectable match.

But I do not care for a respectable *match*, thought Sarah, press-ing her lips together tightly; I want to be able to respect the *man* I spend my life with. In fact, I will not accept anything less than that.

She turned to her sister again. 'How many assemblies will it take before you admit that the men want money rather than a pretty face?'

Alice hunched a shoulder and looked away without answering.

Sarah fanned herself. Why could Alice not admit the obvious fact? Sarah had dutifully gone walking in Hyde Park at the fash-ionable hour, attended various exhibitions and lectures, taken tea with friends of her sister and accepted all invitations to dancing parties.

She attracted plenty of admiring glances, for she was extremely pretty, her green eyes lending expression to a perfect oval face and rose-like complexion, framed by silken fair hair. Her smile was very lovely and her figure tall and graceful. But, as she had told her sister, once the gentlemen heard the name of Davenport, they backed away.

All except one man . . . and he certainly was not a person Sarah could envisage as her husband. George Percival, Earl of Ramsdale, was one of those rakes about whom Alice had warned her. He had a most unsavoury reputation, if even just half of what was whispered about him were true. But from the first time he had been introduced to Sarah, he had shown a tendency to admire her.

Sarah wondered why her sister should encourage her to be on good terms with him. Surely he would never consider marriage to someone without a dowry, when it was known that he was both expensive and calculating. He was also a man with powerful friends in the government. Perhaps that was what inspired Alice's admiration for him.

She glanced around the room, hoping that he was not here this evening. But, alas, that was too much to wish for. Her heart sank as she caught sight of him. That rich golden hair, carefully arranged into the windswept style, that rather pink complexion and the head tilted back so that he looked down his prominent nose at everyone. He was stopping to greet various acquaintances as he moved along the room. Was there time to slip away? No, Alice had seen him as well and she laid a hand on Sarah's arm.

'I believe you have one admirer coming to ask for a dance. You see, I knew you would attract attention . . . and he is *very* wealthy,' she hissed, with a meaningful nod.

He certainly cut a fine figure in his expensive evening clothes. He was handsome, in a florid way, Sarah had to admit, but there was something unpleasant in that haughty expression and his eyes were always watchful. His mouth, too, was thin-lipped and habitually set in a sneer. In short, she did not care for him, especially as he had far too much influence over her brother's new way of life. He was James's hero, leading him into the most expensive of gaming hells and encouraging him to live beyond his means.

In desperation she jumped up. 'I do believe I can see Lizzie beckoning to me,' she said and darted away before her sister could command her to wait. Sarah wove her way through the crowd of onlookers around the dance floor, going in the opposite direction from Lord Percival. The crowd was thicker at this point but in her haste to escape, she squeezed and pushed her way through the mass of bodies. Just as she was passing them, a large group of young men split up. One of them, backing away, collided with her.

'A thousand pardons, ma'am,' he exclaimed, turning to face her. 'How clumsy of me.' He looked keenly at her face and hair. 'Why, I do believe we met earlier today.'

Sarah gazed up into those amber eyes. She was achingly conscious of how well he looked in his dress uniform. The blue jacket seemed moulded to his broad chest and the tight white trousers showed off his powerful legs perfectly. It took a moment before she could find the breath to answer him.

'Indeed, we did, Major Thatcham. And it is I who must apologize. I trust I did not catch your injured arm just now,' she added, looking anxiously at it.

'Not at all.' He smiled at her. 'In any case, the wound is not too tender and you are by far too slight and dainty to hurt a great fellow like me.'

Sarah noticed how the smile chased the sorrow out of his face and made him look younger. She wanted to tell him how it grieved her to see the depth of his sorrow, but she hardly knew him, after all. Even so, she could not resist trying to keep him by her side for a little longer.

'Are you staying at home until you are fully recovered, Major Thatcham?'

Immediately his face shadowed once again. His eyes narrowed and his lips compressed. Sarah was wishing the ground would swallow her up when at last he replied, 'As from tomorrow, I shall be plain *Mr* Thatcham, ma'am. I shall resign my commission – so, indeed, I shall now be staying put.'

'I can see how much you regret the loss of your military career,' she faltered. 'I am so sorry to remind you of the matter. . . .'

'There you are – so you and Greg have met again.' Lizzie put a hand' on Sarah's arm. 'Your sister sent me to find you. She is talking to a handsome and *very* stylish gentleman and I can see she is determined you are to be his partner for the next dance.'

Sarah's eyes flashed green fire. 'I know who it is and you have *not* found me, Lizzie. Please go away.'

Lizzie opened her brown eyes very wide. 'A mystery.' She glanced at Greg. He too, seemed struck by Sarah's outburst. She felt angry for betraying her irritation. She tried to smooth the situation. 'It is just that I feel weary and do not wish to dance at present.'

Lizzie shook her head. 'You cannot be tired, it is still early. And I am enjoying my first ball in London – only I do not know many people.' She fluttered her fan and scanned the dancers wistfully, swaying in time to the lively beat of the music.

She cast a sidelong glance at Greg. He laughed. 'Perhaps I can help you there. Ladies' – he swept them a bow – 'please wait here. I shall not be long.'

They watched him move through the crowd. 'I wonder what he is doing,' murmured Lizzie. 'Such a pity he cannot dance at present . . . Uncle Charlie made him promise to be here, just to keep an eye on me.' She fanned herself, her cheeks becomingly flushed by the heat in the room.

Sarah looked her up and down. 'As I said, the blue silk suits you very well.'

'Yes,' said Lizzie happily, patting her ringlets, 'I enjoy knowing I am in the latest mode. And you look very pretty in your pink, it sets off your delicate colouring and, as always, you look fresh and uncrumpled. What a talent you have.'

'I do not feel fresh and cool,' said Sarah crossly, 'I feel extremely anxious and alarmed. My sister is pushing me at a man I cannot like.' She pressed her lips shut in case she might admit too much. Lizzie was inclined to blurt things out without thinking. It would not do to draw any attention to themselves.

'Ladies. . . .'

It was Greg, with another gentleman by his side. This man was decidedly younger, in fact he still had a rather lanky appearance. He also had copper-coloured hair, but his eyes were blue and twinkling. His face was pleasant and friendly and his smile was so warm and infectious that both girls smiled back at him as if they knew him well.

'This is my younger brother, Richard,' said Greg. 'I fear he is a sad rattle but if he does have a talent, it is for dancing.'

Richard looked reproachfully at his brother. 'You make me sound a paltry sort of fellow.' He glanced at the girls and his infectious grin shone out. 'But let me assure you, ladies, that I do perform well on the dance floor.' His gaze turned towards Lizzie.

She nodded eagerly and gave him her hand. Immediately, they took their places in the set. Sarah was left face to face with Greg. He turned his head to watch the other two and she took the opportunity to admire his profile. His nose was straight and his chin firm but not too prominent. Sarah saw again how the smile transformed his face. She thought she could see a likeness to his younger brother.

That lively young gentleman was making Lizzie laugh already as they performed the country dance. Sarah found herself wishing that her own brother was of a similar character. She was sure Richard Thatcham did not waste all his time in horrid gaming hells and seedy taverns.

'Has something upset you?'

She started a little, jerked out of her thoughts by Greg's question. 'No.' She forced a smile.

He looked at her closely. 'Yet your expression was sad. . . . If you were wishing to dance, I am sure one of my friends would oblige you. As you see, I am not fit on two counts.' He gestured towards his sling and then indicated his black armband. 'My bereavement is not recent but only recently learnt by me.'

'Yes,' stammered Sarah, anxious not to upset him again, 'Lizzie did tell me. I am so sorry – such a dreadful loss.'

He nodded, his face rigid. After a short pause he murmured, 'Thank you,' and cleared his throat. They stood quietly together for a little. Suddenly Greg said, 'But I was offering to find you a partner—'

'Oh no, thank you, actually I am trying to—'

A rich drawl interrupted her. 'So I find you at last, Miss

Davenport. Your sister directed me this way. My dance, I believe.'

Sarah almost cringed as Greg swept a glance over the newcomer and then she saw the slight lift of his brows as his gaze swung back to her. She felt a fiery blush creep up from her throat to cover her whole face. Lord Percival took her arm firmly and led her away towards the top of the set. She glanced back to see Greg watching with a puzzled frown.

CHAPTER THREE

Lord Percival was indeed looking handsome and elegant and he was light on his feet, but Sarah took no pleasure in dancing with him. He had intruded on her precious few moments with Greg. The surprised look on Greg's face was mortifying. His expression showed that he was not impressed by her partner, who was a very obvious rake. She found she did not like Greg to have a bad opinion of her.

Lord Percival's sharp eyes gleamed with malice. Each time she looked his way, he was watching her intently. Sarah did her best to conceal her annoyance. He appeared pleased with himself for pulling her away from another man and treating her as though she were his personal property. How hard it was to maintain a polite smile when she wanted to scream with vexation.

Heaven help the lady he did marry, she thought. It was whispered that he had once been engaged, but the young lady's father had learned such shocking things about Lord Percival's conduct with women that he had broken off the match. Rumour said that there had been a duel. In fact, he was supposed to have fought several duels and fatally wounded his man on two occasions. And her sister was pushing her to consider him as a husband!

Sarah swallowed down her distaste as she moved forward in the figure to clasp his hands.

'You are very pensive, Miss Davenport. I do trust I did not interrupt an important conversation.'

She pushed her lips into a smile. 'Not at all.'

'He was, perhaps, a special friend?'

'Indeed, no, sir. I only made his acquaintance today.'

He cast a glance towards Greg, still standing where she had left him. 'One of our Peninsular heroes, I see.'

Sarah detected a sneer in both his words and tone of voice.

'I believe so,' she murmured. Instinctively she knew that any sign of interest or admiration from her would goad this man into fury. Greg already had enough woes to deal with. She remembered that Lord Percival was friendly with two government ministers who were violently opposed to Wellington and his Peninsular Army, so no doubt he shared their opinions. And he certainly had a craving to dominate everyone. She felt a prickle of distaste across her shoulders.

At this point, to her relief, they had to make their way down to the bottom of the set, so he could not say anything for a little while. But when they faced each other once more, she felt those cold eyes boring into hers. He was still on the attack.

'Come, Miss Davenport, it will not do for the prettiest girl in the room to look so glum! Especially not when she is my partner,' he added, showing his teeth in a cold smile. He held her hand in an uncomfortably tight grasp as they completed the figure. Sarah met his eyes, watching her with a cruel gleam in them. He was determined to dominate her and make her feel his superior physical strength.

How did he imagine that such a display would attract her? She kept a rigid smile on her lips. She was not intimidated by his little threats. It was a matter of honour to show him that she was quite at her ease, and if that irritated him, so be it. But it was wearisome. The dance seemed to be going on for such a long time. At last the orchestra scraped the final chord, the dancers bowed and curtsied and there was Lizzie almost jumping up and down with impatience to speak to her.

'I *told* you he was handsome,' said Lizzie, as soon as Sarah came within earshot. Lord Percival overheard her and for the first time, the smile on his face seemed genuine. He bowed to both girls and strutted away. Sarah took Lizzie's arm and gestured towards a bench nearby.

'Why, Sarah, you are shaking.' Lizzie looked closely at her.

'And you have gone quite pale.'

Sarah nodded and sank gratefully on to the bench. 'Hateful man,' she whispered, clenching her fists. Lizzie's eyes were wide with curiosity but she did not say any more, she simply wafted her fan gently in front of Sarah's face. After a moment's seething fury, Sarah took a deep breath. Lord Percival had done nothing dreadful to her, she was simply prejudiced against him. She made a determined effort to be cheerful. 'But you were impatient to tell me something?'

Lizzie's eyes sparkled. 'Richard Thatcham dances divinely. . . .'

'And. . . .'

Her friend laughed. 'And he is so witty and entertaining. He assures me he attends all the balls. So now I can count on one partner. That does help when you are a stranger in Town. And I have you to bear me company as well.'

Sarah shook her head. 'Not for long, I fear. My sister invited me for a month only and it is nearly time for me to return to Russeldene.'

'You cannot mean that! Leave Town! But I have been so looking forward to having your company. Surely you will remain with Lady Tarrant for another week or two? Oh, Greg.' Lizzie jumped up from the bench to stop Greg as he was passing in front of them. He turned quickly towards the two friends and looked enquiringly from one to the other. 'Please tell Sarah she should stay in London.'

Sarah swallowed a sudden lump in her throat. It was truly heart-warming that Lizzie cared enough to want her company, really want her. How different from Alice, trying to marry her off so she would not have to keep Sarah in her own home.

'. . . I have only just met her again,' Lizzie was explaining, 'but now she says she is going home in a day or two.'

Greg was looking embarrassed. 'Come now, Lizzie, you know I have no authority to persuade your friend. Remember we only met for the first time today. I am sure she has good reasons for her decision.' He directed a warm smile at Sarah.

She found herself smiling back. Two kind friends at the same time. After the long, lonely months since her father's death, it seemed a great luxury to Sarah. Then she realized they were both waiting for her to speak.

'Indeed, I cannot stay in Town.' She looked at Lizzie's reproachful face. 'My sister – there are circumstances – I do need to see what is going on at Russeldene. . . .' She pulled at a strand of hair above her left ear and twisted it round her finger into a corkscrew.

Greg's eyes were on the finger twisting the curl. When she stopped, self-conscious, he blinked, then bowed. 'I understand perfectly, Miss Davenport.'

The next moment Lizzie had disappeared. Greg shook his head. 'I already know that you two have been friends for a long time so you will not think it out of place if I say that Lizzie is used to getting her own way. Both her uncle and her two brothers are her slaves.'

Sarah smiled. 'Yes, I do know that. And she is impulsive – and kind-hearted. But I fear I cannot oblige her in this.'

'It does seem hard that you should leave so soon after her arrival. She has been away for such a long period that she has hardly anyone else to call a friend.'

'She has you.' The words were out before she could stop them.

He looked taken aback. 'Me? No indeed. I have been their travelling companion. It was very convenient to have their help.' He nodded at his injured right arm. 'Also, both General Gardiner and I were entrusted with dispatches from Wellington. My last military assignment.' He heaved a sigh. 'But now that job is done, I shall be leaving London tomorrow. I must go to my father.'

Yes, thought Sarah, but even through travelling with them, he had had time to become close to Lizzie. And she knew Lizzie well. Her friend was always susceptible to handsome young men. She bit her lip. Her hand strayed again up to the silken strand of hair. She saw Greg's eyes follow it and at once forced her hand back down to her side. She gave a little smile. 'A foolish habit of mine, I am sorry.'

'On the contrary,' he said, 'it is—'

'Irritating?' she suggested.

His amber eyes glowed at her. 'Charming,' he said firmly. His gaze was hopeful. She clasped her hands firmly in her lap. He waited, smiling at her but suddenly Sarah's attention was riveted on the dance floor. 'Oh, no!' she exclaimed softly.

Greg turned to look. His lips pursed in a soundless whistle. Lizzie was dancing with Lord Percival. 'Is that the same gentleman who claimed your hand for the last dance?' he asked slowly.

'Yes,' replied Sarah in a hollow tone. 'I suppose my sister introduced them. But—' She checked the very imprudent remark she was about to make. She must wait and see what Lizzie's verdict was after the dance. Beside her, Greg seemed happy to stand and wait. His eyes were on her hair, examining the feathery curls about her ears.

Sarah looked up at him.

But. . . ?' he asked, raising an eyebrow.

She blushed. 'Nothing.'

'But you are going to leave London as soon as you can.'

'Yes, sir.'

He gave a tiny chuckle. 'You sound very determined.' He glanced at her and his expression changed. 'I beg your pardon, this matter is distressing you, I can see.' He grasped her hand in his own left one, raised it to his lips and pressed a kiss on it. Sarah blinked at him.

He smiled. 'You see, I have become quite skilful with my left hand. Miss Davenport, I wish you a safe journey. And I will see that Lizzie does not tease you about the matter any more. I am friendly with her brother, Major Jack Gardiner' – he gave a short laugh – 'and have learned from him how to cope with Miss Lizzie!'

As good as his word, he intercepted her as she came tripping back towards them. Fascinated, Sarah watched as Lizzie went from pouting and sulky to smiles. He certainly knew how to handle her, thought Sarah, a little jealous. Unbidden, the thought crept into her mind that she would like to be persuaded by him. He looked so pleasant and so . . . so charming!

It was the last straw. Here was the first man she had seen who really appealed to her and he seemed more than half attached to her best friend. If they made a match of it, she would lose both of them because of the attraction she felt for Greg. Most definitely, the sooner she went back home the better for what little peace of mind she had left.

CHAPTER FOUR

The following morning, Sarah was facing her sister over the breakfast-table in the tiny morning-room of the house in Benton Street. Her green eyes were narrowed as Alice delivered a lengthy scold on Sarah's disobedience and foolishness.

'I was mortified,' she stated, stabbing at a chunk of ham. 'He was coming to ask you to dance; how dared you run away? A title like his is not to be sneezed at! And, if you are not careful, Lizzie Gardiner will cut you out. She was quite willing to dance with him.'

'I do not like Lord Percival.'

Alice paused, her fork halfway to her mouth. 'You do not have much choice. You need a husband and he is your only suitor.'

'Are you sure he means marriage?'

Alice stiffened with outrage. Her fork clattered onto her plate. 'Of course he means marriage. You are fortunate to attract such an eligible bachelor. He is an earl, he has vast estates and he is very good-looking. Why, even I feel a flutter when I see his golden hair and his smart clothes. . . . Such *style!*' she added, cutting up the egg on her plate and inserting a generous forkful between her lips.

Sarah made a little grimace of distaste. She pushed her plate away, the slice of bread and butter untouched. 'He may be good-looking, but there is something unsavoury about the man. From what I hear, his reputation is bad—'

'Reputation! Fie, miss, that is none of your business. He is wealthy and titled. You have had a whole month to find a husband. He is your only prospect for a respectable match.'

'Respectable?' For the first time, Sarah raised her voice. She looked very steadily at Alice's flushed face. Her sister did not quite meet her eyes.

'You know as well as I do that Lord Percival encourages James to go to gaming hells. Is that respectable?'

'It is something most gentlemen do. . . .' huffed Alice, concentrating on cutting up the rest of her ham. There was a silence. Sarah sipped her tea. It seemed that Alice's patience had run out. The four weeks had elapsed and she had had enough of the hectic social life. It was definitely time to go home.

She glanced at Alice. 'If you do not need me this morning, I do have an errand.'

She got a sharp nod as her only answer. Sarah rose. 'Excuse me, then.' She made for the door before Alice could ask any questions.

An hour later she was feeling better as she made her way back towards Benton Street. Her ticket for the afternoon stagecoach was now safely in her reticule. Her spirits rose at the thought of getting back to Russeldene Manor. Mrs Wiggins, the housekeeper, would be truly pleased to have her home and she could relax again after the strain of this hopeless quest to find a husband. It was soul destroying to be paraded around like a beast in the market and to be rejected every time.

It just proved that society's only concern was with fortune – or the lack of it. Not that she wanted to be very wealthy, but it would be reassuring to know there was enough money to maintain the estate. Sarah frowned. Indeed, it was time to get back and check on how things were proceeding there.

It was a wild day and dust and straw whirled along the street as the wind whipped them up. The weather reflected her stormy mood. Battling against the gale would perhaps relieve the frustration that had been growing steadily since yesterday. At that point it occurred to her that she must call on Lizzie to say her farewells. Perhaps she would find Major Thatcham there. She would like one last glimpse of him before she slipped away to her quiet rural life again.

The wind pushed at her bonnet and she put up a hand to hold it in place. She turned the corner into Berkeley Street. An extra strong gust caught her and her pelisse flapped open. With an exclamation of annoyance, she turned her back to the wind and wrapped the pelisse more closely around herself. Then she took a deep breath and set off again.

She had not taken five steps when a tall figure loomed up in front of her and stopped, blocking her way. Sarah was conscious of a large, caped driving coat, billowing in the wind above highly polished Hessian boots. She raised her head slowly and took in the broad shoulders, the handsome face with those sensual lips. She gave a tiny gasp. It felt as if she had conjured up an illusion.

'Miss Davenport.' It was indeed Greg. And his clear voice sent a shiver down her back that had nothing to do with the chilly weather. He was smiling down at her. 'You are out very early. Are you quite alone? It is a rough old day for a walk.'

'I am quite accustomed to going out alone, sir. And I had an errand that would not wait,' she replied, trying not to stare at his amber eyes. How easily she could fall under their spell. Her heart thumped as she told herself *too late*! She already had fallen. But that did not change her plans. She took another look at him. Now she noticed signs of strain. His smile was a little rigid, there were lines around his eyes as if he had not slept. He was in civilian clothes – and that meant. . . .

'I see you know why I am out early,' he said, his voice husky now. 'I am just returning from Horseguards.' He cleared his throat. 'And that is the end of my military career.'

Sarah felt his pain at this unavoidable step. Impulsively, she grabbed his hand and squeezed it. 'You had no choice,' she murmured.

He returned the pressure of her fingers. 'You are very kind.'

For what seemed a long time they stood there, both deep in thought. Sarah found her eyes had drifted to that heartbreaking mouth. Her own lips parted on a sigh. Greg gave a start and dropped her hand.

'Well,' he croaked, 'it is done. And I must get down to Chesneys – my father's estate in Hampshire,' he explained, seeing her puzzled look. 'But first, may I escort you home?'

Sarah shook her head. 'No, thank you. It is only a couple of minutes from here.' She needed that time alone to digest all the feelings he had aroused. She took a last look at him, saw the strain in his face and blurted out, 'I am sure you will soon be too busy to feel the change so deeply as you do just now.'

'Why, thank you.' He inclined his head and seized her hand again, raising it to his lips. She gave him a quick smile, then turned and forced herself to walk away up the street, her head bent against the wind. She knew he was watching her as she crossed the road and turned the corner. Her hand was tingling and her heart was racing. Sarah scolded herself for feeling so elated. He had shown her a little courtesy, that was all.

When she reached her sister's house again, it was to find Lizzie just arriving from the opposite direction.

'I received a bouquet this morning,' Lizzie told her, 'from Lord Percival.'

Sarah raised her delicate brows and wrinkled her nose. 'Then I know you received lilies. Lord Percival always sends lilies. He sent me some last week. That is what made Alice decide—' She broke off in confusion, then added, 'He must be addicted to the scent. Personally, I find it too sickly.'

'Yes, but it is a compliment,' insisted Lizzie, 'don't spoil my pleasure. My first bouquet. Uncle Charlie is teasing me about making such a hit. He says it is all down to my new blue gown. Oh, but I have some other news for you. . . .'

By now the butler had let them into the house. Sarah looked at him enquiringly.

Peascombe smiled at her in a fatherly way. 'Her ladyship has gone out, miss.' He moved to the door of the drawing-room and opened it. Sarah nodded her thanks and hastily took Lizzie into the room before she said anything indiscreet where she could be heard.

'Now then.' Lizzie threw her bonnet down on to the table and gave Sarah her most coaxing smile. 'I have such a good scheme to suggest to you and you must promise to say yes to it.'

Sarah had to laugh. 'Lizzie, if this is anything like the madcap ideas you used to have at school, I cannot promise anything of the sort.'

'No, no, this is something really splendid. Uncle Charlie

29

thought of it, all planned with military precision. The doctor has ordered him to Bath. His gout is very painful, so he will be glad to obey. That means I have to go as well and we hope, dear Sarah, that you will come to keep me company there.'

Sarah's hands stilled in the act of lifting off her bonnet. The idea was tempting. She liked Bath, where she and Lizzie had spent several happy years at school. She put her bonnet down carefully and ran a hand through her curls. Could she afford to go? Her small stock of money had shrunk almost to nothing after buying her ticket just now.

Lizzie's voice broke into her thoughts. 'Oh, Sarah, you must say yes. How could I manage without your company? I do not want to have to ask Aunt Augusta. She is by far too decrepit to go out in the evenings.'

Sarah tried to smile. 'It is a very kind offer, but I have just bought my ticket home. I leave on this afternoon's stage. And then, I do not know what I shall find at Russeldene.' She began to twist her curls round her forefinger.

'Well, we shall be in Town for several days more while Uncle Charlie has talks with various politicians. And then, on our way to Bath, we can easily call at Russeldene and collect you. It is all planned out.'

Sarah threw caution to the winds. 'Then I accept – and thank you.'

CHAPTER FIVE

He should have been ready to set out, but Greg was still seated at the desk in his library, frowning absently out of the window. His left hand rested on the letter just delivered from his man of business. A deep frown furrowed his brow and the look of sadness had intensified. He turned his head as he heard a knock on the street door, followed by a murmur of voices. His valet, Preston, until yesterday his batman, knew he was not to be disturbed.

But the door opened. Greg darted an angry glance towards the person intruding on him. Then, as a tall, dark-haired man entered the room, his expression changed and he leapt to his feet.

'Theo!'

Theo Weston strode quickly across the room, his hand held out. 'Heard you were in London from my cousin Tom at Horseguards. Greg, old man, I cannot begin to say how sorry I am about your tragic loss.'

Greg swallowed hard before managing to growl, 'Thank you.' He took a swift glance at his friend's concerned face then turned his head away. Theo could see too much. Yet Greg knew he needed help. He walked away to the fireplace and put a booted foot on the fender. The heavy ticking of the clock was the only sound in the room as he considered. At length he shrugged and caught his breath sharply at the sudden stab of pain from his wounded arm.

He turned back to face Theo and read the sympathy in that blue gaze.

'What else do you know about?'

Theo gave him a frowning look from under his straight black brows. 'Well, for a start, how bad is that arm? Did you get that at Salamanca?'

When Greg nodded, he added, 'Sabre cut?'

Greg nodded again. 'At least I still have my arm. Wellington sent me his own surgeon. Then the sawbones had to open it up again to remove a few chips of bone but they have patched it all up now. It gets me plenty of sympathy,' he said, coming back to the desk.

Theo sighed. 'A wound like that takes time to mend. And now, with this other business I suppose you have had to give up your military career.'

Greg looked at him. He could not trust himself to speak. He gestured to a chair. They both sat down. There was a silence. Eventually, Theo said softly, 'I know – it was the same for me. Took a long time to accept it. But my new life keeps me busy in a different way. And I still work to help Wellington.' He leaned forward, 'But even more amazing is that I am reconciled with my father since the birth of our son.'

'So you and Kitty have a baby son. That is splendid news. I am delighted for you, old fellow.' Greg forced himself to show enthusiasm.

Theo smiled briefly. 'Thank you. Later on you must visit and meet him. But at present you have other concerns, I know. I will not delay you.' Theo stood up. He tapped a hand on the table as a thought struck him. 'But you asked me a question just now. . . ?' He raised an eyebrow.

'Yes,' said Greg slowly, 'maybe I am being foolish but something feels wrong in all this business.' He gestured towards the letter in front of him.

Theo frowned at him and sat down again. 'Good God, man, what kind of business do you mean?'

Greg rubbed his chin. 'Have you heard anything about my brother being massively in debt?'

Theo looked astonished. 'Henry? Your sober brother?'

Greg nodded towards the letter. 'Our family lawyer informs me that a Lord Percival is requesting settlement of gambling debts incurred just before Henry died.'

'Lord Percival?' Theo seemed about to say something, but closed his mouth very firmly. His hand curled into a fist on the table. 'The Earl of Ramsdale is not the sort of person your brother would associate with, surely?'

Greg eyed him suspiciously. 'You know something. . . .'

Theo met his look squarely. 'You have never met Lord Percival?'

'No, indeed; I have never heard the name before. Henry was staying with his friend, Hazelwick, at his hunting lodge when the accident happened. I assume this man was among the guests there.'

'I see.' Theo glanced from the letter to Greg. 'Well, I suppose even Henry would have played cards at such a gathering. And the play can be deep – indeed, if Ramsdale was playing, he would insist on it. But surely there were other players to confirm this claim?' He rose and paced over to the window. 'Massive debts, you say? Lord, what a tangle for you to sort out.'

Greg's only answer was a sigh. He folded the letter clumsily with his left hand and thrust it into a pocket. The chair scraped as he stood up. He glanced down ruefully at his corbeau-coloured jacket and immaculate buckskins. His mouth twisted. 'No more uniform,' his voice grated, 'but Lord Liverpool is retaining me for diplomatic duties.'

Theo spun round. His chiselled face was eager. 'Oh, that is splendid! He knows you are too skilled to let you go. And with Napoleon's current campaign in Russia, there is still much to do. So we shall work together again.' He clapped Greg on his good shoulder.

There was a glimmer of his old smile on Greg's face. 'I look forward to that. But for the present I am off to see my father. If you do discover anything about Lord Percival and that hunting party, you will let me know?'

'I shall set to work at once. I wonder if James Davenport is in town—'

'Davenport?' echoed Greg, frowning at him.

Theo raised his brows. 'Yes, the new Baron Davenport – a weak character, much addicted to gambling and drinking. A close follower of George Percival. I can try to pump him for information.'

'I met a Davenport last night,' said Greg slowly, 'an extremely pretty young lady . . . blonde,' he added softly.

Theo frowned at him. 'That is the youngest sister. Trust you, Greg, you are drawn to the blonde girls like a wasp to honey.'

'She seemed to be in some distress.'

Theo groaned. 'Greg, old man, do you not think you have enough problems of your own at present?' When Greg just looked at him enquiringly, he shrugged and went on, 'The Davenport family is facing ruin, thanks to the brother. Since he came into the title he has gambled most of his inheritance away. There is no money for the girl's dowry.'

'With that face and figure, she does not need a dowry.'

Theo looked at him closely. 'My God, Greg, how can you be so smitten on just seeing her once?'

Greg gave a reminiscent smile. 'Hair like spun silk,' he murmured, 'and those soft golden curls . . . and such clear green eyes.'

'True,' said Theo acidly, 'and a money-wasting brother and a harpy for a sister.'

There was a gleam in Greg's amber eyes as he surveyed his oldest friend. 'Maybe so. But Miss Davenport is still a delight to look at.'

'Egad, you will be writing poetry next!'

Greg shook his head slightly. He had no intention of falling in love again. The last time had been too painful. It had taken him most of the last two years to recover . . . but still, he knew beauty when he saw it. Sarah Davenport was stunning and, in addition, she was kind and intelligent. He remembered her comforting hold on his hand earlier that morning and her attempt to console him. He felt a certain regret that he would not see her any more.

Theo was watching him suspiciously. He sighed. 'I know that look! Just be careful.' He picked up his hat and opened the door.

Greg followed him out into the entrance hall. 'There is no need for that warning,' he said. 'I am allowed to admire a lovely girl, surely. Especially,' he added, 'as I am leaving Town now and expect to be at Chesneys for some time.'

Theo nodded. 'It may take me a while to find out what you want to know. I will write when I have news.' He shook hands firmly and strode away down Cork Street. Greg watched him go; there was no trace of a limp these days. Well, if Theo could recover so well from that severe leg wound of two years ago, his own arm would certainly be back to normal just as soon as the bandages came off.

CHAPTER SIX

Greg fumbled with the pages of the ledger. His left hand was not skilful at such tasks. He managed to turn the page and smoothed it down. He frowned over the columns of figures for a while, then looked up at Wilson, the steward.

'Everything seems to be in order. In fact, from what I have seen this morning, the estate is running well and producing a good return.'

Wilson nodded. His expression was still grim. Greg rubbed a hand across his eyes, weary suddenly from this unaccustomed task.

'Yet you say there is insufficient money to meet all our expenses?'

Wilson nodded again. 'Aye, sir.'

'Well, man, why is that?' He gestured at the pile of ledgers. 'There is no problem with the income from the estate, as I have seen for myself.'

'No, sir.' Wilson's face was wooden.

Greg felt that soldier's instinct for danger. Something was badly wrong, he knew. He shifted his right arm in its sling onto the table and leaned forward.

'Wilson, since I returned, I have been aware that something is bothering you. Not just the grief and upset over my brother's death; my father, too,' he said, keeping his gaze steadily on the burly man facing him across the table, 'I expected to find him grief-stricken by our untimely loss, but there is another matter that seems to be weighing on him.' He heaved a sigh. 'You have been the steward here for as long as I can remember and you know all our affairs. My father cannot speak of the matter, whatever it is.' His chair scraped as he stood up jerkily and walked over to the window.

Greg stared out, feeling all the sorrow flood through him again at the loss of the big brother who had always stood by him. At the same time he was angry at this wall of silence. How could he begin to set things to rights if they wouldn't admit what the problem was? There was a long pause, broken only by the crackle of the log on the fire. Greg brought his fist down hard on the wide windowsill. His mouth compressed with frustration.

At last there was a heavy sigh from the man seated at the table. 'Well, sir,' said Wilson slowly, 'I understand how you feel about this, but it is for Sir Thomas to speak of the matter.'

Without turning round, Greg said, in a low voice, 'Is it the matter of my brother's gambling debt?'

There was no reply. The monotonous tick-tick of the clock seemed loud as the silence drew out. Eventually, Greg twisted round. Wilson was fidgeting with a quill pen. Reluctantly he raised his eyes, looked at Greg and nodded.

Greg came back to the table. 'How much is the sum?'

Wilson drew a deep breath. 'Over forty thousand pounds, sir.'

They stared at each other. A look of disbelief gathered on Greg's face. He shook his head. 'I cannot believe that Henry would ever gamble for such stakes.'

'It never happened before,' admitted the steward, 'which is partly why Sir Thomas has taken it so badly.' He fiddled with the quill again. 'It seems to have shaken him, feeling he did not know his son as well as he thought.'

Greg walked back to the window and looked out at the manicured lawns and the trees, almost bare now with just a few russet leaves remaining on the spreading branches. 'At last, I begin to understand his torment. And I would hazard a guess,' he went on, 'that my father has invested all the money he could spare into some new venture.'

Wilson gave a crack of laughter. 'You guess well, Master Gregory – sir, I should say, excuse me. Always interested in new inventions is Sir Thomas.' He shook his head. 'But it will take time to see a return. And one of his other investments is not doing well, not at all! The canal is not profitable, sir. So, you see—'

'I see quite plainly,' interrupted Greg, coming back to face Wilson. He put his good hand on his hip, 'there is no spare cash.'

The steward nodded agreement. 'We contrive to manage, so long as there is no extra expenditure. We have been trying to see how to raise the necessary funds. . . .' His expression was harassed.

Greg watched the quill suffer another mangling but he made no comment. Suddenly, he remembered the letter from his lawyer and shuffled the papers around until he spotted it. He held it out to Wilson. 'I received this just before I left town. Tell me, when did my father learn of this debt?'

Wilson read through the letter, pursing his lips and tut-tutting. He took off his spectacles and looked up at Greg. 'About a month ago. It is not my place to comment, but it does seem odd for Mr Henry to gamble like that.'

'Yes,' said Greg curtly, 'so odd that I intend to probe the matter further. It is fortunate there were no funds to settle the matter. We will make no payment yet.'

'But, sir, a debt of honour. . . .'

Greg looked at him from under his brows. Wilson's eyes grew round. At last he said in a shocked tone, 'Do you mean you suspect something?'

Greg rubbed his chin. 'As you say, it does not seem like Henry.' He went to the door. 'I must go to my father. I think I will call in the doctor if he is no better by tomorrow.'

Sir Thomas watched disapprovingly as Greg picked up a large mug of tea and drank with obvious enjoyment.

'Never saw such a thing at the breakfast table!' he growled. 'Is this what comes of being a soldier?'

Greg laughed at him. 'Of course, sir. Army habits. We dip our mug in the common pot of boiling water and tea leaves. Wakes us up – and warms us,' he added, 'the nights are cold on those Spanish hills.' The memory of his life on campaign, and the convivial group of men sharing their mugs of tea around the camp-fire in the freezing dawn made him smile. Then he blinked and heaved a sigh. Seeing his father's expression, he added, 'Of course, that is all behind me now.'

Sir Thomas looked from under heavy white brows. He cleared his throat. 'I cannot be sorry, my boy, not when I see you with that wound. Of course, I am immensely proud of your gallantry.'

Greg turned a startled face towards him. 'What—?'

'Cited in Wellington's latest dispatch for bravery beyond the call of duty at the Battle of Salamanca.' He looked at Greg's horrified expression and smiled. 'Preston told me, my boy. He is so proud of you he came to see me right away. He knew you would never say a word about it.'

'He should be more discreet!'

Sir Thomas was amused. 'I am very glad he was not! Thanks to him I know that the Prince Regent spoke to you personally to congratulate you. Later on, I shall get Preston to tell me the full story of what you did in the battle.'

Greg wriggled, embarrassed and picked up his mug of tea again.

There was a short silence, during which Greg tackled his portion of meat and eggs. His first hunger satisfied, he glanced up and again felt shocked. His father had his head propped on his hand and was staring into the distance. There was a deeply worried look on his face. When he realized that Greg was watching him, Sir Thomas sat up and made an effort to speak heartily.

'So Dr Price is sending us to Bath, eh? He says it will speed up your recovery and doubtless the change of scene will benefit us both.' He drummed his fingers on the table and stared at his son fiercely. 'But I do not like to go away with this debt problem unresolved.'

Greg drained his mug. 'Pray do not let the matter trouble you for the present, Father. I have set enquiries afoot. It is such an unlikely amount for Henry to gamble that we need confirmation before we accept that it is true. As we are both invalids and away from home on doctor's orders, it gives us more reason to delay payment.'

Sir Thomas looked as if a weight had dropped from his shoulders. 'Egad, my boy, when you put it like that I begin to feel better.' He looked down at his plate as if noticing for the first time that there was food on it. Greg watched with satisfaction as his father tackled a slice of cold beef with appetite. It had shocked him to find Sir Thomas looking too thin for his clothes. Greg devoutly hoped that this visit to Bath would improve his father's spirits.

'How soon shall we leave?' Sir Thomas enquired, reaching for his tankard of ale.

Greg gave him an affectionate smile. 'Before noon, I believe. I just need to speak with Wilson once more. But may I know, sir, why you have put so much money into the new road scheme?'

'Why? Surely it is obvious that it is the future method of transport. Coach construction is better, the roads are being improved and the trade between London and Portsmouth grows each year.'

'But what about the money you invested in the construction of the Basingstoke canal. . . ?'

Sir Thomas pushed his plate away and dabbed at his lips with the napkin. 'It is not doing as well as I had hoped. I shall sell my share of the project – but such things take time. All my money is tied up at present.'

Greg stood up. 'In some ways that may turn out to be a good thing. Otherwise, you would have settled this debt already.' He held the door open for his father to pass through. 'Will you travel in the coach or in my curricle, sir?'

CHAPTER SEVEN

Sarah dropped thankfully on to the old leather chair in the library and sank her head in the well-worn dip at the back. Then she kicked off her shoes and wriggled her aching toes. It had been a hard day; seeing tenants, discussing crops with the bailiff, going through household matters with Mrs Wiggins. She let out her breath in a long sigh. There were just so many jobs to get through, especially as Lizzie and General Gardiner would arrive in two days to collect her on their way to Bath.

'Just five minutes,' she told herself, 'then I will check the accounts.' Her gaze wandered to the neat rows of books, undisturbed since her father's death the previous year. This had been his favourite room and Sarah could remember often perching in this chair as a small girl to listen to him read a story. More recently, as he became too frail to deal with running the estate, he had spent his days sitting in this chair while she did the accounts and discussed day-to-day matters of business with him.

There was a soft brush against her ankles. She looked down. Misty, the old springer spaniel, was wagging her tail hopefully.

'Not now,' Sarah told her softly, stretching out a hand to caress the dog's head. 'Maybe later. Now I must check the figures for the last month.' With a sigh, she got out of the armchair and went to the desk, where the ledger was already open. She drew up a chair, placed the candle closer and set to work. Outside the light faded; there was silence in the room and the spaniel settled at her feet.

It was the sound of men's voices that woke her. Sarah opened her eyes into darkness. Her head was resting on a cold, hard surface. She felt at it and realized it was the accounts ledger. She moved her hand a little further and encountered a square, solid shape. Then she felt the smooth trail of wax. The candle had burnt completely away. Rather painfully she sat up. She was stiff and very cold.

She rubbed her arms to warm them. From somewhere close by came the sound of liquid being poured into a glass. She turned her head towards the noise and saw a faint light coming from the drawing-room a little way down the hall. Then someone spoke again. It was a voice Sarah recognized. She frowned, suddenly wide awake. The sneering tones of Lord Percival reached her quite clearly.

'Pity you do not manage your estate better, Davenport. With your poor skill at cards, you need a larger income.' This was followed by a braying laugh.

'The luck is bound to turn one day. Th-thass what you t-tol' me. . . .' James's words were slurred. Sarah shook her head in despair. Could he not stay sober, even in his own home?

'You had better pray it does. I hold so many of your vowels that I could claim your estate any time I choose, y'know!'

Shocked at this, Sarah strained her ears to hear her brother's reply.

'You swore you would never do that,' he stammered. 'You said that so long as I backed your story about the . . . the accident—'

'Just see you do,' came the sharp reply, 'His family is taking a cursed long time to pay up. The brother has started making enquiries about the matter. You must be very careful.'

Sarah clutched at the edge of the desk as she listened intently.

Lord Percival went on, 'He will never prove anything. But if he *should* learn any details from you, Davenport, I will have this estate from you. And just to remind you of your obligation, I am minded to have your sister.'

Sarah clamped a hand to her mouth to hide her sudden intake of breath. Her heart thumped heavily in her chest. What had James done to put himself so utterly in the power of this man? And even she was involved in the business. She felt a leaping flame of anger at James. He had not refused the grotesque idea that she was some kind of bargaining counter to settle his debts.

There was the sound of a chair being pushed back. Steps sounded, getting louder. Sarah stared wide-eyed towards the faint light coming from the drawing-room doorway. Did they know she was here? For one wild moment, she feared they would come and drag her out there and then. But whichever one of them it was, he merely pushed the drawing-room door shut.

She breathed again, then realized that she was shaking. She stood up and had to stifle a cry as she stubbed her toes on the chair leg. She groped for her shoes, slipped them on and hesitated for a moment in thought. Would it do any good to confront James and his guest about this matter? At length she shook her head reluctantly. It must be something very serious. First she would try to discover more about it from her brother. She crept silently out of the room, along the corridor and into the main hall.

A lamp burned on the table near the stairs but the hall was empty. Sarah seized a candle and lit it as fast as she could, cross with herself that her hands were trembling. 'It is because I am so cold,' she murmured. A quick glance around to make sure James and his guest were not nearby, then she slipped through a door almost concealed at the back of the hall.

She hurried down a narrow passage and up a flight of stairs, thanking her lucky stars that her room was in the old wing of the house, well away from the guest bedrooms. She darted into her own room and locked the door. Setting the candle down, she pressed her hands to her temples, standing very still and straight.

Then she let her breath out slowly and moved across to the mirror on her dressing-table. She stared at her reflection. A pair of narrowed green eyes stared back at her. Threats and bribes! They are involved in something dishonest. She gave her reflection a firm nod. And I will not be treated as an object to be bartered by a pair of gamblers. I will find a way to escape that evil fate.

'Now, Miss Sarah, you never touched your supper and here you are picking at your breakfast. What your poor mama would say, I dread to think.'

Sarah put the slice of toast back on her plate. 'Mrs Wiggins, you did not tell me we were to have a visit from my brother and his friend.'

'Lord bless you, miss. The first I knew of it was when they arrived here late last evening. As you know, we had not prepared for any such event. But they ordered brandy to the drawing-room and that was the last we saw of them,' she added, 'but we never saw sight nor sound of you, miss.' She fidgeted with the teapot. 'And I thought it best not to mention you was here.'

Sarah nodded. 'You did right. Thank goodness this parlour is tucked away next to your room. But I fear I shall have to appear at the dinner table this evening. Perhaps you will see that the servants are all present.' She got up. 'Meanwhile, there is more than enough to keep me busy and out of the way for today.'

'Now, Miss Sarah,' scolded the housekeeper, 'don't you go wearing yourself out. We've managed this far and the house will not fall down just because you are going away for a short while.' She began gathering up the plates on to a tray. 'I'm that glad Miss Lizzie is taking you to Bath. Time for you to enjoy yourself' – she glanced at Sarah out of the corner of her eye – 'which I'll be bound you did not do in London.'

Sarah smiled at that. Mrs Wiggins knew Alice and her calculating ways all too well. She looked at the motherly housekeeper ruefully. She was still wondering how much to tell her about her visit to London when the door burst open. In stormed a tall and slender young man with dark curly hair and green eyes. As usual, James was scowling, his mouth pulled down.

'So here you are,' he exclaimed in a peevish voice. 'Alice said you had run back home. What the devil do you mean by hiding away last night?' He broke off and frowned at the housekeeper's cluck of disapproval at his bad language. 'And you can take that Friday face away, if you have nothing better to do.'

The door closed behind the housekeeper.

Sarah put her hands on her hips. 'James, that is no way to speak to Mrs Wiggins. Russeldene only keeps going because of her hard work. And you are looking decidedly the worse for wear. You have bags under your eyes and you are as pale as paper.'

'Well, we are going to take guns out very shortly,' he replied

44

with an irritable shrug, 'that will give me plenty of exercise. But you must come and do the pretty to George.'

'Certainly not,' exclaimed Sarah. 'Surely you can see that I am in working clothes; I am on my way to the dairy.'

James gave an angry snort. 'It beats me why you need to bother with such jobs. Leave it to the bailiff.'

Sarah raised her eyebrows. 'Well for you that I do take an interest. How are we to find the money for your pleasures if the estate is neglected? And why are you here? I thought you were fixed in London.' She picked up the linen inventory and looked round for her pencil.

'Sarah!' said her brother explosively. 'Do you not realize what an honour it is when a top-of-the-trees fellow like George wants to visit your home?'

She turned her head and stared at him. Her lip curled. 'Honour?'

He glared at her but said nothing. Sarah remembered the conversation she had overheard.

'James, while you are here, what is the problem about an accident? Is Lord Percival in your debt, or are you in his?'

If James had been pale before, his face was a sickly colour now. 'What accident?' he blustered. 'I-I. . . . Have you been listening at the door?' He looked at her accusingly.

'This matter concerns me, does it not?' she insisted. She held his gaze, her chin up. After a moment his eyes fell. With a muttered oath, he swung on his heel and left the room.

By dinner time Sarah had completed all the urgent tasks on her list. With the help of a maid, she had got her trunk packed and ready for the following day. But all the time, she was puzzling over the conversation she had overheard on the previous night. Why did Lord Percival want her as a hostage? And exactly what kind of hostage was she intended to be?

He had made it plain in London that she was the style of female he preferred. She cursed her blonde hair for that. Her eyes narrowed as she remembered how Alice also wanted her to marry Lord Percival. But her sister could not know anything about this matter of an accident. Alice simply wanted Sarah to find a husband – any husband – as quickly as possible.

She must somehow find the time to talk to James before she left. Maybe a day in the country would have put him in a more reasonable state of mind and he would be more clear-headed in the morning. She pushed a last pin into her tightly pulled back hair, checking that no curls had escaped. Sarah considered her appearance in the mirror. She could not help a mischievous smile at the dowdy picture she presented. Now to see if it had the desired effect.

She blew out the candle and made her way downstairs. Taking a deep breath, she walked into the drawing-room. Both men were already there. They rose as she came in. Her brother looked decidedly better for his day in the open air – or was his colour due to brandy? She took a quick glance at the almost empty glass in his hand.

'Ah, Miss Davenport. Such beauty is well worth the wait.' Lord Percival made her an extravagant bow.

Sarah gritted her teeth and inclined her head politely. Even this remark was barbed. He moved forward to offer her his arm. He was inspecting her in a way that made her feel her dress was too flimsy and low cut, even though she had deliberately chosen a high-necked evening gown of plain blue muslin with no flounces or jewellery and had dressed her hair in a severe knot on top of her head.

In the dining-room, Lord Percival hastened to assist her with her chair. He then took the seat at her right hand. He raised his quizzing glass and surveyed the room. 'So many servants,' he drawled. He gave her an amused look. 'Are you trying to impress me, Miss Davenport, or are they here for your own support?'

Sarah nodded to Barnes, the elderly butler, to begin serving the meal. She forced herself to linger over her food, making the meal last as long as possible. James was obviously too much in awe of his guest to support her properly. Sarah watched James push his food around the plate. She was vexed at how readily he gulped down his wine. Already he was ordering another bottle to be opened. And it soon became obvious to her that Lord Percival was encouraging her brother to drink. He did it so naturally, at the same time topping up her glass.

Sarah came to the conclusion that he wanted both of them to be drunk. He himself seemed to be quite sober although he frequently refreshed himself from his glass and accepted refill after refill. He kept up a flow of small talk about the pleasures of life in the country and the particular beauties of Russeldene and its surroundings. In view of his remarks about claiming the estate, Sarah was obliged to bite back a number of sharp retorts. Had he spent the day assessing what the manor was worth?

At last the covers were removed. Sarah stood up, glad to escape. Lord Percival gave her a meaningful look. 'I do look forward to hearing you play and sing shortly.'

She inclined her head, giving him a tight-lipped smile. Now she would have to appear in the drawing-room for a while. Well, whatever plans he had made, he would be thwarted by finding Mrs Wiggins there to chaperon her. Sarah thought she could foil his intentions for that evening. And the next day she would be gone.

CHAPTER EIGHT

'Thank you!' Sarah turned to Mrs Wiggins as they climbed the stairs at the end of a very long evening. The two women exchanged a glance full of meaning. Mrs Wiggins shook her head. 'I'm that relieved you will be away from here tomorrow, Miss Sarah.'

Sarah squeezed the housekeeper's hands. 'Please keep an eye on James.'

'I'll do my best.' Mrs Wiggins gave a determined nod. 'Be sure to lock your door now.'

Sarah went straight to the dressing-table, and pulled the pins out of her tightly braided hair with a sigh of relief. She rubbed her sore head. She did not think that Lord Percival had been repulsed by her plain clothes and scraped back hair. However, she was more deeply concerned by what she had observed of his hold over James. Mrs Wiggins had seen it as well.

There had been a brief respite while the two men lingered over their port in the dining-room. All too soon, however, Lord Percival had led the way into the drawing-room with James following at his heels, like a little dog, instead of acting like the master of the house, thought Sarah, angrily.

Lord Percival took the seat closest to her own. He sat down and turned towards her with a predatory look on his face. Then he spotted Mrs Wiggins, quietly knitting in the corner just behind Sarah. His lips compressed and he darted a dagger look at the housekeeper. James came towards him with a glass of brandy, which he took and set down sharply on the small table close by.

'So, Miss Davenport, do not tell me you prefer the rural life to the excitement of living in Town?'

Sarah forced herself to meet his gaze calmly. 'When there is an estate to run, it cannot be left for too long.'

'But do you not have a bailiff for that work? How many servants are there? How large is the estate?'

He seems to think it is all his already, she thought. Aloud, she said, 'We have owned Russeldene for many generations and we are closely intertwined with the life of the manor – as well as the local village, Ellerscombe.' He seemed ready to ask more questions so she added hastily, 'What kind of property do you possess, Lord Percival?'

He picked up his brandy glass and took a sip. 'I have a large estate in Essex.' He nodded importantly. 'Extremely large, I think I may say ... as well as a hunting lodge in Leicestershire.' He surveyed the room, his beaky nose rising and falling as his attention went from painting to ornament or item of furniture. Something on the mantelpiece caught his eye. He set down his glass and rose. Walking over to the fireplace he picked up a porcelain vase and turned it from side to side in the candlelight.

'Exquisite,' he purred, replacing it at last. 'Sèvres – and the best workmanship. I do appreciate such items.' He gazed around the room again. 'I must look at your paintings by daylight. Perhaps you would show them to me tomorrow.' He smiled at Sarah, but it sounded more like an order than a request. He resumed his seat and leant back, one arm draped over the side of his chair. He crossed his elegantly shod legs and turned his beaky nose in her direction.

Did he consider her to be a part of the collection? Her bosom swelled with wrath. To avoid responding to his suggestion, she tried a change of topic.

'You are fond of hunting, Lord Percival?' It was an ordinary enough question but his reaction surprised her.

'Why do you ask?' he snapped. His usually rich voice had become much sharper. He jerked up in the chair. The look he gave her almost burned through her. Sarah maintained a politely enquiring look, but inside she wondered why he should be so alarmed. Then she caught sight of James. He was sitting bolt upright and glaring at her. Could there be a connection between hunting and the accident they had mentioned? The accident about which a brother was asking questions. Sarah looked at James. Was he mixed up in something even worse than the loss of all his money and estate?

Lord Percival was certainly uneasy. She gave him her sweetest smile. 'I believe I have heard that you are a keen sportsman in every field, sir.'

He visibly relaxed. His smile was catlike. 'That is so. It is no exaggeration to say that I enjoy all forms of sport, eh, James?' He swung round to look at the younger man.

James nodded eagerly. 'Quite so. You are a real goer, whether with the horses or . . . or any form of exercise.'

Lord Percival turned back to Sarah. 'You admire sporting prowess, Miss Davenport?'

She inclined her head. 'Of course, sir.' Really, he was the most conceited man she had ever met. But he was dangerous and so she must appear to flatter him.

'Do you ride?' he asked her.

'Certainly, but sadly, there are no horses here at present apart from one for the gig.' She cast a glance at her brother, who was just picking up the brandy bottle. He shrugged, as if to say her needs did not matter. He walked over to Lord Percival.

'More brandy, George?'

'By all means.' He held out his glass but looked towards Sarah. 'Your brother assures me that you play, Miss Davenport.'

Sarah stared at him. Did he mean cards? With another smile that did not reach his eyes he indicated the pianoforte.

'Oh. . . . Yes, but not very well. I do not practise as I should.'

'Nevertheless, it would give me great pleasure to hear you perform. . . .'

He rose and walked over to the instrument, opened it and fetched a branch of candles. Sarah walked round on the far side of the pianoforte to him and seated herself. She flicked through the sheets of music, frowning slightly. He was still there, observing her. She would not be intimidated. She chose a jolly marching song and played it with as much dash as she could manage. It was annoying when he joined in the chorus, in a rather fine baritone.

'What other songs do you have here?' he enquired, moving close to her and reaching over to examine the pile of music. His sleeve brushed against her arm. Sarah drew back a little and rearranged her shawl to cover her arms. Eventually he selected another song and handed her the sheet. She took it and waited until he moved a step back before she played the tune. She could not help striking the keys with rather more force than usual.

But when that song was ended, he returned to his seat. James went over to him. Sarah watched them as she began to play a sonata. The card table was set up and the two of them were soon playing piquet. It was obvious to her that James was more than a little castaway, but Lord Percival seemed as sharp as if he had not drunk at all. He was encouraging James to refill his glass very frequently. Was this how he made money? These were not the actions of a man of honour.

Eventually she stopped playing. Neither of them took the least notice. She looked at her brother, frowning and nervous. Lord Percival was concentrating on the game, smiling again. He was winning, increasing his hold over James and thus his claim to gain possession of Russeldene – and of her! Her chin went up. He was not going to get either.

She indicated to Mrs Wiggins to come closer. The two of them sat down to observe the play. James was fidgety and uncertain. He was muddling his cards and losing each time. However, now the two women were there, Lord Percival stopped filling the glasses so frequently. Gradually James managed to win a game, then another and at last he settled down to play more steadily. The pile of coins on his side of the table grew and he seemed to be judging his cards better.

When they finally parted for the night, James was almost cheerful. But Sarah felt more anxious than ever about what would become of him.

*

'Be careful what you are about,' she told James the next morning when he again sought her out in the back parlour. 'Your *friend* – she stressed the word – 'appears uncommonly interested in our home.'

James flushed angrily. 'What is it to you? I hope I can invite a friend here without you criticizing everything I do. You are the younger, anyway.'

Sarah gave him a warning look. 'I did not care to see you losing money to him at such a rate last night. He was sober but you. . . .' She shook her head. 'James, matters are serious. It will take years to restore the estate and make up the money you have lost this last year. We have no more horses to sell. You cannot afford to continue like this.'

He gave that irritable twitch of his shoulders. 'What is a fellow to do, dash it? Besides – got to entertain George and he likes to play high.' His eyes narrowed as he watched her shake her head again. 'It is my choice. Just see that you serve up a good dinner this evening. And be a bit more welcoming. You were like an iceberg last night. Dashed embarrassing.'

Sarah walked towards the door. She reached for the handle and said over her shoulder, 'I regret I will not be here for dinner.'

'What the deuce do you mean? You have to be present, I mean, George will expect—'

Sarah let go of the door handle and turned back to face him. 'I mean that Lizzie and her uncle will arrive during the course of the afternoon.'

'What!' But instead of being angry, James sounded eager. 'Lizzie is coming here? Well, by Jove! I shall be very happy to see her again.'

'Yes but only for a short while. They have invited me to go with them on a visit.' She stopped abruptly. If she told him where they were going, he would inform Lord Percival. However, it was good to see James taking an interest in someone other than that evil creature he thought was his friend. Perhaps if he wanted to impress Lizzie he would stay sober and smarten himself up.

She considered his appearance. He was tall and wiry, his dark curly hair falling over his forehead. He was quite good-looking but his skin was pasty, his eyes bloodshot and shadowed by dark circles.

'James,' she said impulsively, 'it would do you good to stay here at Russeldene for at least a month. The fresh air and a quieter way of life would benefit you. Indeed, you do not look well.' She put a hand on his arm.

For a moment he stared at her then shook her off with a sharp laugh. 'Pray do not worry about me, little sister. I assure you I am perfectly well.'

Without another word, she left the room. There was still a long list of jobs to complete before she could leave things in Mrs Wiggins's hands.

It seemed as if she had been busy for a week, not a day, when at last she took her seat in the coach with Lizzie and General Gardiner, waving goodbye to Mrs Wiggins and bowling down the avenue to join the main road from London to Bath.

The general settled his gouty foot on a cushion. 'We should arrive before nightfall,' he remarked, and pulled his hat over his eyes. When he began to snore Lizzie leaned forward and whispered, 'Fancy Lord Percival being a guest at Russeldene! And you left town to avoid him, did you not?'

'He has come for the shooting.' Sarah whispered back.

'Oh.' Lizzie was silent for a while, then, 'Your brother was very welcoming.'

Sarah had to smile. James had indeed made every effort to please. It was plain he admired Lizzie even more now than when she used to come on visits as a schoolgirl. Lord Percival had also been very attentive to Lizzie. Under all this masculine admiration she had prattled on, giving away the details that Sarah had managed to keep secret until that moment.

How Lord Percival had smirked when Lizzie innocently revealed their destination and even that they would be staying in Milsom Street. She gave an inward shrug. At least for the moment she had escaped a very awkward situation. And in Bath, perhaps she could find a solution to her problems. A certain plan began to take form in her mind as the well-sprung carriage rolled on, covering the miles at a good rate.

CHAPTER NINE

It was at a rather late hour that they gathered round the breakfast-table in their smart lodging the following morning.

'We must make haste to go to the Pump Room and sign the Visitors' Book,' said Lizzie, pouring out her coffee, 'then we can see who else is already in Bath.'

Her uncle looked up from his newspaper. 'I doubt if there is much society of your age, my dear. It is a little early in the season yet. The place is likely to be full of dowagers and gouty old fellows like me.'

'I hope that with treatment at the hot bath, sir, you will soon recover your usual health,' said Sarah warmly.

'Well, Uncle Charlie, even if there is no company at all – which I doubt – you know how much we both like this city.' Lizzie turned to Sarah. 'Do you remember our walks with Miss Pickering after church service on Sunday afternoons?'

Sarah laughed. 'Our weekly escape from our lessons. And there was always something to admire as we walked around the streets.'

'We were never allowed to look in the shop windows properly. But now I mean to put that right.' Lizzie gave a peal of laughter, as her uncle clutched his head in mock dismay.

They were both excited to be back in the city where they had spent happy years at their school in Queen Square. Now, however, they were in a much more luxurious setting, in a handsome apartment in Milsom Street. The idea of elegant shops on her very doorstep made Lizzie impatient to go out. Even Sarah, with so little money in her purse, knew she would enjoy examining the fashions. With a bit of ribbon and a few artificial flowers, she could copy what she saw and refresh her bonnets and gowns.

It was not that her clothes were shabby and worn, simply that they had been bought for her intended come-out two years previously. But then her father had become too ill for her to leave him. So the gowns had remained in the closet and Sarah had remained at home to nurse her father. Then there had been the time of mourning, so that the clothes, which had been in the latest fashion then, were still unworn but now rather out of date.

Today the weather seemed quite mild. She selected a blue spencer, which echoed the blue ribbon trimming at the bottom of her cambric gown. In response to a shout from Lizzie, she whisked on her bonnet, tied the matching blue ribbons and rushed downstairs. Lizzie was a picture in soft pink, with cherry-red ribbons tied under one ear. 'We shall take the town by storm,' she said in a satisfied tone.

Their progress down Milsom Street was slow but eventually they had looked in all the shop windows. They then walked faster, weaving through the constant traffic of sedan chairs as they drew closer to the Pump Room. The girls ventured in, but as General Gardiner had predicted, it seemed to be full of elderly dowagers and their companions, mostly promenading around slowly or gathering in little knots for conversation.

A few heads turned when the two girls walked in. They knew they were being inspected in minute detail. Nobody showed any sign of recognition, however. Sarah glanced at Lizzie and raised her eyebrows. Lizzie nodded agreement. There was no reason to linger. They went over to add their names to the book and to examine the list showing who was presently in town.

Lizzie was running her finger down the page as she read. Suddenly she stopped and gave an exclamation of surprise. 'Just look at this!'

The fair head and the dark one bent closer. They looked at the page, then at each other.

'It has to be Major Thatcham,' said Sarah. 'presumably Sir Thomas is his father?'

'Yes, I am certain that is his name,' nodded Lizzie. 'What a coincidence. He said nothing about coming here when last I saw him, but lucky for us that he has.'

Sarah kept a slight smile on her lips but she felt her heart sink. Could she cope with this? She had just escaped a most unwelcome admirer and she wanted a respite from all her private emotions. The sight of Greg Thatcham becoming ever closer to Lizzie was going to be very hard to endure.

'As we are not intending to drink the waters today,' she said, 'I suggest that while the weather is so fine, we should go back up to the lending library and take out our subscription there.'

They had just reached Milsom Street again with their arms full of books when a gentleman crossed from the other side of the road and stopped in front of them, lifting off his hat. Sarah looked up and when she saw who it was, her spirits rose in spite of her attempt to keep a firm control of her unruly heart.

Greg Thatcham was smiling very broadly at both of them. 'What a charming surprise.' His eyes went from one to the other appreciatively. 'Let me guess . . . General Gardiner's gout!'

'Of course,' laughed Lizzie. 'Poor dear, he will be better for some treatment. But how do you come to be here?'

'My father needed a change of scene, but he thinks he is here to help me recover from this.' He indicated his arm, still in a sling. He turned to Sarah. 'I trust you feel better pleased with Bath than with London, Miss Davenport?'

Sarah gazed into those dancing eyes. She felt a blush creep up her cheeks. 'Yes, certainly. I am very fond of Bath. Lizzie and I were at school here.'

'It must have been a good school if you retain such happy memories,' he remarked. 'It certainly could not be from drinking the waters. Have you *tasted* them?' He grimaced.

Sarah laughed. 'You soon become accustomed,' she assured him.

He looked disbelieving. 'But they recommend such a huge amount – and three times a day!'

The girls laughed at him.

A smile crossed his face, and he added, 'May I assist you? You are both very laden.'

He took the books in spite of their protests, tucking a couple into his sling and gripping the others in his left hand. 'I believe I said before that I have become quite skilful with this arm.'

'Yes, but how will you knock on the door?' gurgled Lizzie.

'With my foot of course,' he grinned. 'Now, ladies, which way?'

Sarah indicated the top of Milsom Street. They set off again. It was a very short way to the house where General Gardiner had taken lodgings.

'Do come in,' Lizzie urged, 'my uncle will be pleased to see you again.'

Greg handed the books over one at a time. 'If you will excuse me, I was on my way to meet my father at the Lower Rooms. He has gone to get tickets for this evening's concert.' He looked from one to the other. 'Would you like me to get tickets for you as well? And then, on my return, perhaps I may bring my father to call?'

This was agreed to and the girls hastened inside to inform the general of the expected visit. Sarah flew up to her room to remove her bonnet and tidy her hair. 'You fool,' she scolded herself, 'this is idle vanity. He is coming to see Lizzie, not you.' Yet somewhere deep inside, she felt that he liked her very well also. At all events, he was a much needed friendly face in a difficult world.

She heard the sounds of an arrival and made haste to go back down to the drawing-room. The gentlemen were all standing. They turned as she entered the room and Greg stepped forward with a smile.

'Miss Davenport, may I introduce my father, Sir Thomas Thatcham.'

Sarah curtsied and looked up at the lined face and the white hair. He had the same eyes as his son and was nearly as tall. He held himself very erect and was smartly dressed. She warmed to him instinctively. He looked to be a kindly person and also had an air of culture. For an instant, she thought of her own father.

'I trust you are all music lovers,' said Sir Thomas, as he sat down opposite the general. 'The performers at this evening's concert are very well spoken of; there will be quite a varied programme.'

General Gardiner looked a little embarrassed. 'I fear you must excuse me. I will not be able to cope with those hard seats, or the length of the performance. . . . Perhaps when I have recovered.' He looked towards his niece.

'Now, Uncle Charlie,' she laughed, 'I am sure you would manage an evening of card-playing well enough, without noticing the hard chairs.' She looked across at Greg with her twinkling smile.

'In that case,' said Greg, smiling back at her warmly, Sarah noticed, 'I will see if there are still tickets for the assembly tomorrow evening. There will also be cards – so everyone can be happy. And of course' – he turned to the general – 'if you permit, sir, you can all be conveyed there in our carriage.'

The concert was excellent. Sarah gave herself up to the pleasure of the music and the fine singing. It was such a haven of culture in the desert of her recent life. She sat through the whole event quietly, her eyes shining. She was lost in the melodies and could scarcely believe it when the evening's entertainment drew to a close. Sir Thomas turned to her with a smile.

'They are a fine bunch of musicians, are they not?'

Sarah nodded, reluctantly coming back to the present.

His smile broadened. 'I have to say that it was as much a pleasure to see your enjoyment as to listen to the music, excellent though it was.'

'It is not often that I have the opportunity to attend a concert,' she told him, rising to her feet and pulling her wrap closely around her shoulders. 'I would have taken pleasure in any musical entertainment. But this was certainly superior.'

They followed the others out into the chilly night air. It was only a short distance to their lodgings and they set off on foot, waving aside the offers of a sedan chair. Sarah accepted Sir Thomas's arm. She was able to admire Greg's tall figure as he walked in front with Lizzie. Again she felt the pang of longing. He looked so solid and dependable. She stifled a sigh.

On their doorstep, as they said their goodnights, Greg clapped a hand to his brow. 'I was forgetting – I have obtained tickets for tomorrow evening's assembly.' He looked from one to the other, 'and I think my arm is useful enough for me to be able to ask if you will both stand up with me?'

Sarah felt she was slipping deeper and deeper into a quicksand. Of course she would dance with him and it would do nothing to strengthen her resolve to keep him at a distance. She must remember that he was already attached to Lizzie. Was there nowhere she could be at peace?

CHAPTER TEN

As Greg had promised, the coach collected General Gardiner, Lizzie and Sarah and delivered them safely to the Assembly Rooms on the following evening. The girls had dressed in simple muslin gowns, Sarah in white with pleated white satin trimming and Lizzie in pomona green. Sir Thomas and Greg were waiting for them in the spacious entrance hall. The strains of a lively dance tune reached them while they greeted each other. Sir Thomas and General Gardiner immediately agreed to go to the card room. Sarah followed Lizzie and Greg into the ballroom.

'Why, there is hardly anyone here!' Lizzie's face fell as she looked around the vast room. In the centre, a small line of couples was dancing but there was a wide, empty stretch of floor all around them. Along the walls the rows of chairs stood empty. Here and there a family group clustered or a chaperon sat watching the dancers.

'It is a little bare,' agreed Sarah, 'but we shall still manage to dance.'

'I cannot see a single person that I know,' remarked Greg, 'but then, I have spent most of the last seven years out of the country.'

'Well,' said Sarah, 'I must admit I cannot see anyone *I* know – and I was at school in this town for a number of years.'

'We will have to find the Master of Ceremonies and ask him for some introductions.' Greg glanced up and down. 'I do believe that he is over there. Excuse me.' He strode off.

'Have you noticed,' whispered Lizzie, 'he has left off his sling?'

'He really intends to dance, then.' Sarah began to twist the curl above her left ear. Her eyes widened as she considered her situation. She was tired of always struggling against events. This evening she would behave like any other girl at a ball and just enjoy herself. And if Greg asked her to dance, surely she was able to stand up with him without doing any damage to her heart?

But her heart was already beating faster than it should. No doubt she was excited by the prospect of a pleasant evening's entertainment with no Alice on the look-out for a possible husband for her. She drew a deep, calming breath. Her heart was still fluttering! She became aware of someone approaching and looked up.

It was the Master of Ceremonies bringing two gentlemen with him. Sarah hastily pulled her finger out of the curl and glanced guiltily towards Greg. His face was quite bland, but he was looking in her direction. Blushing slightly, she curtsied as the newcomers were introduced. They were two unexceptionable young men and the problem of partners was now solved.

The next dance was just being announced and the taller of the two gentlemen, Mr Keating, invited Sarah to join in. She accepted readily and discovered that he was a light and skilful dancer as well as an amusing companion. She found it easy to make conversation with him and on several occasions he made her laugh.

She relaxed and began to feel her cares slipping away. Mr Keating was a good-looking young man with wavy brown hair and an amiable smile. Sarah judged him to be in his mid twenties. At the end of the dance, he asked permission to introduce her to his mother and sister.

Sarah was delighted to discover that Mrs Keating was a plump, kindly little lady. She greeted Sarah warmly and introduced her daughter, Lavinia, a petite brunette with lively blue eyes. Sarah could see she was a very young debutante, dressed in the usual demure white dress and pearl necklet but there was a sparkle of intelligence and a look of mischief about her. She probably kept her mother and brother quite busy, looking after her.

'I am very glad to meet you, Miss Davenport,' smiled Mrs Keating. 'You and your friend make a welcome addition to our society. We ourselves only arrived this week but I confess I was disappointed to find Bath so sadly empty of young people. No doubt this dry weather has kept everyone in the country for the hunting.'

'It will soon become busy once we get into November,' Sarah replied. How refreshing it was, just to meet kind people and spend a few hours in agreeable company. Miss Keating was well mannered and pleasant, like her brother. Sarah introduced Lizzie and her new partner, Mr Wilden.

'You see,' she murmured to Mrs Keating, 'we have formed quite a group already.'

'Indeed,' replied the lady, 'it is so much more comfortable than just sitting here in this great empty ballroom.'

'By the end of another month you will be longing for more space even in this room,' laughed Sarah.

'Well, Lavinia needs to become accustomed to living in Society before I take her to London in December, so you will not hear me complain about crowds.'

They were all still busy talking when the bell rang to announce the supper interval.

'Goodness, nine o'clock already!' exclaimed Lizzie, 'I do hope there are ices.'

They began to move towards the refreshment area. Sarah looked around to see if General Gardiner had ventured from the card room. Across the crowd, her eyes met Greg's and she could not help but smile. At once a smile spread over his face. In a moment he was by her side.

'All well so far, Miss Davenport?'

'Oh, yes, I much prefer this to London assemblies.'

He lifted an eyebrow but made no comment.

Sarah looked round again. 'I was wondering about your father and the general. . . .'

'Pray do not worry. They have already been attended to.'

Sarah looked her surprise. He smiled. 'There are waiters to serve the infirm card players at their tables.'

'Well,' she said, 'that could be a good thing or a bad one – if they are very addicted to cards.'

'If they are very addicted, I doubt they would stop for refreshments anyway. Do you play, Miss Davenport?'

'No, not at all.'

Greg cast her a glance. 'That was very gravely said.'

She looked away. Did she need to tell him how low her family had sunk through James's addiction to gaming? Fortunately, he did not press the matter. They moved up to the table in silence. She accepted the ice he offered her. Lizzie, already eating her ice, beckoned them to follow her back to Mrs and Miss Keating.

Soon it was time for the dancing to begin again. Lizzie and Mr Keating were already joining the set. Sarah found Greg looking enquiringly at her.

'I do hope you will not snub me,' he murmured.

She put her head on one side. 'Why would I do that?'

He offered his arm and she laid her hand on it. They walked towards the line of dancers. 'Well,' he said, 'I had the feeling you were cutting me off just now.'

Sarah felt her colour rise. 'Please forget that. It – it's just my – a. . . .' She floundered to a stop.

He pressed her hand slightly as they joined hands for the turn. 'Not the moment to twist your curls, is it?' He grinned at her. 'Yes, I did notice.'

She cast him a rueful look and bit her lip. When next they came together he asked her, 'Does your sister remain in London?'

'Oh, yes. She is settled there, I think for the whole season.'

He nodded. 'Do you have any other brothers or sisters?'

Why was he asking? Sarah did not think he could possibly be interested in James. He did not seem like a gambling man.

'I have one brother. He is usually to be found in London.' She did not add 'in a gaming hell' but perhaps someone had told him that already. Or maybe not, as he was still being friendly. She wondered if the Davenport reputation was known in Bath. If it was, maybe the Keatings would not be so friendly the next time they met. Sarah swallowed hard, there seemed to be a lump in her throat. How was she to find a way out of her disgrace by association? Even more important, how was she to save Russeldene from Lord Percival?

Certainly not by gambling. She almost had to repress a shudder at the idea. She gave herself a mental shake. This was not the moment for such thoughts. She gave Greg a smile as she stepped towards him again and found he was considering her with a grave look in those fine eyes. Before she could think of anything to say the musicians gave a final flourish and the dancers all made their bow or curtsy.

Greg surprised her by taking her arm and preventing her from returning to her new friends. He looked at her very meaningfully. 'Pray let us take a turn round the room,' he said. 'There can be no objection, can there?'

'N-no,' she stammered. Now what was he going to say?

He drew her hand firmly under his arm and walked her over to the most deserted part of the hall. She gave him a questioning look.

'This is perhaps the best chance I shall have to understand the problem,' he said, indicating a chair. Sarah ignored it. She fixed her eyes on his.

'What problem?'

He rubbed his chin. 'It is obvious that something is troubling you deeply. I saw it at the assembly in London. And even here, you are still blue-devilled.' He gave her a very kind smile. 'I would be glad to help you if I can.'

Sarah's lip trembled. She lowered her gaze, afraid he would see too much. She was not used to sympathy. At the same time, she was puzzled by his insistent questions. Why was he so interested in her brother and sister? Well, she would try a direct question in her turn.

'Are you acquainted with any of my family, sir?'

He gave a short laugh. 'I believe I may have danced with your sister once or twice, when she was a debutante in London for the season. That was before I joined the army. I do not know your brother.'

But I need to know him! Dancing with Sarah Davenport was every bit as much pleasure as he had expected. She was very lovely with her pale oval face and long, slender neck. And that silken fair hair, twisted into a topknot and with little curls over her ears, with wispy tendrils escaping down her neck – his fingers itched to caress them and the creamy skin underneath. And her pretty pink lips – better not think about them!

He had other matters to deal with. Why was he preoccupied with her to the point that it was interfering with his quest to deal with the mystery of Henry's debt? Had he not sworn never to let another woman get close to him? *So, he warned himself, just stick to your plan! Get the information now, while you have the chance.*

However, as soon as he asked questions about her family, the hunted look returned to those jewel-green eyes. In spite of his determination, Greg hated himself for upsetting her. But he must persevere. When the dance came to an end, he walked her firmly to a quiet corner. 'I do not know your brother,' he said, 'but perhaps he is in Bath as well?'

She gave him a wary look. Greg remembered what Theo had said about James Davenport being a wastrel. It was clear that she felt ashamed of her brother. No doubt she was aware that Society would be gossiping about his impending ruin and speculating on her future as well. How could he not feel pity for her? It was pity that drew him to her, made him want to help her when any fool could see how forlorn she was. The fact that she was very lovely did not enter into it.

He cleared his throat. 'Miss Davenport, I do not wish to intrude but, if I can be of service, please tell me.'

This time there were definitely tears in her eyes. Then she bent her head, giving him the chance to admire the fine blonde hair so cleverly swept into the knot on top of her head. He wanted to pull the pins out and bury his face in those silken strands. He took a deep breath and caught the fragrance of her lavender perfume.

She raised her head. 'You are very kind,' she said in a husky voice, 'but it is time to rejoin our friends.' Her expression changed as she saw him rubbing his right arm. 'Is your wound troubling you? You should still be wearing your sling to rest it.'

'We soldiers are tough enough to withstand such trifling things as an aching arm. The muscles need exercise, that is all. Come.' He offered that arm for her to place her hand on it and encouraged her to do so with a nod. As they walked towards the Keatings he murmured, 'You did not answer my question about your brother.'

He caught the flash of green as she threw him an angry glance. 'He is at Russeldene for the shooting, but he will probably return to London shortly.'

Then she was talking to Miss Keating and he was definitely being cold-shouldered. He looked at her lovely profile. He would have to charm her again, without insulting her fine intelligence.

CHAPTER ELEVEN

It was raining the next morning and the two girls arrived at the Pump Room rather wet. When they entered, it was fairly crowded and there was a cheerful buzz of conversation. Lizzie spotted the Keatings and started in their direction. Sarah was following when she saw Sir Thomas Thatcham and stopped to exchange a few words. He smiled courteously on seeing her and bowed with old-fashioned elegance.

'Are the waters doing you good, sir?' she asked, with a mischievous glance.

He gave her a sharp look from under his brows then chuckled. 'It is to be hoped they have some positive effect. They taste even worse than their reputation.'

'In that case, they are certainly beneficial,' she assured him. They were both laughing when a figure suddenly appeared at her side. It was Greg. Her wayward heart beat faster and she had to struggle to hide her pleasure as she acknowledged his greeting. She looked from him to his father. How closely they resembled each other, not only in their features, but with the same tall, broad-shouldered frame. They both had the same open, direct look.

But while Sir Thomas had the more elaborate manners of her own parents' generation, Greg was every inch the bluff soldier. So far he had seemed very straightforward in his dealings with her. Yet now she had the suspicion that he was seeking her out simply to enquire about her family. Why was he interested in James? There could be no connection through gambling.

Like a bolt of lightning, a phrase she had overheard shot

through her: *the brother is making enquiries*. Could it be. . . ? Was it possible that there was a link? The idea made her feel breathless with suspense. She had to find out more from James.

In the whirl of these unpleasant ideas, she did not hear Greg speak to her. He cleared his throat and tried again. 'Miss Davenport. . . .'

At this she looked up and he went on, 'You seem rather cast down. I trust last night's exertions were not too fatiguing for you?'

She made an effort to appear at ease. 'I am not such a fragile creature as to be worn down by one assembly. In fact, it was very enjoyable.'

His amber eyes shone. 'I am glad to hear it. I already know how energetic Lizzie is. So, if you also enjoy exercise, perhaps I can suggest that we all take a walk around the Beechen Cliff – on the next fine day, that is.' He looked ruefully at his father. 'I will reserve the offer of a drive until I have strengthened my arm. My father has made me promise that I will be cautious.'

The older man nodded gravely. 'We are here to get you well, so we will stick to the doctor's advice.'

Greg caught Sarah's eye before looking away hastily. She saw the darker colour stain his cheekbones. He had been an officer in the bloody war being fought in Spain and no doubt had faced terrible danger and hardship countless times. But he could not say a word. Sarah understood. Sir Thomas was reacting to the loss of his eldest son by watching over this one with over-protective care.

She smiled at both of them. 'How fortunate you are, sir, to have such a loving parent.'

Sir Thomas gave her a nod, bowed and walked away to return his glass to the attendant. She watched him greet an elderly lady and, as he lingered, chatting to her, another dowager joined them. Sarah's eyes narrowed in amusement.

'Your father seems to be quite at home in Bath.' She turned back to Greg, who had recovered his usual poise by now. He glanced at his father and smiled. 'It seems half of his old London friends are here. I am glad of it.'

While he watched his father, Sarah inspected him. As always he had a splendid appearance. Today he wore a smart russet jacket and snowy cravat. His buckskins emphasized the powerful muscles of a man who spent many hours in the saddle and his boots were dazzling. Her eyes travelled up to his lean face and coppery hair. She felt like a fly being relentlessly attracted into a spider's web.

Then suddenly, the spell was broken. She gave a gasp of horror. Not two yards away Lord Percival was in conversation with another very rakish-looking man. She heard his bray of laughter. She stiffened with dismay. Her escape had been short indeed!

At length she heard Greg's voice as if from far away. 'Miss Davenport? Are you quite well? You have gone very pale.'

Slowly she raised her eyes to his. There was no way she could explain the problem. He put a hand under her elbow. 'Come,' he said, I think you need to find a seat.' He gently pulled her along, out of the Pump Room and into the wide entrance area. Here he found a bench and pushed her down on to it.

Sarah was angry with herself for being so weak. Her knees were trembling and she was finding it hard to focus her thoughts. She was conscious of Greg's kind help and made a pitiful attempt to smile. 'Thank you, I am well again now. I am sorry to be so troublesome.'

He bent over her. 'What happened? It seemed you received a terrible shock.'

She nodded. 'Yes. I – I saw someone I did not expect to find in Bath.' She drew a shuddering breath. 'I cannot say more.'

Greg frowned down at her, looking very like his father. 'Is this person likely to cause you annoyance?'

She looked at him miserably. What could she say? There was a long silence.

'Will you not tell me his name?'

Sarah hesitated. Unconsciously, she started twisting a curl. This time, Greg took no notice.

'I will soon discover it, you know,' he said quietly. 'Is it the same person who claimed you for the dance at the ball in London two weeks ago?'

Sarah clasped her hands firmly. It was foolish to act like a vapourish little miss. And Greg was only trying to help.

'He is Lord Percival, the Earl of Ramsdale.'

If she had thrown a bucket of cold water over him it could not have had a greater effect. Sarah almost forgot her own woes as she watched Greg's head jerk back in shock. He definitely went pale. Then his face hardened. Sarah glimpsed the steel that underlay his usual pleasant expression. He stared at her out of narrowed eyes. She sensed a withdrawal. And that was the last straw.

'I do try to avoid him,' she said in a low voice, 'but he is my brother's particular friend. I cannot ignore him.'

He nodded slowly. 'I understand,' he said at last. 'You are in a difficult situation.'

She stood up and squared her shoulders. 'At least I am prepared now. But I prefer to keep away from him if I can. Would you be kind enough to tell Lizzie I forgot something and returned home?'

'I can escort you if you wish. Indeed, you still look pale.'

And so do you! But why should that name have such an effect on him? Sarah forced a smile to her lips. 'Thank you but I am perfectly well. It is a very short walk to Milsom Street.'

It was clear she wanted to be alone. Greg watched as she set off, a slender figure under her umbrella, picking her way round the puddles. Now he had the key to her anxieties. But it was going to be a tricky matter to help her. He turned back towards the Pump Room. It would only be a question of time before someone introduced him to Lord Percival and then the subject of the gaming debt would arise.

Sarah's reaction to Lord Percival was most instructive. It made Greg more determined than ever to discover just what had happened at that hunting party where his brother had died. As he wove a path through the crowd in search of Lizzie, he decided that his first task was to make the acquaintance of Sarah's brother and see what he could find out from him.

Lizzie was at the far end of the room, in the midst of a group of people and chattering happily. Greg paused for a moment. He was shaken at how savagely the bitter anger over the loss of his brother had surged up again. He must not show any sign of that.

As if to remind him of his other woe, his arm was aching like the devil after the previous night's exertions on the dance floor. He tucked his elbow into his side and moved towards Lizzie, summoning up a polite smile.

Lizzie caught sight of him and stepped forward. The group of people all turned as she did so. 'Here you are at last,' she said brightly. 'Let me introduce you to the Earl of Ramsdale. Lord Percival, this is Major Thatcham.'

CHAPTER TWELVE

'Sarah! Where are you going in such a hurry?'

That peevish voice could only belong to James. Reluctantly, Sarah stopped and waited for him to cross the street. It was busy with carriages and he had to dodge and run to get across, which did not improve his temper. His face was just as pale and haggard as when she had last seen him.

'You have scarcely tired of the shooting at Russeldene so soon?' she asked, by way of greeting.

A passing coach threw up a spray of water. James cursed and moved away, brushing at his greatcoat. 'Just look at that. What a damn— dashed place Bath is for weather.'

'Well, you should have stayed in the country, then.'

He scowled at her. 'George took a fancy to come here. Thing is, Sarah, he wants to pay court to you. And there is no need to look like that!' he added explosively.

'Like what?' she challenged.

'As if you had seen something disgusting. George is a great fellow and my particular friend, y'know. I insist you give him a chance.'

She shook her head.

'Sarah,' he pleaded, 'dash it, Alice thinks he is suitable—'

'Alice does not want the expense of an unmarried sister living with her,' she flashed. 'And she knows I am soon to be a pauper if you go on wasting all our inheritance.' She turned away, took a deep breath and set off again in the direction of Milsom Street.

'Hey!' James came scurrying after her. He took her by the arm

73

and forced her to stop.

'Let – me – go!' she said through her teeth. She tried to pull away but he kept a firm hold.

'I mean it, Sis. You must make yourself agreeable to George. Thing is, I owe him the devil of a lot of money. He will not heed it, however, if you let him pay court to you.'

Sarah gave him a withering look. 'How dare you! How could you sink so low as to gamble even your sister. Have you taken leave of your senses?'

He blinked at her. 'It is not like that. Why do you put it in such a way? George is—'

'Spare me,' she interrupted. 'He is ruthless and people hint at very dark things in his background. But are you so deep in his debt you have bribed him with me? James, is there no end to your gambling fever? You were not like this before you got drawn into this man's circle.'

Under the fire of her gaze, his bloodshot eyes sank. He shuffled his feet then jerked his shoulder and shot her a quick glance. 'There is no other way now. He could turn us out of our home if he wished. It all depends on you to save us.'

It was a clear statement of how matters stood. The blood turned to ice in Sarah's veins. The horror must have shown in her face because James shifted uncomfortably. Then, as usual, his temper snapped. Sarah knew from experience that if he could not easily gain his own way, he would resort to threats and bullying.

'You might at least give him a fair hearing,' James continued. 'Dash it, he is very well set up. Most of the ladies are falling over themselves to be noticed by him. What ails you? Come on! Let us get out of this curst wet.' He forcibly pulled her in the direction of the Pump Room.

They were attracting glances and some whispered comments. Sarah allowed herself to be walked back down Union Street. The rain was falling heavily and the hem of her dress was soaked. It clung unpleasantly to her ankles as she hurried to keep up with her brother's long strides.

Her umbrella wobbled due to her hasty steps. The drips landed on James and made him curse. He swept her up the entrance step and into the wide hall that she had left so short a time before. There she stopped and wrenched her arm free of his hold.

'James, just look at me. My gown is sodden from the knees down. I can feel that my hair is damp. Even the ribbons of my bonnet are dripping. I am in no state to be exchanging social chit-chat. I shall catch an inflammation of the lungs.'

He scowled. 'Deuce take it, Sarah—'

But she was no longer listening. She had spotted Greg walking in her direction. He had an unusually grim frown on his face. She felt a little shiver down her back that had nothing to do with the cold and damp. Here was another side to this man's character. He was dangerous in his anger.

When he noticed her he stopped in his tracks, made a visible effort to adjust his expression and then came up to her.

'Whatever has happened, Miss Davenport? Have you fallen in the river?'

'It feels like it,' she admitted. 'Oh, this is my brother, Lord Davenport. James, this is Major Thatcham.'

In the act of bowing, James jerked upright again. 'Thatcham!' he ejaculated. 'Oh, Lord!'

Greg looked at the dissipated young man. He was tall and slender, with regular features and dark, curly hair, at present rather flattened by the rain. He could be handsome if he did not have that unhealthy pallor and irritable expression. He was almost as wet as his sister. Only ten minutes ago she had been desperate to get away from the Pump Room. Why had her brother forced her to return here?

Greg strove to calm his own inner turmoil in order to concentrate on this problem. It was strange that in the space of a mere ten minutes, he had met the two men he most needed to find. And it seemed that his instinct was right. On learning his identity, this young man immediately betrayed a consciousness of something. Greg eyed him keenly. 'You already seem to have heard of me.'

James opened and shut his mouth. His hat dropped from his hand. 'Er . . . no, no – that is, believe you have a brother in Town. . . .'

Greg nodded. He would pursue this later. At present, if this creature could not see that his sister was shivering with cold, Greg could.

'Miss Davenport, this time I insist on calling a chair for you. You need to change those wet clothes.'

The look she gave him was thanks enough. In a very short space of time, Greg had summoned a sedan and handed her carefully into it.

'Be sure to hurry,' he urged the porters as he closed the door. He nodded to her and watched her on her way before turning back into the entrance hall. He shook the raindrops off his face. Now for a word with her negligent brother, but, not entirely to Greg's surprise, the wretched fellow had disappeared. Greg's lip curled. How typical. No doubt James Davenport had fled to his crony, Lord Percival.

His face hardened as he saw again the moment Lizzie had presented him to that man. The arrogance seeped from every pore. Here was a man who trod over the feelings and lives of others for his own selfish gain. The sneering voice, the hint of contempt and yet – and yet, Greg mused, the eyes were wary, defensive, watching him for any sign of weakness or emotion, or could it be that Lord Percival had something to conceal?

Greg puzzled to understand why Henry had ever consented to play cards with this type of gamester? Why, Theo had said that Lord Percival was well known as a deep player. After seeing James Davenport, Greg suspected that Lord Percival was the type to lead young men into gaming hells and relieve them of their fortunes.

He would test that theory when the right opportunity offered. For now, he must observe the habits and favourite haunts of his quarry. He strolled back into the Pump Room and made his way slowly across to the long counter where the girl was serving glasses of the spa water. Greg took a glass and leaned his back against the counter. He looked at the gently moving crowd while he sipped the foul tasting stuff.

Across the room Lizzie was still chatting in her lively way to a group of young ladies. A smile curved Greg's lips as he watched her. Such vivacity and sweetness. She was a pearl. His expression changed as he made out James Davenport in the group surrounding her. So he was interested in Lizzie, was he? Greg determined to increase his guard on her.

His survey continued. The room was definitely more crowded today. The people were still mainly elderly and infirm. Groups formed and then drifted on, so that there was a continual murmur of voices and footsteps, together with the clink of glasses. At length he saw his quarry. Lord Percival was with a couple of other overdressed gentlemen. Their dandified appearance was earning them many glances. Well, it would be easy to pick out the fellow at any function.

Satisfied, Greg set down his half-full glass on the counter. But he had forgotten that his arm was weak and a spasm of cramp seized it. The glass wobbled and tipped over. Recollecting his surroundings just in time, he swallowed down the curse that rose to his lips. It was time to find a sporting salon and start strengthening his arm again.

CHAPTER THIRTEEN

Sarah was curled up on the sofa with a novel when Lizzie arrived home. She burst into the sitting-room, still wearing her outdoor clothes.

'You see, she is quite all right,' she announced over her shoulder. James appeared in the doorway. He cast his sister an angry glance.

'Good heavens, James,' she said, before he could begin his reproaches. 'I wonder if it is possible for you to get any wetter. If you mean to stay in Bath you should get yourself an umbrella.'

'Never mind that,' he snapped, 'just see you remember what I told you earlier. We shall be at the Pump Room at the same time tomorrow.'

There was a distinct emphasis on the *we*. Sarah looked at him very levelly but said nothing. He glared at her and opened his mouth, then glanced at Lizzie and snapped his mouth closed without speaking.

'You are dripping on to the carpet,' Sarah pointed out. With an exasperated snort, James swung round and went out.

'It all depends on the weather,' Lizzie said, following him into the hallway. 'Perhaps we shall go for a walk if it is fine tomorrow. You might like to join us? And, oh, James, what do you think of. . . .'

The rest of her words were too faint for Sarah to make out. She heard James say something in reply, then the front door slammed shut and Lizzie came back into the cosy sitting-room. Sarah raised her brows enquiringly. 'What schemes have you been planning?'

Lizzie took off her wet cloak and set it on a chairback in front of the fire. She peered into the mirror over the mantelpiece and adjusted her curls. 'The Keatings went to visit Wells last week. It is something we never did when we were at school here. They are full of admiration for the fine architecture of the cathedral and the beauties of the countryside. I am sure I can persuade Greg to drive us there.'

Sarah felt the now familiar lurch in her chest. She longed to see him yet dreaded it because every time she did, his good qualities made her even more aware of how much she liked him. There was no pleasure in being a bystander while he and Lizzie seemed to be growing ever closer.

'Do you not want to go?'

She could hear the disappointment in Lizzie's voice. She tried to summon up a cheerful look. 'Who else is likely to join us?'

'Well, I did hope to persuade your brother, but he seems to be a little out of sorts this morning.'

'I fear James is often like that. And it would be miraculous if you could persuade him to be up and out at the time we would need to set off if we are to travel to Wells and back in daylight at this time of year.'

Lizzie settled in an armchair by the fire. She raised a foot to examine her boot. 'How wet everything is today,' she said crossly. 'I shall have to change these now. I did want to go for a proper walk. It is no distance to the Pump Room.'

Sarah smiled. 'It is if you are General Gardiner with a gouty foot. Thank goodness for sedan chairs. I take it you have left him there?'

'*Left* him! Just try and winkle him out. He has met some old friends and I think they will be there all day, talking and playing cards.'

The door knocker sounded just as Lizzie had got the first boot off. She thrust it behind her chair and tucked her foot under her dress. Then the door opened and Greg made his way into the room. Sarah noticed that he now looked as pleasant and good-humoured as ever. Whatever had caused that grim expression, he had overcome it.

79

'I was passing and decided to see if you were safe and dry again,' he said to Sarah. 'I am glad to find you looking more relaxed than you were earlier.'

'Yes, what did happen to prevent you from joining me?' Lizzie chimed in. 'I had quite forgotten in all the excitement.' She glanced from Greg to Sarah a little suspiciously. 'What have you been getting up to?'

Sarah was twisting her curl before she could stop herself. 'Nothing at all, I got very wet and was so cold I could not stay at the Pump Room.' She cast a sideways glance at Greg. There was a gleam in his eyes. She forced her hand out of her hair and smoothed the neck of her gown. Greg's eyes followed her fingers. To her annoyance, Sarah felt a blush creep up her cheeks. She deliberately folded her hands in her lap and raised her chin.

Greg waited a few minutes, his eyes hopeful. When she did not move he heaved a sigh and moved towards the door. 'Since all is well and you are so cosy, I will not intrude further on your time, ladies.' He was already turning the handle when Sarah remembered her manners.

'Mr Thatcham, thank you for your help this morning. . . .'

His eyes glinted at her. 'Glad to be of service. Now or indeed, at any time.'

'Oh, that reminds me,' Lizzie exclaimed, 'we are planning a visit to Wells. Would you like to join the party?'

'Lizzie, you are a minx,' he said. 'You mean, will I drive you?'

She nodded and grinned at him.

He shook his head. 'We cannot go three in one curricle. And until the weather improves, it is out of the question.'

'Oh,' she pouted, 'I do so want to see the cathedral.'

'You will,' he promised. 'Just have a little patience.' The door closed behind him.

'Well!' said Lizzie with another pout, as she returned to pulling off her other boot, 'if he is going to be so disobliging, I shall ask Lord Percival to take us.'

Sarah had been lost in a little dream, but at this she sat up with a jerk. 'How could you even consider going on such an expedition with him?'

'Just because you do not like him it does not mean everyone must do so. I find him very polished and handsome.'

'Oh Lizzie, beware.'

Lizzie wriggled her toes towards the blaze in the hearth. She gave Sarah a long look. 'You really do dislike him so much?'

'I mistrust him. Truly, Lizzie, he is the last man to make into a friend. He has a dreadful reputation—'

'So, someone will reform him.' Lizzie tossed her head. 'Would that not be a good idea?'

'I fear he is past redemption,' Sarah snapped. She bent her head over her book. The words would not make sense, however. This was an intolerable situation. Between Greg on the one hand and Lord Percival on the other, her days were a constant source of misery and problems. She frowned at the page but the letters just blurred.

'Sarah.' It was a very little voice.

Sarah shook her head and kept her face bent over her novel. The next instant, Lizzie flew across the room and slipped an arm round her neck.

'Oh, Sarah, dear, I promise not to tease you. I can see you are upset.'

Sarah blinked and sniffed. 'Never mind me, Lizzie. I am fine again now. But please do not ask Lord Percival to join any outings you plan to make. It would do your reputation a great deal of damage.' She had to smile at her friend's disappointed face. 'I daresay you can stand up with him for a dance now and then without causing any scandal.'

Lizzie considered this. 'Why is that acceptable?'

'Because he can hardly do you any harm in a ballroom, with all the chaperons looking on.' She tilted her head on one side. 'Do you remember how you used to fall in love with all the singing and drawing masters who came to the school?'

'I was young then,' said Lizzie indignantly.

'You still are. This is no different. But why do you not feel enthusiastic about Mr Keating? He is a very pleasant young man.'

Lizzie considered the question. She went back to her seat and held her hands out to the warm blaze in the hearth. 'I suppose,' she said at length, 'that he is very good-looking . . . and pleasant but . . . not exciting.' After another pause, she gave Sarah a side-ways glance. 'And, in any event, I noticed at the assembly that he was very taken with you.'

CHAPTER FOURTEEN

'Bath is really living up to its name,' remarked General Gardiner. He took off his spectacles and laid aside his newspaper. 'What do you girls plan to do today in this wet weather? Apart from getting a bath in the street, of course?' He beamed proudly at his mild joke.

Lizzie buttered another slice of bread and reached for the honey pot. 'All our plans have to wait,' she said with a little sigh. 'A walk to Beechen Cliff, a ride to Wells . . . we cannot do either in this endless rain.'

Her uncle shook his head. 'No rides out of town without a proper chaperon,' he said firmly. 'Is that understood?'

Lizzie gave him an innocent look. 'But if we go in a group, surely there is nothing wrong in that.'

'Miss Lizzie,' said her fond uncle in a despairing tone, 'I allow you a great deal of freedom. But I will not have you giving the Bath tabbies anything on which to speculate. You can be sure that your Aunt Augusta is getting regular reports from some of them.'

'Oh no!' gasped Lizzie. 'I had not thought of her. She never stirs from Sussex. Why should she take an interest in what I do here?'

'You would do well to remember that she has friends everywhere. Any hint of gossip about you and we shall have her descending on us with her parrot and that pug dog she dotes on.'

Lizzie looked horrified. 'But the pug is smelly. And Aunt is much too strict—'

'Aha!' General Gardiner pushed back his chair and rose painfully to his feet. He nodded at her. 'So you do acknowledge that I am easier to deal with, hey, miss? Well, while it is so wet, perhaps you can make the time to write her a civil letter. Tell her how you are improving your mind with serious reading.' He winked at Sarah. 'I assume it is serious reading . . . I can see by the way you turn the pages so eagerly. But the titles of some of 'em leave me wondering. What was that last one I saw you with? *Umberto and the Maiden. . . .'* He pursed his lips. 'Clanking chains and ghostly apparitions, kidnapped damsels and highwaymen, if I know anything about it.'

'Have you been reading my book when I was not there?' exclaimed his niece, her eyes open very wide.

Her uncle burst out laughing. 'No, but I know the style of thing you enjoy.'

There came a discreet tap at the door and his valet entered, a twist of paper in his hand.

'Your sedan chair is here, sir, to convey you to the Pump Room. And this message has just been delivered for Miss Sarah.'

The general had not reached the door when Sarah exclaimed, 'Here is the answer to your desire for exercise, Lizzie. Mrs Keating invites us to Laura Place for dancing practice at two o'clock. She writes that she wishes to be certain Lavinia can dance the waltz, even if she may not do so in public.'

Lizzie brightened up at once. 'Oh, that will be an agreeable way to spend the day.' She looked at her uncle. 'But do you think Aunt Augusta would approve?'

He waved a hand airily. 'It sounds unexceptionable to me. But do not forget the letter, now.'

Mrs Keating had found two other young ladies to invite. 'But we are a little short of gentlemen,' she told Sarah and Lizzie when they arrived. 'However, Monsieur Lebrun will no doubt partner one young lady as he demonstrates the steps. He is the best dancing master in Bath.'

Everyone soon found that Monsieur Lebrun had an eagle eye for the smallest fault and he demanded perfection. He himself moved with such grace that all the young couples exerted themselves to copy his movements. He kept them hard at work for an hour before he allowed them a brief pause to catch their breath.

At this point Mrs Keating signed to her butler to bring in refreshments. She engaged Monsieur Lebrun in conversation while the young people tried to cool down. Sarah willingly accepted the glass of lemonade brought to her by John Keating.

'It is very good of you to give your time, Miss Davenport.' He smiled at her warmly. 'One has only to see you dance to realize you do not need any tuition.'

'Why, thank you. But you flatter me. I assure you, I do not have many opportunities to take part in dances and this extra practice is most useful.' She sipped her lemonade. 'Particularly with such an excellent teacher.'

He nodded. 'My mother is most anxious that Lavinia should feel confident before she goes to London next month.'

Sarah's eyes went to where Lavinia was talking to Lizzie and Lucas Wilden.

'I am sure she will be a credit to you. You are a careful brother.' Unlike mine, she thought. His eyes met hers and she knew the same thought was going through his mind. She set her glass down and glanced across at Lavinia once more. 'It seems to me that your sister simply needed to find companions of her own age. Just see how she is enjoying herself now.'

He inclined his head. 'You are quite right. And what about yourself, Miss Davenport? Are you comfortably settled in Bath?'

She gave him a quick glance, but his face when he looked up from refilling her glass was merely polite. Could there be any ulterior motive behind his question? Probably not. Even so, her hand stole up to pull at a curl by her ear.

'You are aware that I know the town well, sir. . . .' she was saying, when the butler came in and spoke to his mistress. Mrs Keating rose. Her son's attention was diverted. A moment later, Greg walked into the room. He bowed to Mrs Keating who led him towards the dancing master. They spoke together for a few minutes.

'You will be able to take a rest, now we have reinforcements,' said Sarah.

John Keating gave her a steady look. A smile curved his mouth.

85

'I do not think I want to take a rest. I am enjoying myself far more than I had anticipated.'

Sarah's breath came a little faster. Her lips parted but she could not think how to reply to this. He moved closer. 'We shall soon start dancing again,' he said. 'We have done with the cotillion, and the quadrille. Now we shall waltz.' His eyes gleamed, 'I do look forward to that.'

Then a voice spoke from behind them. 'I must apologize for my late arrival, Keating. I was out of town this morning and only found my invitation when I arrived home just now. I have come in all haste to bear my part. I understand I am in time to join in the waltzing.'

'Ah yes, I recall Miss Gardiner said you were a member of Wellington's staff. They are all famous for their dancing ability.' Mr Keating's voice was not so cordial now.

Greg laughed. 'I do not know if I deserve the label of being a famous dancer. But it was a good way to spend evenings in camp when there was no prospect of military action.' He glanced away for a moment. Sarah thought she could see regret in his face, but the next second he was smiling at her.

'Might I ask you to be my partner?'

She would have loved to accept but Mr Keating had asked first. 'Perhaps after the first dance,' she said, 'or perhaps I should say the first attempt. You will find that Monsieur Lebrun is very exacting.'

When they took the floor shortly afterwards, Greg was partnering Lavinia. Sarah's eyes kept straying to them as she twirled around with John Keating. Sarah bit back a smile as she noticed that Lavinia was very shy and her cheeks were scarlet at having Greg's hand actually on her waist. Monsieur Lebrun's frequent instructions soon diverted her mind to her steps, however.

'Your sister is an apt pupil,' she told Mr Keating.

'I am very glad to learn that you were observing her,' he replied. 'I rather thought it was her partner who was holding your attention.'

Sarah raised her eyes quickly to his face. He gave her a rueful smile. The colour crept into her cheeks. Was she so easy to read?

She made some comment about Monsieur Lebrun's perfection-ism. Mr Keating allowed this diversion. But when the dance came to an end, he kissed her hand and gave her a keen look before turning to his sister.

'Well done,' he told her. 'Miss Davenport and I have been observing your progress. Now I feel you should try with Lucas. You need to feel confident with a variety of partners.' His eyes were on Sarah as he spoke.

Greg came over to Sarah. His eyes shone at her. 'I do like it when you do that,' he grinned.

'Do what? Oh!' she exclaimed, vexed. She was twisting her curls again.

Before she could put her hair to rights Monsieur Lebrun was tapping his cane for everyone to begin the next dance. Greg held out his hand and she placed hers in it. She felt his other hand lightly clasping her waist. Then the music began and the rhythm flowed through her. Greg danced perfectly and they twirled and stepped lightly into a dream of sound and motion. They stepped and spun in a wordless harmony until the music stopped – far too soon for Sarah, who now seemed to herself to be dropping back down to earth from a great height.

She met Greg's eyes. His were heavy-lidded, dreamy. He was standing so close his broad chest almost touched her when he drew a slow, deep breath. He leaned even closer. For a heart stop-ping second it seemed as if he was going to kiss her. And if he did, she knew she would kiss him back, in spite of the other people in the room.

Then one of the girls laughed and the sound shattered the spell. Greg turned his head as if realizing where he was. His eyes opened wide. He took a step back and made her a bow. Somewhere behind him, Sarah saw John Keating watching them. His face was serious. When he caught her eye, he gave her a long look.

CHAPTER FIFTEEN

Greg forced up his right arm to adjust his neckcloth. His hand accomplished the task but the protesting muscles in his upper arm made him grit his teeth. He surveyed himself in the mirror and nodded. It would do. His valet held up the coat of dark-blue cloth.

'There you are, Major,' he said, as he assisted Greg into it. His tone was reproachful. 'This one is nice and dry an' brushed again.' He smoothed away a wrinkle from across the shoulders. 'All this watchin' an' walkin' you be doin' in the rain, it makes life difficult, sir. Tryin' to get your coats dry and your boots to shine. . . .' He pursed his lips and cast a shrewd glance at his master. 'An' that arm of yours not right yet by a long way, as I can see.'

Greg frowned at him. 'You disrespectful old dog, Preston. Just stick to being a gentleman's gentleman. We are not in the army now.'

'No, sir,' agreed Preston regretfully. He sighed. 'Life is uncommon quiet at present, as one would expect in Bath. And yet. . . .' He gave his master a keen look as he held out a dazzlingly white handkerchief.

Greg pocketed it. 'You never know,' he said, 'we might just be about to have an adventure.'

Preston's leathery face brightened. 'I knew it! You can call on me, Major.'

'In the meanwhile,' said Greg, turning round in the open doorway, 'there is another set of wet clothes to attend to.' He laughed at the sudden change of expression on his valet's face and left the room.

He was still smiling as he ran down the stairs. Preston was a useful man in a fight. He had been Greg's loyal companion on a variety of missions during their years in Wellington's Army. It was due to Preston's efforts that Greg had escaped from more than one trap laid by the French during his many secret journeys between the two armies.

Greg stepped outside and looked up at the night sky. A few stars showed overhead. Thank heavens the rain had stopped at last. He set off down Great Pulteney Street at a brisk pace. From time to time he checked but could not see that anyone was following him. It was very quiet at this time. There were a few well-lit windows but the majority were in darkness, signalling that people were still out, making the most of Bath's pleasures.

He had spent the past two days getting soaked as he discreetly followed James Davenport and George Percival during their outings round the town. It was no surprise to discover that Lord Percival was lodging in the elegant Circus. A man of his arrogance obviously wished to impress all his acquaintance by demonstrating his wealth and taste for high living. Lord Davenport, on the other hand, was staying in Westgate Buildings. That indicated how short of funds he must be.

Greg sighed as he considered the probable situation. Here was another young man, dazzled by being admitted into the circle of a more experienced man of fashion, obviously wealthy and with a taste for rakish pleasures. No doubt young Davenport was in the throes of hero worship. And when he finally woke up to the truth, he would be penniless. Well, he would not be the first to suffer from such a sad lack of judgement.

Greg crossed the Pulteney Bridge and strode on towards the Parade Gardens. A cheerful noise came from the taverns, which were full tonight.

Greg paused for a moment, tempted to go in and join the crowd, forget his quest and simply enjoy a few tankards of ale. Then he shook his head and forced himself to continue on his way.

His own interest seemed now to be entwined with Sarah's

problems. At the thought of her he felt his heart beat faster. How foolish! How many times these last two years had he sworn not to allow any woman to get close to him again. It was simply that she was a lovely young woman and he was a red-blooded male. But she was also a damsel in distress and he was a gentleman . . . and it was clear that she was being pursued by Lord Percival against her wishes.

Of course he must do what he could to help her. How could he do otherwise, when her own brother seemed intent on pushing her into the arms of that devil Percival? Only today, Greg had seen James call at General Gardiner's lodgings twice and then emerge, obviously in a bad temper, to go and report back to Lord Percival at the Pump Room.

Greg thought of Sarah, struggling to keep her dignity as her brother persisted in pushing her at the man she disliked so intensely. And, now he thought about it, he remembered that in London, she had been avoiding Lord Percival – and then her sister had also tried to throw her at the fellow. God help any woman who fell into his clutches!

When he entered the Lower Rooms, Greg was pleased to hear music. As he had hoped, the tea interval was over and the dancing had begun again. The entrance was almost deserted. He began by sauntering into the ballroom. There he exchanged a word of greeting with one or two acquaintances of his father while he made a careful but unobtrusive survey of the people there. It was noticeably more crowded tonight than at any previous gathering. No doubt the poor weather had decided people to leave their country homes to seek the many pleasures of life in town.

By degrees he reached the card room. Here he wandered slowly around, watching the play at different tables but declining to join in. At last he spied his quarry and casually wandered up to watch the play at that table. When at last the game broke up, Greg moved forward and addressed James Davenport.

'A game of piquet with you, my lord?'

James looked up. He frowned blankly, then recognized Greg. His eyes widened. He gave a convulsive swallow. Greg was blocking the way out of the room. Reluctantly, James rose and moved to the small table that Greg was indicating. A waiter brought fresh cards and Greg ordered port. James cut the pack. Greg picked up the cards and fumbled a little as he dealt them.

'You will have to excuse me,' he drawled. 'Until I can get the muscles in my upper arm working properly again my hand is clumsy.'

'Of course,' mumbled James, flicking him a nervous look.

They played the first rubber. James began to relax, getting absorbed in the game. The second rubber eventually fell to Greg. James tossed off his drink and dealt the cards impatiently. He scowled at his hand, made a discard and drew another card from the stack. Greg went to put down his own card but dropped it.

'Sorry,' he said cheerfully, 'my hand is tired, I think. He laid down his remaining cards and refilled both their glasses, using his left hand. 'What a pity I cannot use my left hand to play,' he remarked.

James was looking angry at the interruption. He nodded but said nothing.

Greg looked at him over the rim of his glass. 'If you will be kind enough to allow me five minutes or so, I shall endeavour not to do that again.' He leaned forward. 'Cards are your great passion, are they not?'

James looked at him warily. 'Yes.'

'Did you ever play with my brother? I mean my older brother, Henry?'

James seemed to shrink in his chair. He shook his head. 'No. Never.'

'But you did know my brother?'

James looked away. He licked his lips. 'Not very well.'

Greg affected surprise. 'Yet you were both guests of Lord Hazelwick at his hunting lodge back in the spring.'

James nodded. His hands were gripping the edge of the table so hard that his knuckles showed white.

'So you must have had some degree of acquaintance. My brother was a very easy-going fellow.' He sighed, then brought his attention firmly back to James. 'And, at Hazelwick's party, I would wager cards were the usual evening's pastime?'

'Cards ... or billiards,' stammered James. His skin, always pasty, had gone grey.

'And which did my brother prefer?' Greg's eyes hardened as he watched the perspiration bead on James's forehead. His voice was quiet but insistent. 'You do appreciate that I want to know how my brother spent his last days.'

James's eyes bulged. He was staring at something behind Greg's shoulder. Greg heard his sharp intake of breath and turned round himself. Across the room Lord Percival was watching them. His left hand rested on his hip. There was a distinct menace in his gaze.

Greg turned back. 'Well?'

But James shook his head and rose. 'Excuse me ... have to abandon the game. ...' His bloodshot eyes did not meet Greg's as he scuttled away.

Greg finished his wine. He was not totally dissatisfied. James had shown that there was definitely some mystery concerning Henry's end. As for that damned George Percival. ... Then the helpless anger swept over him again at the loss of his brother – especially if his death had not been accidental. Greg stared grimly at his clenched fists. He would get to the bottom of it!

CHAPTER SIXTEEN

Sarah let herself out of the house quietly. It was early and she was almost the only person in the street. She took a deep breath of fresh air and lifted her face towards the pale blue of the sky above the rooftops. The last two days of rain had given her an excuse to stay at home. Now she was angry with herself for such cowardice. She was going to meet Lord Percival some time and she would make it plain that she was not interested in his attentions.

She walked up Milsom Street to the top and then turned left. In a couple of minutes she reached Queen Square, where she walked around, enjoying the quiet open space. Apart from a few servants there was nobody out at this early hour. She smiled as she reached the building that housed her old school. No doubt the same teachers were still giving the same instruction to a new generation of young ladies. She looked at the windows but could see no sign of activity there. Well, her schooldays had been happier times, when her parents were alive and life seemed more secure.

Now she had to face the fact that she was alone in the world. The tiny annuity left to her by her mother would not be enough for her to live on. The future seemed bleak. Sarah knew she could make Russeldene profitable again, given time, but only if James stopped taking every penny and more out of the estate. But far worse was the nagging fear of what would happen if, as James kept saying, Lord Percival had now won all his assets. If Russeldene passed into his hands, she would be cast adrift in the world.

She would face endless reproaches from Alice and James, both seeming to think that she should sacrifice herself and accept Lord Percival in order to save the family home. Sarah shuddered. Even for Russeldene, she could not endure to sell herself to someone she instinctively knew was a villain.

So she could not live with Alice – who did not want her anyway – and therefore she would have to earn her living in some way. Deep in weighing up the possibilities open to her, Sarah kept walking. She felt too much anxiety to stay still. She did not even notice that the streets were filling up with people and carts. Eventually she turned a corner and walked straight into a large woman with a basket of apples.

'I am so sorry,' she apologized, waking up to her surroundings. She had reached Union Passage. The main street ahead was busy with coaches and carts. Sarah shook her head to clear it. She decided to continue her walk around the abbey and towards the river. To do that, she would have to cross Cheap Street, but there was such a press of traffic she remained on the pavement for some time, waiting for a gap between the fast-moving coaches.

Then, as she gazed across the street through the constant procession of carriages and a mail coach going in the direction of Bristol, she saw a tall, familiar figure. It was Greg, waiting to cross from the other side. He had not seen her as he was looking for a gap in the traffic. It gave Sarah a chance to observe him. She dwelt admiringly on the clean lines of his face and his very masculine outline with his splendid height and broad shoulders. Yet she knew it was foolish to feed her longing.

She then saw that he was holding his right arm across his chest and rubbing it with his left hand. So his arm was still troubling him. Another coach rumbled past, then a tilbury appeared, driven by a very young gentleman and going much too fast for a city street. Just then a rough-looking man in a green jacket came racing from the archway. Sarah saw him run up behind Greg and push him hard into the path of the tilbury. Greg stumbled and fell forwards. Sarah pressed her hands to her cheeks in horror.

'Stop!' she screeched at the young driver. He sawed on the reins, pulling his horses further out into the road. But at the same instant Sarah watched helplessly as Greg struck against the side of the vehicle and then slumped down in a heap into the roadway.

Sarah darted across the street. She caught a glimpse of the rough man hurrying away down Cheap Street. Then she reached Greg and bent over him. There was blood trickling down the left side of his face. His eyes were open but not focusing. Sarah could hear the next coach approaching fast. She glanced up in a panic. To her relief, a couple of men were waving handkerchiefs and shouting to divert it away from the accident. Another man stepped forward and helped her haul Greg off the road. They pulled him back against the wall but he slid down sideways until his head was on the paving stones.

Sarah knelt beside him and raised him, laying his head against her bosom. She pulled out her handkerchief and pressed it against the cut on the side of his forehead. She was panting from her rush across the road and from the effort of heaving such a large man on to the pavement. How badly was he hurt? Suppose he. . . ? No, just at that moment she felt him give a sigh and move his head a bit.

'What. . . ? Where am I?' He turned his head and nestled closer against her. His eyes were closed now.

'Are you badly hurt?' she asked. Her voice came out as a squeak.

He seemed to think about it. 'Bruised my shoulder,' he managed.

'Which one?'

'Left side.'

He made no effort to move. Sarah looked down at the thick copper hair streaked with mud and blood. 'Can you sit up now?' she asked. 'I need to see to your injuries.'

He sighed again and struggled into a sitting position. Sarah hastily stood up and came round in front of him. She bit her lip. The left side of his face was already swollen, the skin scraped and raw. He winced as he tried to raise his left hand to feel his cheek. Then he struggled to get up but it seemed he had no strength in either arm. Helped by the same man who had pulled him out of the road, Greg finally scrambled upright. He leaned against the wall and looked at Sarah.

'Someone pushed me.' He frowned. 'Can't believe it!' He

paused for a moment. 'How do you come to be here, Sarah – I mean Miss Dav—?'

'Sarah will do,' she interrupted him. 'I was just taking a walk. I was waiting to cross the street and then I saw a man run at you and deliberately push you. He made off that way.' She pointed up Cheap Street. She looked back at Greg. He stared at her frowningly.

'You are bleeding,' she pointed out, 'and it is going to spoil your clothes.' She offered him the handkerchief. He took it and dabbed at his forehead. Then another thought occurred to him. 'Where is my hat?'

'It's ruined, gov',' said another voice. The squashed and muddy hat was handed forward by the crowd. Sarah looked at it and shuddered. That could have been him. That was what the man had tried to do.

The young man from the tilbury had by now pushed his way through the crowd to reach them. 'How bad is it?' he enquired. 'Awfully sorry, sir, but it just happened so fast. . . .'

'It was not your fault,' said Greg. He dabbed his face again and looked at the blood on the cloth. 'I will have to return home.'

'Happy to drive you,' said the young man, 'Insist! Least I can do.'

He indicated the way through the onlookers to his coach. While he turned his horses, Sarah stood beside Greg. She could see that he was far more shaken than he wanted to admit.

'I fear you are going to discover a number of other injuries when you have recovered from the first shock,' she said. 'How about your right arm.'

He grimaced and moved it gingerly. 'It has not helped, but I do not think I struck it against the carriage.' He gave her a keen look. 'Miss Da— Sarah, I mean – this was an accident.'

'It was not!' she began hotly, but he silenced her with a small gesture.

'No, please say nothing yet. I do not want to alarm my father.'

She nodded reluctantly. 'I understand. But if he sees you, he will be alarmed. Your face is swelling fast.'

'Well, I shall not attend the assemblies for a few days – wouldn't do to frighten the young ladies.' The good side of his mouth lifted in a grin. 'What a blessing you were here. You must call me Greg from now on,' he told her as he climbed stiffly into the tilbury. 'It is across the bridge,' he directed the young man. 'I am staying in Sydney Place.'

He looked down at Sarah. 'Thank you,' he said simply. His face was ghastly with a livid bruise growing rapidly and blood smeared across the left side. But his eyes glowed at her and Sarah felt her heartbeat quicken. She stood watching until the tilbury was quite out of sight.

Why did Greg not want to tell his father that someone had tried to injure him? Perhaps there was some quarrel between Greg and another man. The ghost of a smile touched her lips. Greg was big and powerfully built but in general he seemed to be the most pleasant-tempered of men. She knew he had a more dangerous side to him, which was natural, given his years in the army. But, on the whole, it was difficult to imagine him quarrelling. Could this be a case of mistaken identity? Somehow, she knew that it was not.

Now that he had gone and the urgency was over, she found she was shaking. It had been a lucky escape. Sarah stood there for a moment longer, then turned back up Cheap Street. Perhaps she could find the man in the green jacket. She walked briskly, looking in every doorway and side alley. There was no sign of him, however. She went as far as Westgate Buildings, but on her own she could not venture any further into this area full of alehouses and smoky, rubbish-laden dens. Already she was attracting attention. Ragged children were following her and men in the alehouses were whistling as she passed by.

Disappointed at her failure to find the villain, she retraced her steps to Union Passage. She was standing waiting to cross the street again in order to go back home when a hated voice addressed her.

'Why, Miss Davenport, what an age since I last saw you.' Lord Percival swept off his hat, revealing his pomaded curls. He was looking at her with those cold eyes that seemed to miss nothing. They narrowed now. 'Do you know that there is blood on your clothes?' His voice was sharp, almost eager, quite different from his usual languid drawl.

Sarah glanced down. There were two bloodstains on the bosom of her spencer, together with a smear of mud. 'It is not mine. I have been helping at the scene of an accident.'

He swung round, his beaky nose quivering as he surveyed the pavement. 'And where is the victim?'

'He has been conveyed home.'

'Was he . . . ah . . . very badly hurt?'

Sarah nodded. 'Quite badly shaken and bruised. And bleeding.'

He raised his brows. 'Bleeding, eh?' He nodded slowly. Then he returned his attention to her. 'How is it that he has gone home and left you here to fend for yourself?'

She gave a short laugh. 'I could not help him any further. There is nothing amiss with me beyond the stain on my wrap. Excuse me, sir, I must return home and change.' She saw a gap in the traffic and set off quickly across the street. 'Good day to you,' she called over her shoulder. To her relief he did not follow her. She was able to slip inside and up to her room before anybody saw her. She decided not to mention the 'accident' until Greg himself spoke of it.

Later that afternoon, when the two girls were sitting sewing and talking by the window in the sitting-room, they heard someone knock on the front door. Then a maid came in with a small packet.

'For you, miss,' She handed the package to Sarah, who took it, mystified.

Inside she found six exquisite lawn handkerchiefs. A card fell out. She picked it up and saw Greg's name. On the back he had scrawled, 'With my thanks for your help'.

'Handkerchiefs? From Greg?' Lizzie stared at Sarah's reddening cheeks. 'Whatever is going on?'

CHAPTER SEVENTEEN

'Ah, Miss Davenport. How delightful to find you – and not engaged to dance at present. What a crowd there is tonight. May I join you?' The words were scarcely out of his mouth when Lord Percival sat down beside her. He surveyed her with a look of approval, his eyes going from the top of her head, dwelling a moment on her face, her mouth and the curve of her neck, before dropping to linger on her white bosom. Sarah's flesh was tingling with dislike at this inspection. His gaze took in her pink muslin gown, travelled down to her feet, then back to her face.

She forced herself to meet his eyes, her own sparkling with anger. He was looking at her hungrily. 'Once again you are undoubtedly the loveliest lady here tonight.'

Sarah forced a little laugh. 'I fear you cannot have looked very far, sir.'

'Oh, no, you mistake.' He gave a bray of laughter. 'Believe me, ma'am, I am a connoisseur.' He raised his quizzing glass and inspected the couples on the floor. He turned back to her with a satisfied smirk. 'Indeed, you outshine them all.'

Sarah hated exaggerated compliments, but she decided to say nothing. It seemed he wanted always to be right, so he would continue to argue. She looked up and saw James, watching her from the other side of the ballroom. He gave her a tiny nod. Mrs Keating was close by but she was busy discussing something in an undertone with another chaperon.

Sarah sat very straight. She plied her fan, looking at the dancers and willing Lord Percival to go away. She became aware that he was saying something. She glanced at him. 'I beg your pardon?'

He leaned forward. 'Did you feel no ill effects after helping your injured friend this morning?'

'Oh,' she exclaimed, 'I had almost forgotten about it – except of course, I do hope the gentleman is not too badly hurt.'

'Indeed,' he said with a smirk. 'That would be unfortunate for him.' His voice was a purr.

How could he take such pleasure in someone being injured? Sarah looked at his cold eyes and a chill went down her spine, like an icy trickle of water. Then she realized just what he had said.

'Why did you call the injured gentleman my friend, sir?'

'I did not suppose you would go to so much trouble for a stranger.'

'Of course – I would help anyone in such a dangerous situation,' she exclaimed hotly.

He raised his brows in disbelief.

'Surely you would do the same?' she protested, but someone was calling his name and he turned his head away.

Another dandified gentleman strolled up to them. This person was indeed something out of the ordinary. The shoulders of his wasp-waisted jacket were obviously padded to emphasize his hourglass figure. His coat tails were very long and his pantaloons fitted him so tightly she thought he could not dare to sit down. His shirt collar was so high it reached his cheeks and his cravat was extremely intricate and large. He looked to be of a similar age to Lord Percival. He had a dissipated air, but lacked that vicious undertone that she was aware of in his friend.

'George, you dog,' drawled the newcomer as he reached them, 'trust you to find the prettiest gal in the room and monopolize her. Pray introduce me.'

'I was before you, Monty,' replied Lord Percival. His tone was not cordial.

The other gentleman gave a shrill laugh. 'Maybe, maybe, but if you will not, I shall just find someone else to do the job.' He pulled out his quizzing glass and stood looking at Sarah, or more precisely, at her bosom, she noticed with indignation.

'Miss Davenport, may I name my old friend, Lord Montallan,' snapped Lord Percival.

'Oh, by Jove,' said the dandy, letting his quizzing glass fall, 'you are the sister of young James Davenport. Fancy that!'

Sarah inclined her head slightly. She was trying to stifle a giggle at the man's appalling lisp and his foppish air. The music stopped before he had finished his examination of her figure. Shortly afterwards, Lizzie arrived with Miss Keating and her brother. Lizzie greeted Lord Percival with a warm smile. It was obvious that she had already met Lord Montallan. Sarah decided she must have another word with Lizzie about suitable new friends. Perhaps they did need a chaperon after all.

After a quick look at these two dandies, John Keating bowed and escorted his sister away. Sarah wished that she could do the same. The next dance was announced. Suddenly, James appeared and was asking Lizzie to be his partner. Sarah faced the inevitable and allowed Lord Percival to lead her into the same set. Again she struggled with her revulsion at taking his hand in the moves of the dance, but she tried to keep her expression neutral. He was watching her keenly. She willed herself to show no emotion. That became more and more difficult as he made it plain he was inspecting her very thoroughly. Face, figure and dress, all were subjected to his keen scrutiny. It made her burn with frustrated anger.

In her turn, she examined him. She would be fair and admit all his good points – if she could find them. His fair hair was cut and curled into the windswept style. It was too florid for her taste, she preferred short, thick copper-coloured hair, brushed back neatly. His shirt was shining white but, again, his cravat was tied in a complicated way and his waistcoat was rather too bright. The man was a dandy. That was his choice, of course, but she did resent the amount of money he must have spent to appear in such expensive glory. Money he had won from James. She remembered how he had encouraged James to drink, while keeping sober himself. It brought a bitter taste to her mouth.

'Your brother seems very taken with Miss Gardiner,' he remarked, breaking the long silence.

Sarah glanced at them. 'We have been friends since our school-days,' she said. 'James used to consider us both to be a nuisance.'

He gave a snort of laughter. 'You certainly could not say that now.'

She stifled a sigh. James was in no position to make up to any girl. He needed to bring some order into his life and then to restore Russeldene.

The following morning, General Gardiner kept giving Sarah puzzled glances when he thought she was not looking. He shook his head and gave the matter up when his sedan chair arrived to convey him to the Pump Room.

He had not been gone long when Lizzie came into the room with her arms full of sewing materials. She spread some new ribbons out on the table, ready to trim her blue muslin dress. She looked up from the task of smoothing out the ribbon. 'Why have you braided your hair so severely? It makes you look like a governess.' She pinned a length of ribbon to the neckline of the dress, adding, 'And that grey gown is dowdy.'

Sarah was pleased. 'Just what I intended,' She peeped at her reflection in the mirror over the fireplace. No dandy would look twice at such an unfashionable creature. Or so she hoped.

'Now what are you planning?' Lizzie looked at her suspiciously. 'Are you disturbed by Lord Montallan? I wager there is no harm in him.'

'I would not be too certain of that. And most definitely, we must steer clear of Lord Percival.'

Lizzie pushed her sewing aside and clasped her hands together on the table. 'Sarah, you keep giving me dark hints. Please tell me why you dislike the poor man so much. I find him handsome and charming, that is all.'

Sarah clutched at her head in dismay. 'Can you not see how dissipated he is? There are many dark stories about his past life. It can do us no good to be in his company. He is a friend of my brother's, but I try my best to avoid him.' She sighed. 'I do wonder if we ought to engage a chaperon: we are so unprotected.'

'We are managing well enough so far,' retorted Lizzie, 'and we certainly do not want Aunt Augusta and her smelly pug to come here. Even if Uncle Charlie spends his days at the Pump Room, we can always rely on Greg to escort us.'

Sarah made no comment. She wondered if Greg was still waiting for his bruised face to heal and what he had told his father.

CHAPTER EIGHTEEN

Greg examined his face in his bedroom mirror. He grimaced at the ugly bruises and cautiously felt his cheekbone. The flesh was tender but definitely less swollen. The grazes were healing as well. Perhaps he could go for a drive. His horses needed the exercise and he wanted a change of scene. He felt more cheerful at this prospect and suddenly knew he was hungry. The smell of fresh coffee wafted up the stairs and further brightened his mood.

He walked into the dining-room and stopped short in surprise. Richard was sitting there, devouring a large plateful of ham and eggs. Greg raised his brows enquiringly. Richard grinned his crooked grin and stood up to shake hands.

'Came on the night stage,' he said. 'Nothing like it for giving a man an appetite.' He picked up his knife and fork again as if he had not a minute to lose. Busy slicing up another generous mouthful, he glanced up. 'What *have* you done to your face?'

Greg poured coffee and selected a more modest helping of food for himself. 'Accident,' he said briefly. He cast an amused glance at lanky Richard's heaped plate. 'I am surprised Lord Liverpool could spare you from your duties.'

Richard disposed of a mouthful of ham and mustard. 'Ah, but I am here in the performance of said duties. He has charged me with a message for you. And I have a letter from Theo as well.'

In the act of swallowing some hot coffee, Greg choked. 'Well, little brother, do not keep me waiting,' he gasped, when he could speak again.

Richard left the table. He fumbled in a leather satchel thrown on to a chair and produced a sealed letter. Greg seized it.

'At last,' he muttered, breaking open the seal. The note was short.

I am at Weston Parcombe for the moment and beg you to do me the honour of spending a couple of days here at your earliest convenience. T.W.

Greg's breakfast was forgotten as he pondered the meaning of this bland message. Whatever Theo wanted to tell him, it was too important to commit to paper. His face took on the hard look that had disturbed Sarah. Richard glanced at him thoughtfully, but knew better than to interrupt his brother in that mood.

At last Greg recollected himself, downed his coffee and turned an enquiring gaze on Richard. He indicated the letter. 'What do you know about this?'

Richard shook his head. 'Nothing. Assure you. Theo gave it to me yesterday, just after Lord Liverpool had informed me I might come to Bath to see how you are doing.' He got up to refill his plate. 'He simply charged me to say he hopes you are recovering well. I expect he has a mission for you as soon as you are fit. Of course, he does not know about your latest accident.' He set his plate down and added, 'Can I get you something else?'

Greg glanced at the cold food on his plate. He pushed it aside. 'Some more coffee, if you please.' He looked at his brother and grinned. 'You could do with a shave.'

The stubble rasped as Richard rubbed his chin. 'By and by.' He nodded towards the letter, 'I hope I have not brought bad news?'

'Not at all. But it means I shall be off to see Theo today. I shall be away overnight. Which means I shall have to entrust you with a few jobs.'

Richard looked horrified. 'Do I have to go and drink the waters with Father?'

Greg chuckled. 'Father has a very robust opinion about the waters. But he goes to the Pump Room to meet a wide circle of friends. It has done a lot to raise his spirits. You will also find

General Gardiner and Lizzie in Bath, as well as her friend, Sarah Davenport.'

'Now that sounds more interesting.' But Richard could not stifle a huge yawn. 'If you do not need me now, I think I will turn in for a couple of hours.'

Greg nodded. 'I shall see you tomorrow evening.' With a wave of his hand, Richard left the room. Almost at once Greg heard voices on the stairs. Shortly after that Sir Thomas came into the room. Greg stood up.

'Here's a surprise,' exclaimed Sir Thomas.

'But a pleasant one, sir. And Richard has brought me an invitation from Theo, who is at his home in Oxfordshire. It is just what I want. A curricle ride, fresh air and a good chinwag at the end of it. And by the time I return, these bruises will have faded.'

Sir Thomas looked from under his brows. 'Have a care, my boy. No more accidents, if you please.'

'Indeed, sir. I shall have Preston with me, of course.'

It was mid afternoon when Greg bowled up the drive at Weston Parcombe. The butler informed him that Theo was to be found at the Dower House, a short distance further on. Greg smiled as he considered the difference in his friend's life since his marriage. Once the black sheep of the family, now Theo was the valued older son, learning how to manage the family estate. Just as he himself was now going to do, he realized with mixed feelings.

As he drove up to the front door of the mellow old house, Theo and Kitty appeared in the entrance to greet him. Grinning from ear to ear, Greg bounded up the steps to a warm welcome from both of them. They drew him inside and, laughing and talking, took him into the pleasant sitting-room.

'How did you manage to get another black eye?' Kitty asked him. 'When last I saw you in London, you had a black eye then as well.'

Greg nodded as he recalled the evening at the opera and then being hit round the head by a spy. 'Either I am prone to suffer accidents or I am constantly being mistaken for someone else,' he joked. 'I apologize, Kitty, for not looking my best.' He looked from her to Theo. 'But I must say how radiant you both look. It is a great pleasure to see it.'

'Oh, you have not seen the best yet,' smiled Theo. He beckoned forward the nurse who had just entered the room and took the little bundle from her arms. He advanced towards Greg and held the infant out to him. Greg backed away a step, his expression alarmed.

'No, really, old fellow, never done this in my life. . . .' Gingerly he received the baby and held him at arm's length.

'He will not break,' said Theo, grinning. Master Arthur Weston considered Greg solemnly from large blue eyes. Greg looked down in silence at the tiny human being in his arms. He drew the baby closer and smiled at him.

'That is better,' encouraged Kitty. 'You look very well like that.'

Greg gave her a glance of awe. 'Miraculous,' he murmured.

She held out her arms to take her son. 'I know you must be anxious to exchange all your news with Theo, so we will leave you in peace now.'

In the library, they settled in armchairs one each side of the fire. Theo leaned forward. 'Now, old man, what is the true story of this accident?'

Greg told him about his attempt to question James Davenport and of that young man's fear of Lord Percival.

'So you are being warned off. . . .' Theo struck his fist against the arm of his chair. 'It ties in with what I have discovered about the man.'

Now it was Greg's turn to lean forward attentively. He listened to Theo's account with painful eagerness.

'Hazelwick was most reluctant to discuss the matter, but I told him I had also spoken with a couple of the other men who were in that hunting party. He only had to confirm what I already knew.'

Greg nodded and Theo went on, 'It appears Henry did spend his evenings in the bookroom playing cards with George Percival. However, from Percival's foul temper, Hazelwick assumed he had been the loser and was trying to win his money back. He said that James Davenport would know; he was always to be found near

107

George. Obviously, Hazelwick feels badly about such a tragic accident to his friend, but he seems to have no suspicion of anything
underhand.'

Greg considered this news. 'Very well. Let us suppose that
Henry won, rather than lost, a considerable sum of money. But is
it . . . can it be' – he swallowed, then forced himself to continue –
'can it be connected to his death?'

They looked at each other. 'Everyone I asked said the same
thing,' said Theo. 'They were all spread out following a stag. A
few shots were fired. Henry was in the act of leaping a fence when
one gun went off. His horse panicked and Henry fell and broke
his neck.'

'Oh God!' Greg dashed a hand through his hair. There was a
long silence. Theo rose and poured out brandy. He set a glass
down by Greg's side and resumed his own seat.

Eventually, Greg said, 'Each time I see George Percival, he
strikes me as being wary. He is definitely hiding something, so I
have to suspect the worst.' His face was grimmer than Theo had
ever seen it.

'I am inclined to agree,' replied the latter, after a short interval.
'But I have more to tell you. Lord Liverpool sent your brother to
Bath so that we could get you here and give you this information.
I am afraid that, fully recovered or not, you are now officially on
a mission.'

Greg took a large sip of brandy and nodded. 'Fire away.'

'It is generally known that George Percival buys the finest
clothes and horses and is altogether a very expensive dandy. He
frequents some of the highest playing gaming hells in London. He
has both lost and won enormous sums of money and it is noted
that he befriends young men of wealth and brings them to his
gaming clubs, where they mostly lose their money to him.

At least two wealthy women have disappeared from Society
after their names were linked to his – and there are rumours of
duels with their husbands. One source says Percival has twice
killed his man.'

Greg tossed off the rest of his brandy and set the glass down. 'I
assume this information is leading up to some other matter. . . ?'

'Of course,' nodded Theo, 'but it shows the man's character and why he might be desperate if he lost money. Now, this is the matter that concerns you. For a number of years, the government has been losing huge sums of gold bullion and other valuable goods. This happens when it arrives by ship at certain ports. Someone is selling information about the movements of such cargo – and with the war continuing, it is becoming critical to stop this loss of revenue. You and I both know that Wellington is careful of every penny, but it costs a fortune to keep the army going.' He scowled very much in his old style. 'The money that would help him win the war is being lost before it even reaches government coffers.'

'So' – Greg stared frowningly at Theo – 'are you saying that George Percival is involved in stealing government funds?'

Theo sighed. 'From our enquiries he is definitely a suspect. He is friendly with two Cabinet ministers, one of whom is Lord Dalbeagh – and you know how *he* hates Wellington. It is certain that George Percival is fearfully extravagant but he is never without funds. He has much more money than his estates can produce. And his lifestyle bears witness to his ruthless streak. We have been investigating him – as well as others – but we are now satisfied that he is the most likely one.' He paused and savoured his brandy.

Greg picked up his own glass. 'But just how does he carry this piracy off? It must require a lot of men to steal sacks of bullion and then store them secretly.'

Theo went to stoke up the fire. When the new log started to blaze, he straightened up and brought the brandy decanter over to refill both their glasses. 'We have placed an agent in the village of Seldon, not far from Bath, on the Bristol road. His name is Josiah Whitby and you will find him at the Three Bells hostelry. There is a convoy of ships due to arrive from the Americas laden with tobacco and gold.' He raised his brows. 'If George Percival is our man, I feel sure we will see him attempt to get his share from such a tempting cargo.'

'The fact that Percival is currently in Bath does make him look suspicious.' Greg rubbed his chin thoughtfully. 'So my job is to get the evidence.' He smiled. 'Preston will be delighted to have some action.'

They sat in silence as the light outside faded. The log hissed and shifted, sending out sparks. The room was warm, the brandy good. Greg felt himself relax as he had not done since his return from Spain. Better than anyone, Theo understood what these changes in his life meant.

But his oldest friend also understood another side of Greg's character.

'Tell me,' said Theo, his blue eyes glinting in the firelight, 'is James Davenport's sister in Bath?'

For a long time Greg remained silent. His face was unreadable in the dim light. At last his lips twisted in a wry smile. 'Sarah Davenport is a charming young lady and I like her very well,' he said carefully. 'But I am utterly determined to solve the mystery of Henry's debt and his accident before I get involved in any other kind of . . . er . . . relationship.'

CHAPTER NINETEEN

'Surely that is enough for the first session,' panted Richard. He wiped an arm across his sweating forehead and looked in appeal at his older brother. 'We have been here for well over an hour.'

'Come on, one last bout.' Greg took up the *en garde* position and flicked his foil menacingly in front of Richard. They fenced energetically for a few minutes until Richard parried a thrust from his brother and saw Greg wince.

'That really is it!' he declared, lowering his blade. 'In any case, I cannot wait any longer to pay my respects to Miss Gardiner.'

Greg raised his eyebrows. 'Oho. Taken a fancy to Lizzie, have you? Well, little brother, I hope you have the energy to keep up with her.'

'I shall be very glad to dance with her at the assemblies, if that is what you mean.' Richard towelled his face vigorously. 'Who is the other young lady you mentioned?'

'Her old schoolfriend, Sarah Davenport.'

'Is she the blonde ice maiden we met at the ball in London?'

'*Ice maiden* . . .' spluttered Greg.

Richard gave his lopsided grin. 'You have made her thaw, have you?' He shook his head. 'Wish I knew how you do it, Brother. I always get treated like a badly behaved puppy.'

'That is because you are one.' Greg dodged his brother's mock punch and laughed. He realized it was the first time he had laughed with sheer enjoyment in a long while. Richard's easy temper was doing him good. Even though he had enjoyed his short visit to Theo and Kitty, it had not been without its darker side. He snatched the towel from Richard and wiped his own face. Yes, he also was anxious to see the girls again. Who knew what they had been up to since he had had his 'accident'?

The brothers were in luck. Both girls were at home and very glad to put aside their sewing when they heard Greg and Richard announced.

'What a welcome surprise,' exclaimed Lizzie, jumping up. 'And Mr Richard as well. You must stay for tea.' She inspected Greg's face. 'Oh, my goodness! You certainly did bruise yourself.'

Greg brushed her concern aside. 'It is not so bad, Lizzie. Just a foolish accident.' He was looking beyond her to where Sarah stood quietly by the window. 'Excuse me,' he smiled, 'I must say my thanks to my rescuer.'

He left Richard to talk to Lizzie and turned towards Sarah with a gleam in his eyes. At once he noticed something different about her. As he came close, he took in the dull frock and the hair scraped back severely. However, nothing could disguise that translucent skin or the lovely oval of her face. She watched him come towards her, and in response to his smile her lips curved and her eyes sparkled.

Greg took her hand and pressed a kiss onto it. 'I have not yet told you how very grateful I am for the help you gave me,' he murmured. 'It could have been a lot worse if you had not acted so promptly.'

A delicate rose coloured her cheeks. 'I wish I could have done more,' she said, looking at his bruises, 'I am happy to see that you are so well recovered. But have you wondered why such a thing should happen to you?'

He glanced round. Richard and Lizzie were chatting happily and most certainly not listening. Even so. . . .

'Perhaps we could discuss this at a more convenient time?'

He received a very sharp look from those jewel green eyes. She nodded. 'Of course.' They sat down and, after a slight hesitation, Sarah gave him a shy smile, 'I must thank you for the gift you sent.'

'Please do not mention it.' Greg waved his hand and stopped in mid gesture. He gave a sharp intake of breath at the stab of pain.

The muscles in his arm were protesting at the violent exercise they had endured that day. He knew that Sarah had heard him but before she could say anything, Lizzie called across.

'Greg, your brother says you have started strengthening your arm. Does that mean it is completely healed now?'

'As good as ever,' he said stoutly, 'just a little more exercise needed to get the muscles back in practice.'

'Yes, but does that mean you are ready to drive us to Wells?' persisted Lizzie.

Greg shook his head in mock despair. 'You never give up, do you? Grant me a little longer. You know very well that we need to make a big party and persuade someone to act as chaperon.' He turned back to Sarah. He inspected her drab clothes and severe hairstyle. She lifted her chin and met his gaze gravely. Greg thought he could guess what she was trying to achieve. She was a determined fighter and he admired her spirit. He hoped his own mission would be the means to solve Sarah's problems as well. If he could catch Lord Percival red-handed in his criminal activities she would never have to see the villain again.

Somehow he had clenched his fists and all his muscles were tense as if for a fight. He made himself lean back in the chair and gave Sarah a conspiratorial smile. 'Have you been very busy over these last few days?'

She understood what he was asking. Her finger began to tease out a strand of hair and wind it as she answered. 'I have not been out much. There has been plenty to occupy me here. However, we went to the last assembly. It was quite a squeeze; suddenly everyone is arriving in Bath.'

'Mostly old people,' chipped in Lizzie with a sigh. She poured out the tea and brought a cup to Greg. 'Lord Percival was there. He introduced us to a newly arrived friend of his. You never saw such a quiz of a man . . . so wasp-waisted . . . such a high collar to his jacket that he could scarcely move his head!'

'I would lay a monkey that is Lord Montallan,' said Richard. He grinned as both girls burst out laughing and nodded agreement. 'He is well known at all the London balls. Fancies himself on the dance floor. We shall have to cut him out at the next assembly, hey, Greg?'

'Perhaps Lizzie is secretly looking forward to dancing with her new acquaintance.' Greg gave her that teasing look that Sarah had noticed so often. At once Lizzie protested and they both laughed. Greg downed his tea then rose to take leave. Everything seemed well with Sarah and Lizzie for the moment.

Now he was anxious to talk to Preston. He had sent his valet in disguise to spy out the mysterious Josiah Whitby at the Three Bells Inn at Seldon. It was not until he was nearly home again that he recalled how cool Sarah had been when he said goodbye. Perhaps Richard's name for her was appropriate. And yet he could have sworn she had been truly pleased to see him when he first arrived at the house.

CHAPTER TWENTY

When the two brothers had bowed themselves out, Sarah took up her sewing again. She sat and stared at it absently as she thought about the conversation. Greg had seemed really pleased to sit and talk to her but then, without being aware of it, he had shown how warmly attached he was to Lizzie. Sarah could not mistake the evidence of her own eyes. In addition, Lizzie was comfortable in his company and the general already seemed to consider him a member of the family.

She stabbed her needle into the cuff she was hemming and pricked her finger. That woke her up to her surroundings. Lizzie was devouring a thick novel, curled up in a huge armchair. The teacups were still dotted around on the side tables, where their guests had left them. Sarah knew she was being foolish but she went and picked up Greg's cup. It rattled in its saucer as she carried it over to the tray. Lizzie stirred.

'Are you tired of your needlework?' she asked. 'Sorry I am poor company but I have reached a really exciting part of my story.' She plunged back into her reading. Sarah wandered over to the window. She put up a hand to her hair and realized she had made several ringlets down one side. She hastened over to the mirror and bit her lip at her image with one side so severe and the other all tendrils and curls. She must cure herself of this silly habit!

She quickly smoothed her hair back again and surveyed herself once more. The quakerish image looked back at her gravely. Had it had the desired effect on the brothers? Sarah rather thought so. Richard had hardly spoken to her and she had caught Greg's eyes on her grey gown more than once. If only it would have the same sobering effect on Lord Percival. Perhaps she should blacken her teeth with soot from the fireplace. . . .

The following day was sunny and the girls ventured into the park for a refreshing walk after dawdling along Milsom Street window shopping. Lizzie was complaining about Sarah's appearance.

'Just what is your scheme?' she demanded. 'You have even taken the trimming off your bonnet. And that grey dress is giving me the dismals!'

Sarah nodded. 'That is just what I wanted to hear. I wish to pass unnoticed.'

'What ... you mean like a governess, or a companion? But why?' Lizzie's voice rose to a squeak of frustration.

'Hmm,' Sarah looked at her thoughtfully. 'That gives me another idea. Perhaps I could find a pair of spectacles.'

Lizzie sank down on a bench. She shook her head angrily. 'You are the strangest creature. You are deceiving yourself if you think that any of this disguises your good looks.'

'Oh, I think it does – at least, it sends a message that I am not very interesting.'

'I assure you that you are wrong,' snapped Lizzie. 'Come, let us put it to the test.' She slipped an arm through Sarah's and started marching her firmly towards the Pump Room. 'You will see,' she said, rather breathless from the rapid walk, 'you will not pass unnoticed.'

They reached the Abbey Churchyard and were making for the entrance to the Pump Room when James came hurrying up to them. He scarcely had time for a civil greeting.

'Need to speak to you,' he told his sister, 'in private.'

'I shall see you inside then,' Lizzie walked on.

Sarah examined her brother. He looked even more haggard and a little untidy. His eyes were heavy and his mouth grim. He put a hand under her elbow and steered her towards the abbey, out of the way of the main flow of people.

'Has something happened to Alice?' asked Sarah, alarmed at this manoeuvre.

James shook his head. He grimaced, shot her a glance then looked away. 'Fact is, I . . . er . . . I lost a deal of money to George last night. Now he really could claim pretty well everything I own.'

Sarah felt the blood drain from her face. 'D-do you mean Russeldene as well. . . ?' she faltered.

He shifted uneasily and nodded.

'How could you?' Her voice was like a whip and he flinched at the anger in it. 'Do you have *no* control over yourself? How do you think so much money is to be found? Why do you waste your time in such a way?' A tear ran unheeded down her cheek.

'For the Lord's sake, do not cry here,' muttered James. 'And no need to behave like a shrew. George is top of the trees, plays high, y'know.' He gave his irritable shrug. 'What is a fellow to do when he invites you to play?'

'When he sets out to fleece you, more like!' she hissed. 'Now he has taken all your worldly goods, perhaps he will drop you. When he has the keys to our home, no doubt!' Two great tears rolled down her cheeks. Her stomach churned with the fear of what would happen to them now, cast adrift in the world.

James shifted again. 'Do not look so stricken,' he managed to say. 'Know for a fact that George is mighty taken with you. Won't demand payment if you will entertain the idea of letting him court you – with a view to marriage,' he added hastily.

Her green eyes flashed. The look she gave him made James take a step back. 'Lizzie likes him well enough,' he protested feebly.

'Can you not see that he is a villain? He has robbed you. Do not mix me up in your schemes. I would rather starve than entertain such a grotesque idea.' She turned on her heel and walked blindly away from him.

'Miss Davenport? Sarah, whatever is wrong?' A hand touched her arm.

She dashed away the tears and darted a glance upwards. It was Greg standing in front of her. At that moment, Sarah could not

117

have uttered a word. She was holding back heavy sobs of anger and despair at the way her whole life had crumbled. She shook her head. The next moment a handkerchief was thrust into her hand.

'Come,' said Greg, his voice gentle, 'let us walk down towards the river. You can sit in the Parade Gardens and recover your composure. Perhaps this time I can be of more help.'

She let him guide her, too preoccupied with the storm of feelings raging inside her to give any attention to the way they went. Just putting one foot in front of the other was hard enough. Images of Russeldene and the people there came into her head. The lump in her throat was almost choking her. She was conscious of Greg by her side, his arm firmly supporting her. He seemed like the only solid and secure thing left to her.

At length she felt herself being pressed gently down on to a seat. She looked around and saw she was on a park bench. There were bushes on both sides. Sarah wiped her wet cheeks and heaved a sigh. She attempted a smile.

'Once again you have come to my rescue, Major Thatcham.'

'Not Major any longer, alas,' he replied, 'but that is of no importance. And, by the way, I thought we agreed to use our given names.' He sat down beside her, leaned his elbow on his knee and examined her face. Sarah looked back steadily, breathless at the closeness of those wonderful amber eyes. His lean face was so open and honest, she felt a rush of longing to lean her head against his broad shoulder and shelter from her problems. Then she remembered Lizzie and her heart contracted again. She raised her chin.

Greg swept off his hat and ran a hand through his coppery hair. His jaw clenched. He frowned, looked at Sarah from under his brows then, with a little difficulty, he said, 'This is perhaps not my affair, but I cannot see you reduced to this state and not ask what the problem is? Please tell me how I may be of service to you.'

Sarah plucked at her skirt. It was some time before she could answer. She cleared her throat. 'I am most grateful for your kind help. I always seem to meet you at a . . . a difficult moment in my life.'

Greg shifted his long legs. He took her hand. It was quite swallowed up in his large one. 'No young lady should have to be so very distressed. It makes me imagine all kinds of dreadful things.'

She shot him a scared look and knew her cheeks were going red. She could not explain the problem without disgracing her brother. 'It is not so bad,' she murmured, sliding her hand out of his. 'I was angry as well as upset.' She gave her eyes a final wipe. 'You must think I am nothing but a watering pot.'

'Certainly not,' he replied promptly. 'If you are in need of help that I can give you, you have only to say the word.'

She gazed at his face, read in it his kind concern and wished with all her heart that she could lean on his strength. Since her father's death there was nobody in her own family who paid any attention to her concerns. She suppressed a sigh and nodded, forcing her lips into a smile. 'You are very good.'

She rose and shook out her grey skirts. The time for sentiment was over. She would not give in to such weakness again. She was going to make it clear to Lord Percival that his suit was unacceptable. Greg again offered his arm and they set off back towards the Abbey churchyard.

'Do you know,' he said, escorting her safely across the road, 'I did expect you to twist a few curls.'

She put up a hand to her cheek. 'I must stop that foolish habit.' But she smiled and he smiled back, obviously pleased to have diverted her thoughts.

They went up the step and into the Pump Room. James was lounging in the wide entrance hall. When he saw them, he gave a start and moved forward. Sarah frowned at him to keep his distance.

She glanced at Greg and saw that hard expression on his face as he spotted her brother. He placed his other hand over hers, still tucked in his arm and kept walking through into the crowded Pump Room.

'No doubt we shall find Lizzie here,' he remarked in a bland tone. 'Ah, there is my brother as well.' He glanced down with a faint smile. 'A cheerful group of friends to give your thoughts a new direction.'

Sarah drew a shuddering breath and nodded. She had seen Lord Percival. He was standing very erect, his hand on his hip, eyes narrowed as he watched Greg and Sarah advance into the room.

CHAPTER TWENTY-ONE

Greg felt Sarah's arm stiffen as she looked at Lord Percival. Damn that arrogant swine, glaring at them! Why was he standing in a pose suggestive of drawing a sword? Greg was now certain that Sarah's distress had a lot to do with this man. And her brother seemed to be adding to her problems. He felt an instinctive urge to protect her, so delicate and lovely a creature, from the web in which she was caught.

He kept his grip on her hand and steered her towards Lizzie. As usual this lively young lady had managed to assemble a group of friends around herself. Greg's mouth quirked as he saw his brother by her side. Lizzie was introducing Richard to everyone. Greg winked at his brother and was rewarded with the lopsided grin. Richard's eyes moved to survey Greg's companion. His eyebrows lifted, but he made no comment, merely exchanging a bow.

'I have discovered that your brother is a notable whip,' began Lizzie, fixing Greg with her most appealing smile.

'Did he tell you so?' Greg raised one eyebrow.

Richard grinned. 'Don't let me down, Brother. I have promised to drive her to Wells.'

Greg stared at both of them forbiddingly. 'As I said, Lizzie, you are a minx. We will go to Wells when I can organize a proper party for the journey. Please be a little patient.' He waited until she nodded, then turned to Sarah. 'I take it you would join the party?'

'Certainly,' she said in her usual voice. 'I should very much like to see the cathedral.' Greg noticed the shadows under her eyes.

Again he felt the urge to smash his fist into Lord Percival's hard, sneering face. The man was sauntering past, in company with a fellow dressed in an extremely tight-waisted jacket and with shirt points touching his cheeks. This had to be the Lord Montallan the others had been laughing about.

Lord Percival caught Greg's eye and then he stared pointedly at the bruises still so obvious on Greg's face. He curled his lip and moved away. Greg's various aches all throbbed as he remembered the moment he had been hurled against the tilbury. Was the man threatening him? He glanced round at Sarah but she had gone.

Then he saw her with her brother. James had a hand on her back, pushing her towards Lord Percival. Greg manoeuvred himself so that while he talked to the others in the group he could see what would happen. He saw Lord Percival take Sarah's hand and bow deeply over it. He held on to it for far too long. Greg clenched his teeth.

'Did you hear what I said?' asked Lizzie, breaking in on his concentration.

'Mmm? Er . . . yes,' he answered vaguely. Now the blackguard had pulled her arm through his and was strolling round the vast room with her by his side.

'. . . so that is agreed,' Lizzie's voice broke in again. 'Perhaps we should go this afternoon. The weather here is so unsettled, if we wait for tomorrow it may rain. . . .'

Greg grunted and gave a nod. He shifted to keep an eye on Sarah but the crowd now hid her from sight. He gave an impatient sigh and looked down at Lizzie. She eyed him severely. 'You were not listening,' she told him, 'but it is no matter. You said yes.'

'Did I?' He looked at his brother in appeal.

Richard laughed. 'You agreed to let me drive Miss Elizabeth round the town in your curricle. We are going this very afternoon.'

Sarah walked unwillingly round the room side by side with Lord Percival. He had drawn her hand to rest on his arm and she felt she was his latest trophy being put on display. The contrast with Greg could not have been brought home more strongly. Then she had felt his warm concern and attention to her welfare; now she had the distinct feeling that she was a prisoner.

She was aware that Lord Percival was scrutinizing her closely.

'You have changed your style of dress, Miss Davenport. Permit me to tell you that it is not becoming. A little more dash would suit you far better.'

She looked away. It was not his affair. A tiny smile tilted her lips at the knowledge that her clothes displeased him.

'I cannot wait for the day when I will decide what you wear,' he continued in his rich drawl. 'I prefer to see a woman displaying her charms.' His eyes went insolently to her bosom. He gave a bark of amusement as she tried to jerk her hand out of his arm. He caught her wrist in a vice-like grip and forced her hand back into place. His expression changed, warning her not to defy him.

'Your pardon, sir,' she said coldly, for all her voice trembled. 'Mrs Keating is signalling that she wishes to speak to me.'

'Then we will go together,' he hissed. 'We are going to do everything together from now on. You know that.'

'I cannot imagine where you got such a notion,' she said through clenched teeth. 'Have the goodness to let me go.' She stopped walking and pulled against him, trying to free her hand.

He swung round towards her. There was a dangerous gleam in his eyes. His thin lips compressed. She thought he would strike her, he looked so furious. Then his friend Lord Montallan appeared and Percival turned the glare on him instead.

'Thought I recognized you, George – and Miss . . . ah . . . er. . . .' The dandy's eyes kindled with pleasure. 'By Jove!' He gave Lord Percival a meaningful look, then swept off his hat with an exaggerated flourish. Lord Percival loosened his grip to bow in his turn.

Sarah seized her chance and pulled her hand free. She stepped back out of reach. 'Gentlemen,' she said icily, with a brief inclination of her head. She whisked herself away, darting through the many groups of people, back towards Lizzie and Greg.

But, as she approached, she saw Lizzie, with a hand on Greg's, looking up at him and saying something with a winning smile. Then Greg laughed and nodded. Sarah's heart, already bruised, seemed to wither inside her chest. She lowered her head, afraid her face might betray her pain and so she failed to see another gentleman who was quietly observing her from a short way away. John Keating raised his brows and sighed heavily.

CHAPTER TWENTY-TWO

It was growing dusk when Lizzie returned from the drive with Richard. She shed her pelisse and bonnet and gratefully accepted the cup of tea that Sarah poured for her.

'So, is he a good whip?' asked Sarah, keeping her back to the window. She had been thinking over the events of the morning and all Greg's good qualities. It was somehow more melancholy than if he were a rake. The outcome had been a few tears and she was not sure whether or not Lizzie would notice.

Lizzie took a gulp of warm tea. 'Ah, that is so nice.' She glanced up, 'why have you not rung for candles? It is getting dark in here.'

'I was wool-gathering and only roused when Polly brought in the tea tray. It is quite cosy with just the firelight. But tell me, where did you go? Have you set the Bath gossips in a roar?'

Lizzie waved an airy hand. 'Not at all. Everything was most proper and correct – a tour of the King's Circus, the Royal Crescent and most of the main avenues. Those horses are very high bred and strong but Richard handles them well. It was a very pleasant afternoon.'

She giggled and got up to pour herself another cup of tea. 'As luck would have it, we nearly did have a collision with a coarse fellow in a gig. I just do not know how Richard managed to stop the horses in time. Fortunately we were in Great Pulteney Street at the time and the road is wide there. The other driver was so rude. Goodness, how he did curse and shout. I never heard such *language*! And he looked as horrible as he sounded, what with his red face and green jacket—'

'Green jacket?' Sarah's cup clattered into the saucer. 'Was he a big, rough-looking man?'

'Indeed, he was. He looked like a labourer.'

'But this is extraordinary.' Sarah forgot her own pressing worries as she remembered the man who had pushed Greg into the road. Could it be the same person? She determined to speak to Greg about the matter when next they met.

There was no assembly that evening. Sarah played backgammon with General Gardiner while Lizzie continued reading her Gothic novel. The evening was passing quietly. Sarah felt secure in the company of these two old friends. But who knew what tomorrow would bring? Lord Percival was hunting her now. It would take all her determination to convince him that he was not going to succeed.

The clock had struck ten when they were all startled by a knock at the front door.

'Were we expecting anyone?' asked the general. When both girls shook their heads, he grumbled, 'Deuced strange time for a visit.' He had shed his jacket and loosened his cravat. His feet were in soft slippers and he was too tired and too comfortable to make the effort to tidy himself up. They all sat with their heads turned towards the door, listening.

'It cannot be Aunt Augusta . . . can it?' whispered Lizzie. She clasped her hands in a silent prayer.

A footstep was heard, then the servant knocked and entered.

'If you please, sir, Lord Davenport wishes to speak to his sister.'

'Well, show him in,' sighed General Gardiner.

'He says it is a private matter, sir.'

Sarah stood up hastily. She pulled her shawl round her shoulders and went out into the entrance hall. James was there, swaying a little. His face looked grey and his eyes sunken. Her anger with him forgotten, Sarah clasped his hand and rubbed it.

'James, whatever is wrong?'

'You know very well,' he pronounced, slurring his words.

She smelled the brandy on his breath. Her shoulders slumped. How could he break free of his destructive behaviour?

'Please, James, go back to Russeldene. You need some time to rest and clear your head of all these mad schemes.'

He shook her hand off. 'Mad?' His voice rose. 'Unless you do as I ask we are ruined.'

She clenched her fists. 'You are ruined! I will not submit to this plan; it is preposterous.'

'Alice thinks you should accept,' He backed away, ready to leave. 'Warn you, Sister, no other choice now. He will talk to you tomorrow.'

'James . . . wait – there is something else I need to ask you.' Sarah watched his face intently. 'Why is Mr Thatcham so angry with you?'

He snarled at her, wrenched the door open and walked out.

It took Sarah a moment before she moved forward to close the door and shoot the bolts. Then she stood with her back against it, staring into space with a frown on her brow. Lizzie eventually came out and found her there.

'Why, Sarah, did he bring bad news? You are so white. You look quite strange.'

Sarah shook herself. 'I must admit James worries me. He gambles too much – and drinks,' she added.

Lizzie laughed. 'Why, my two brothers do that. He will reform when he gets older.'

'I wish I could think so.' Sarah let Lizzie draw her back into the sitting-room. She sat down and stared into the fire. It was some time before she realized that her two companions were sitting in silence, waiting. She looked from one to the other. Lizzie gave her an encouraging smile. General Gardiner was looking at her very carefully. He raised his brows when she turned his way.

'You are very pensive, my dear. Is everything well with your brother?'

Sarah opened her mouth and closed it again. No words would come out. She shook her head.

'James has been gambling and drinking,' put in Lizzie.

'Like most young men,' remarked the general wryly. 'But he is worrying his careful sister.' He watched her with a sympathetic eye. 'Perhaps I should have a word with him about that.'

Sarah could feel her eyes filling with tears. She bent her head down and so did not see Lizzie shake her head at her uncle.

'Well,' continued the general, 'I expect things will seem better after a good night's sleep. I think we have finished our match for tonight. If you will ring the bell for Hughes, I shall retire.'

He struggled to his feet and in the business of helping him with his stick and his snuffbox, Sarah was able to appear more like herself and wish him goodnight in her usual manner. She then busied herself with putting the backgammon away before turning to find Lizzie waiting, her arms folded firmly and a gleam in her eye.

'Are you going to tell me why James has upset you so?'

Sarah twisted her curls furiously. This was too big a problem to reveal.

'Whatever it is,' went on Lizzie softly, 'please do not go away and leave me here alone.'

Sarah swallowed a sob. Suddenly, the burden seemed too great to carry all alone. Twisting her shawl between her fingers, she said, 'James has gambled away everything.' She looked at Lizzie. 'Everything!' she repeated in a trembling voice. 'I fear that I no longer have a home to go to.' She gulped and stared at her friend. There was a shocked silence. Then Lizzie leaped up and came to put her arms round her.

'It does happen. How can they be so reckless? This is shocking news, poor Sarah. But you always have a home here with us, you know that.'

Sarah made a pitiful attempt at a smile. 'Dear Lizzie, that is so kind. For the moment I accept, but of course, I shall have to find some way of earning my living.' She drew a painful breath.

'Surely not,' said Lizzie in horror. 'There must be some gentleman for whom you feel a partiality. Or if not now,' she added, as Sarah shook her head vehemently, 'you will soon meet someone suitable.'

'That is not a good solution,' said Sarah wearily. 'I think now that I prefer to trust to my own skills. Suppose I married a gambler.' She moved towards the door. 'Come, it is late now. Your uncle is right. Perhaps the night will bring counsel.'

Much later, as she lay staring at the ceiling, Sarah was no nearer finding a solution to her problem. If she went to Alice, it would only be until that lady pushed her into the arms of a husband – the first man willing to take her. For the moment she was safe with Lizzie and General Gardiner but her pride would not allow her to remain with them when their stay in Bath came to an end. And in any case, she must leave them before Lizzie married Greg. It was already so hard to see them smiling and laughing so cosily. She did not want to hate her best friend but the pangs of jealousy did shoot through her far too often already.

She shifted restlessly. Now it was time to consider the plan she had first thought of at Russeldene. She had always been a good scholar and had made the most of her education. Perhaps her old headmistress would consider giving her a post, or else recommending her as a governess. Sarah grimaced. The grey gown and tightly braided hair had indeed been a taste of her future. But if it freed her from James's wicked plot, it would be worth it.

As long as Lord Percival thought he could coerce her into marriage, he would keep James dangling on a string, taking the very clothes from his back. Once she disappeared, perhaps he would drop him. Then James might come to his senses. She remembered him as a rather shy and awkward young man, but on inheriting the title and estate, he had gone to London and been swept up into a dissipated way of life by new friends.

Sarah wished with all her heart that he could be more like the Thatcham brothers; energetic, open and interested in sports rather than gaming. She pummelled her pillow angrily. She must not think about Greg. She had seen with her own eyes on so many occasions that he was close to Lizzie. She could not blame him for that. Lizzie was one of the sweetest and most generous persons she knew, as well as a very pretty girl and an heiress.

Eventually she drifted off to sleep and dreamed of walking in the Parade Gardens with Greg. She was trying to explain why she could never marry him but it became so involved she woke up. There were tears on her cheeks.

CHAPTER TWENTY-THREE

In spite of her mainly sleepless night, Sarah found she was unable to stay in bed once dawn showed in the sky. She dressed and slipped downstairs. In no time she was out in the street, walking up to the top of the road and then turning blindly into the street up towards the grand new Royal Crescent with the open fields below it. There she could get some much needed fresh air.

It was so early that she could not see very far yet but the day was fine and dry. The brisk walk helped to soothe her aching head but it brought no solution to her woes. On one thing, however, she was absolutely determined: bitter as it was to lose Russeldene, she was not prepared to save it by selling herself to a scoundrel like Lord Percival. He had already shown that he would be a cruel master and would expect obedience to all his whims. To be his wife and obliged to obey him in everything would be to make her life intolerable.

A laden cart rumbled past, on its way to the market. That put Sarah in mind of the man in the green coat. She must speak to Greg about her suspicions. But her mind was immediately taken up again with the sad loss of her home. She walked on, not noticing where she was, only wanting to feel the wind in her face and open space all around.

Eventually she realized that she had crossed the park and she was passing a row of cottages in a little lane leading out of the town. Ahead of her she could hear a shepherd, driving his flock out to pasture. She must turn back. Reluctantly, she did so, feeling suddenly exhausted. By now it was full daylight. She reached

Royal Crescent again and made her way along the wide pavement. But already there was an increase in the number of carts and
riders on the road below.

It seemed a long way back but at last she turned into the Circus,
crossing it on her way down to Milsom Street. Just before she
came to the road out of the Circus, a gentleman on a splendid bay
horse appeared, trotting towards her. She gaped in astonishment
at Lord Percival. His many caped driving coat was liberally caked
with mud, as were his boots. He spotted her and an expression of
fury crossed his face. She was so astonished that she did not turn
away in time.

Lord Percival reined in and stepped his horse towards her. The
beast looked as if he had been ridden hard. 'This is a strange time
and place to find you, Miss Davenport.' He sounded put out. 'Do
you have some purpose in being here?' He frowned at her.

Even in her surprise and dismay, Sarah found that a strange
question. She noticed that he was dishevelled and his eyes were
red-rimmed. In addition, his clothes were much plainer than
usual. He needed a shave. In fact, he looked as if he had been up
all night. He was still glaring, waiting for an answer.

'I have been on an errand, sir, and am taking a short cut to
return home.'

'An errand?' He seemed uneasy. 'To do with me?'

She frowned. 'Not at all. A household matter.'

'Oh!' He sounded relieved. Then, assuming his usual swagger-
ing manner, he said, 'I shall expect to see you later on, in the Pump
Room. You know what I shall ask.'

Sarah shot him a scornful look. She marched off, head held
high, her spine ramrod straight. Behind her, she could hear him
cursing in a low voice. She judged that both he and his horse were
too weary to follow her. How could she have known that he was
lodging in this place? Of course, given his taste for extravagance,
he would want to be in an expensive location. Sarah pressed her
lips together in a grimace. No more walking through the Circus.

She had hardly gone twenty steps when she found another man
in front of her, blocking her way. She glanced up to say 'Excuse
me' and realized it was Greg. He was staring at her as if he could

not believe his eyes.

'What an early bird!' he said, by way of greeting. He looked at her keenly and then glanced up the road towards the Circus. Suddenly, she knew that he had seen Lord Percival ride past. Surely he did not think she had deliberately been to meet the man? But there was nothing she could say in her own defence. Even the sight of Greg could not cheer her spirits. As he continued to stare at her, she attempted a wan little smile.

'We all seem to have business in town this morning.'

His hat was tipped forward and under it his face was in shadow. But she made out the black bar of his brows above his nose. A muscle moved in his jaw. 'Are you out quite alone?'

She nodded, raising a hand to her forehead. 'I needed some fresh air – I have the headache. It was too early to ask anyone else to accompany me, but I could not sleep.'

He was still watching her. The expression on his face was hard to read. Sarah felt uncomfortable. He was not as friendly as he had been. But she was too tired now to care very much. She just wanted to get home and rest.

He was still blocking her way, so she said, 'Excuse me, I must not linger now. Lizzie will be looking for me at the breakfast table.'

'I will see you home.' His voice was harsh. He glanced up the road towards the Circus again. She had the feeling he wanted to go after Lord Percival.

'Really,' she protested, 'there is no need to go out of your way. It is just along George Street. I will wish you good morning.'

She held out her hand. He was still frowning. He took her hand and tucked it in his arm. 'Come,' he said, in a sort of growl and looked both ways before pulling her to cross the road. After a moment's resistance, Sarah leaned gratefully on his arm. It was such pleasure to feel that strength supporting her. Suddenly her legs would hardly carry her.

Neither of them spoke until they reached the door of General Gardiner's lodging. Greg beat a tattoo on the knocker and withdrew his arm from hers. As the door opened, he said, 'My compliments to the general – and to Lizzie, of course.' Then he gave her a nod and turned and strode away.

Sarah was mortified. He had never been so curt before. She felt bereft at the loss of his goodwill. She went into the parlour, where Lizzie was nibbling at some bread and butter and the general was stirring his tea with a great clinking of the teaspoon. She could not face food. Suddenly her headache was agonizing. She made an excuse to go up to her room and fled up the stairs.

Lizzie very soon followed her up with a cup of tea and lavender water to bathe her temples. When a maid came in, bringing a warming pan, Sarah protested. 'Please, Lizzie, all I need is an hour on my bed. I will be better after that, I assure you.'

'Where have you been?' asked Lizzie in a whisper.

Sarah sighed. 'I was awake so early, and could not get back to sleep. I just wanted some fresh air. Now, of course, I am tired out.'

Lizzie drew the curtains and left her in peace at last.

CHAPTER TWENTY-FOUR

Greg strode away down Milsom Street. The rage that had gripped him on seeing Sarah talking to Lord Percival still threatened to burst out. He had contained it until he had seen her safely home. Now he desperately wanted to kick something or punch someone very hard. How could she talk to the man, actually stop and hold a conversation with him?

Even worse, what was she doing out wandering the streets alone at such an early hour? Anything could happen. She just did not realize how tempting she was to men, with that lovely face and soft blonde hair. He ground his teeth. He cast a speculative glance at a passer-by, a serving-man by the look of him. The man looked warily at Greg and crossed the street.

'Spoilsport,' muttered Greg. His fists were clenched. He shook his head in frustration. This was ridiculous. He must get his priorities back in order. But Sarah had ruined his concentration. Just when he had discovered Lord Percival returning from what looked like a night meeting, as well! He had raced up towards the Circus to get a closer look at Percival's horse, to judge how far the man had ridden. But he simply could not leave Sarah alone in the street. God knows where else she had planned to go.

Greg thumped his hand hard against his forehead. Time to think the matter through. He dived into the first decent-looking ale-house in the street and called for a tankard of home-brewed. Had he been mistaken about Sarah all along, deceived by that lovely face into thinking her an innocent? Theo had warned him to have nothing to do with the Davenport family. And, as far as

James and Alice were concerned, he agreed with him.

Absently, Greg took a pull at his beer. Conversations stopped and heads turned as he strode over to a table and sat down. Nobody came near him. He glowered down at the tiny table and saw again Sarah's face. Now it occurred to him how pale she was with violet shadows under her eyes. He remembered the way she had clutched her head. It was not an act.

Why did he feel so angry? Why was she filling his mind when he was on the verge of proving that Lord Percival was the crook that Theo suspected him to be? This was not the time to be side-tracked by a lovely face. The gossips were whispering that her brother was penniless, having lost everything at play. So was he forcing his sister to entice Lord Percival into cancelling the debt?

At this idea, Greg clutched his hair. It seemed to be the most likely solution. And what choice did she have, a mere woman with – according to gossip – no fortune. She had resisted, but there would come a point where she might break under the relentless pressure. And he had seen how Lord Percival coveted her. Those lascivious eyes – the swine almost drooled each time he managed to get close to her.

Frantic with anger and worry, Greg seized his tankard, but it was empty. How long had he sat here? The tavern had filled up with farmers and market traders so the morning must be getting on. He spent a few moments checking on the people in the ale-house, then rose and went out. He entered a shop, bought a fob that he really did not need and meanwhile kept an eye on the tavern. Nobody came out, so Greg set off again, twisting and turn-ing through several other streets before he came to a coaching inn on the Bristol Road.

Jenkins, his groom, was waiting here with Greg's horse. In no time, Greg was trotting off along the Bristol road towards Seldon. As soon as he was clear of the town he coaxed his mount to a gallop. He reached the Three Bells feeling better for the fresh air and exercise. He thought of his many horseback journeys across the arid mountains of Spain and smiled at the contrast with this green and gentle landscape.

The ostler at the inn received Greg's horse with every sign of pleasure.

'Cor, 'e's a prime un, sir. I'll be sure to rub 'im down, an' that at once, sir.'

'See you do,' responded Greg, noting that there was only one other horse in the stables. It was a large, rangy beast. Greg wondered if it belonged to Mr Josiah Whitby. He had not yet met this person but had a description of him from Preston.

Greg walked round to the front entrance and entered the taproom. It was clean and spacious. The landlord was a burly, middle-aged man. He came bustling forward to greet his new customer and promised that the meal would be well worth the wait.

'I can believe you,' said Greg, 'for the smell of the cooking is making me hungry already.' He accepted the large mug of home-brewed ale and added, 'but you have no other customers?'

The landlord laughed. 'When the Bristol Stage comes through, we shall be busy enough, I warrant you, sir. Would you be wanting a private parlour?'

Greg shook his head. 'I shall be fine in here, Landlord.' He went over to a small alcove at the back of the room where there was a window seat and a small round table. He took out a pencil and a notebook and laid the book down, open, with the pencil lying across it. Then he savoured his beer and waited.

As the landlord had said, it was not long before the stagecoach drew up. The passengers came in, eager for their meal. The coach driver walked through and disappeared into a back room. A couple of serving-boys came in and began to set out the food. The landlord himself brought Greg a tray laden with dishes.

A tall man came and sat at the next table and he also was served by the landlord. This man was gentlemanly in appearance and dressed very soberly in a dark jacket and buckskins. As they reached the end of their meal he turned to Greg.

'Excuse me for addressing you, sir,' he said, 'but I came through the stables and very much admired your splendid grey horse.'

Greg considered the speaker. He was perhaps in his late thirties, with a thin face, enhanced by a pair of intelligent brown eyes.

'Thank you,' he replied, 'he is indeed a strong fellow and with a good disposition.'

'He certainly looks as if he could go all day. A really fine piece of horseflesh.'

'Would you care to see him properly?'

The other man nodded eagerly. They went out to the stables and as soon as they were in the open air, the man said in a low voice, 'You have guessed I am Lord Liverpool's agent?'

Greg nodded. 'I know the emblem as well.' He indicated the signet ring on Whitby's little finger. 'Any news?'

'There was a big gathering of men last night. A convoy is due from the Americas any day. Money changed hands for information about the cargo – tobacco and bullion – and they made arrangements for smuggling goods from the ships before they dock.'

'How do they do that?' asked Greg.

'Some local fishermen are part of their gang,' replied Whitby through his teeth. 'We have not been able to work out how many.'

'Did you see Lord Percival among the plotters last night?'

Whitby shook his head. 'It was dangerous even to be close enough to hear them. They met in a barn and I was able to hide in there.'

'But could you not recognize his voice?' insisted Greg. 'He has a very affected drawl. . . .'

Whitby shook his head. By now they had reached the stables. They spoke more loudly and about their horses as the ostler came to join them. Shortly afterwards, Greg shook hands with his new acquaintance in the taproom, politely wishing him an enjoyable stay in the area.

He set off towards Bath, feeling pretty certain that Lord Percival was the informer about the precious cargo. Whitby had alerted the Riding Officers, so a watch would be set. But Percival had powerful friends in Whitehall. Greg knew it would require very clear evidence before they could arrest the man. He and Josiah Whitby would need to witness him taking part in the smuggling operation and get proof that he had accepted the goods.

CHAPTER TWENTY-FIVE

Late that afternoon Greg called on Lizzie and Sarah. He had left Jupiter, his grey horse, at home and come back into town in his curricle. Lizzie was alone in the sitting-room when he arrived. She was all smiles as she told him about the driving expedition of the previous day.

'The main thing is that Richard did not mistreat my horses . . . or let them get away with you,' said Greg, a teasing light in his eye, 'but I am glad you found it enjoyable as well.'

Lizzie frowned indignantly at him. 'I declare you are even more disagreeable than Sarah.'

Greg looked round. 'Where is she, by the way?'

Lizzie shrugged. 'She was asleep when last I peeped into her room.' She twisted her fingers in her lap, hesitating, then glanced up. 'Oh, Greg, I am very worried about Sarah.' She moved to a seat next to him. 'I shall have to whisper this very quietly. Her brother keeps losing money at cards and now he says he has even lost his estate. It does not seem possible. It has been in their family forever and Sarah loves her home so much. I love it too. You know, I used to stay there in my school holidays.' She stared at him, her eyes round with horror.

'Does she have any money of her own?' he whispered back. He thought of the haunting sadness in Sarah's eyes and found he was clenching his hands into fists. He wished he could wrap them round that worthless brother's scrawny neck and choke some sense into him.

'Very little – not enough to live on. What choices does she have now?' Lizzie murmured in his ear.

At that instant the door opened and Sarah walked in. She stopped short, her eyes widening. 'Oh, I b-beg your pardon,' she stuttered, 'I did not realize there was anyone here.' She turned her gaze to Lizzie. 'Shall I go away?'

Both Greg and Lizzie jumped up guiltily. There was a tinge of colour along Greg's cheekbones. He felt embarrassed to have been caught gossiping about Sarah and wondered how much she had heard. Beside him, Lizzie bit her lip and, for once, had nothing to say.

Sarah cast an anguished look from one to the other. 'Excuse me,' she whispered and fled. They heard her running up the stairs. The next moment, somebody knocked hard on the front door. Lizzie darted back to her seat on the other side of the fireplace.

The maidservant tapped and announced, 'Lord Davenport.'

James walked into the room and started violently when he saw Greg. It was all Greg could do not to pin the fellow against the wall and vent his anger on him for his selfish behaviour towards his sister. But since this was the general's home and he was in the presence of a lady, he forced himself to stay still and acknowledge James's greeting with a very slight inclination of his head.

His face, however, told another tale and James could see it. He cast a wary look at Greg even as he asked, 'What has happened to Sarah? We have been waiting for her at the Pump Room this age.'

Lizzie's eyes sparkled with anger. 'James, whatever you told her last night made her unwell. She is still in her room.'

James scowled. 'How can that be? George particularly wishes to speak with her.'

'Well, she is not leaving the house today,' snapped Lizzie.

James digested this. He looked round rather desperately. 'Can I see her?' he asked.

'No!' said Lizzie and Greg together. They glanced at each other, startled by each other's determination to protect Sarah. James gave his twitch of the shoulder. 'In that case, there is nothing to keep me here any longer. Good day.' He swished around and pulled the door open violently. Greg strode after him.

'Just a moment, Davenport,' he called, snatching up his hat and following James out into the street, 'we will walk together.'

James looked over his shoulder in dismay.

'You must know that Hazelwick says you can confirm a few details about my brother's last days,' said Greg, striding along in step with James.

James shook his head. ' 'Fraid not,' he mumbled, walking even faster.

Greg caught him by the arm, forcing him to stop.

'What the devil? Let go of me,' protested James, trying to pull free.

Greg's nostrils flared. He slammed James back against a wall and held him there, then he pushed his face close to James's. 'I said,' he growled through clenched teeth, 'Hazelwick says you know the truth of what happened in the card room, when Henry played with your friend, Percival. So will you tell me what sum was lost and by whom?'

There was real terror in James's eyes. He wet his lips, hesitated and finally shook his head. 'There is nothing I can tell you.' His eyes dilated as Greg bared his teeth in fury. This was not the polite society gentleman but the battle-hardened warrior. James shrank away with a moan of fear.

'By God, you will tell me the truth. Your very silence is an admission of foul play,' snarled Greg.

James stared at him helplessly. He shook his head. 'I can say nothing,' he croaked.

Greg glared at him through narrowed eyes. This weak-minded creature was so in thrall to a flashy gamester that he dared not go against his wishes. The anger flared up again as he remembered how James was seeking to use Sarah to pay off his own debts. Greg had seen such things before and always found these deals contemptible. His eyes burned in his set face as he stepped back.

'Go then,' he growled, 'but be sure the next time I ask you, it will be in a place where you will have to give me a true answer.'

James drew a shaking hand across his mouth. He eyed Greg for an instant, then sidled away. When he judged he was out of reach, he set off at a smart pace, glancing back over his shoulder several times. Greg drew a deep breath and willed himself to be calm. He turned and walked back up the street. By the time he reached Lizzie's house he had decided against calling again so he went on up to the inn where he had left his curricle. It had been an eventful day. The intrigue was definitely thickening.

CHAPTER TWENTY-SIX

The next morning dawned bright and sunny, although very cold. Greg and Richard had their usual fencing match, under the sharp eye of the master. This time, Greg knew his arm was more skilful and his moves were faster. When Maitre Henri signed to him that he had won, he shook his right arm in a little victory salute and grinned at his brother.

Richard mopped his forehead. 'There was no way I could keep up with you there.'

Greg nodded. He stretched out his arms and gave a laugh. 'It feels good to be getting back to normal. But the foil is just to help me regain movement and speed. Next, little brother, we need to try with sabres.'

Richard groaned. 'I have no skill with those weapons. They are for cavalrymen.'

'I shall soon teach you,' promised Greg, walking over to select a suitable pair of swords. He handed one to Richard. 'Once I can handle this properly, I shall progress to the shooting range.'

'This is all very warlike,' said Richard, giving him a curious look. 'I thought you had resigned from the army for good.'

'Of course,' said Greg, with a little grimace, 'but I do not plan to let my skills get rusty. It is always wise to be prepared.'

'Prepared for what?' asked Richard, leaping into the salute as Greg advanced on him with the sabre.

Sarah excused herself from going out with Lizzie that morning.

'You can walk down with Mrs Keating and Lavinia,' she told

Lizzie. 'If you will excuse me, I wish to avoid James for a while longer.'

Reluctantly, Lizzie accepted this. 'I do hope you will find that things are not as bad as you fear . . . with Russeldene, I mean.' She placed a charming new bonnet with a turned-back brim and long pink ribbons over her dark curls and turned to the mirror as she tied the bow under her chin.

Sarah watched from the window as Lizzie set off down the street. Once she felt sure that Lizzie would not change her mind and come back, she ran upstairs and surveyed herself in her bedroom mirror. She was dressed neatly in a sober blue gown with no frills or trimming. Her hair was smoothly brushed back and arranged into a neat twist on top of her head.

She made a face at her neat but dowdy image. There was no other way open to her. Through the long night she had tried to quell her longing for a different future, one in which Greg featured. In all honour, she could not stay where she was going to move in the same circles as he and Lizzie. The more she saw him, the more she wanted him. The knowledge that he could never be hers was costing her too many sleepless nights.

Since she had come upon Lizzie and Greg sitting so close together in the sitting-room yesterday, she had been waiting for Lizzie to tell her of her engagement to Greg. But maybe they had to wait while Greg informed his father. Perhaps Sir Thomas was not yet ready to consider a marriage, while still grieving for the loss of his oldest son.

Sarah was sure that General Gardiner would approve of Greg as a suitable husband for his darling niece. Indeed, she thought with a sigh, what was there to disapprove? Handsome, honest, brave and charming, he had every quality. In addition he was wealthy. There was no way she could endure staying with Lizzie when she and Greg became engaged. That would be torment indeed. She looked in the mirror and saw the dark shadows under her eyes.

Giving herself a little shake, she put on her plainest bonnet and her grey cloak. It was time to act! Leaving her room she checked to see that the hallway was empty, then tiptoed downstairs and out. She drew a deep breath. Her heart pounded and her mouth was dry.

It was not far to Queen Square but it seemed to take her a long time to get there. At last she walked across the road into the open centre of the square. Standing under the bare trees, she looked again at her old school. It was a respected academy and Miss Howard was a sensible and just headmistress. Sarah swallowed hard. She walked slowly up to the entrance, but at the last second she swung away and set off to go round the square once more.

That was cowardly, she scolded herself. When she reached the school door again, she would knock and go in. There was no point in lingering. If Russeldene was no longer her home, there was nowhere else to go. She must accept that she had to work to earn her living as a teacher. Yet here she was, dawdling in the middle of the square once more. Clasping her hands together tightly, she took a deep breath and strode forward across the open space. She reached the pavement and was advancing up the broad path to the door when a hand on her arm checked her.

Startled, Sarah jumped and jerked her head round. It was Greg. There was a strange expression on his face. She could almost believe he was angry.

'Come!' he said urgently. 'Let us walk a little.'

Sarah shook her head. 'No, no, I assure you, I must—'

'You must not!' His voice was quiet but he spoke with finality. Helplessly, Sarah felt him pull her away from Miss Howard's Academy. She stole a sideways look up at him. His face was hard, his eyes narrowed and his normally sensual lips were tightly compressed. Yet she felt no fear. This man would never do her any harm.

He drew her up the road and towards the open land on the outskirts of the town. Turning to the right, they reached the Gravel Walk. Greg nodded towards it.

'We will be more sheltered here,' he said. She murmured an assent. For the moment she was overcome by his closeness and his apparent knowledge of what she had been about to do. They paced on slowly. At length, Sarah pulled herself together.

'Why did you stop me just now? How did you know. . . ?' She

looked at him earnestly.

He halted and turned towards her. Again she saw his face harden. His thick brows made a solid bar above his nose and a muscle moved along his jaw. Then, as he looked at her, a smile came, his eyes shone and she could not prevent herself from smiling back at him. He took hold of both her hands.

'I just happened to be passing through the square. You seemed to be very agitated so I regret to say I stood and watched. It seemed to me that you were intending to do something you might very soon regret.'

Sarah turned her face away. She blinked and felt a tear slide down her cheek. How could she explain this to him, of all people? 'You cannot know the reasons,' she managed to whisper. 'I have no other choice.'

He squeezed her hands. 'I think I do know why you went there. And I still say you would be making the wrong decision to leave your own world. Heavens above! You cannot become a drudge for troublesome schoolgirls.'

'Well, at least I would be independent and no longer forced to watch my brother bring ruin on us,' she flashed, her eyes stormy. 'I cannot endure to see him following in the steps of that evil man he calls a friend.' She pulled a hand free and pressed it to her lips. 'I am s-sorry,' she gasped. 'Please forget what I just said.'

'You are not telling me anything I did not know,' replied Greg calmly. He caught hold of her hand again. 'And now I will tell you that I also have great reason to suspect that same man of – what shall I call it? – behaviour that is unworthy of a gentleman.' His voice became harsh as he said those last words.

Sarah felt the tension in the hand that was holding hers. She stared wildly up at him. As his meaning sank in, her mouth opened in a gasp of shock. For a second Greg stared at her. His eyes fell to her mouth. He swallowed. Slowly, slowly he lowered his head and pressed his lips to hers. His mouth felt warm and firm yet gentle. It was such a pleasant sensation that Sarah clung to him and tilted her head up to respond.

With a groan, Greg slid a hand to the back of her neck, pulling her closer, deepening his kiss. All Sarah's troubles vanished in the sweet sensation. She ran a hand up his jacket, against the hard muscles of his chest. She leaned closer, closer. . . . Suddenly, both of them recollected where they were and jerked back at the same instant.

Sarah's cheeks became very red but she kept her eyes on him steadily. She raised a trembling hand to touch her lips. Her breath was coming in little gasps. Greg's eyes glowed as he watched her and his mouth curved into a breathtaking smile. They stood there, staring at each other, unaware of the wind, the cold and of various nursemaids and servants passing them in both directions.

It seemed a very long time before Sarah said, 'We should not have done that. It was very wrong of us.'

'I cannot believe that something so pleasant can be entirely wrong,' protested Greg. He raised an eyebrow and grinned at her. After a moment in which she continued to stare at him, he added, 'But if I have distressed you, I apologize.'

She looked down, veiling her eyes with long dark lashes. Her head was whirling. Why had he done it, when he was as good as engaged to her best friend? Why had she responded? And yet, somewhere in her mind, she rejoiced at that sweet contact, oh yes, and she wanted more of it. Which meant she must put herself out of danger, not just from the man she loathed but from the man she loved.

It burst upon her how much she loved him. And with that realization, she knew how desolate her life was going to be. The loss of Greg was more important than the loss of her home. One great sob escaped before she rigidly quelled her emotions. Later, she would find somewhere to deal with that.

Greg looked horrified at that sob. 'Oh, Sarah!' The words burst from him. He seized her hands again. 'I do not want to say sorry for something so beautiful. . . .'

'It is – is only because . . . .' she faltered, blinking away a tear, 'because. . . .'

'Come, you are shivering,' he said when it became obvious she could not get out any more words. 'Let us walk on.'

He tucked her arm under his and drew her on up the slope. She kept her head bent down as she struggled for composure that could not come while he was so close.

Greg also appeared to be deep in thought. They had reached the top of the rise before he roused himself to speak. He tilted his head down to look in her face. 'We were discussing your intention to become a teacher. Promise me you will not do that.'

When she shook her head silently, he added, 'Not yet, anyway. Please give me a little time to sort things out.'

'But how can that make any difference to me?' In her surprise, she forgot to feel embarrassed with him.

'We were speaking of your brother and his *friend*,' Greg's voice was sarcastic as he said that word, 'and I told you I also have an interest in that man.'

They paced on, reaching the top of the walk. 'He has such a hold over my brother,' admitted Sarah with a shudder, 'and I do wonder if James has lost everything to him fairly.'

Greg stopped abruptly. She glanced up in surprise. His face was white and frowning. 'Why do you say that?' he asked, his eyes painfully intense.

Sarah stared at him, puzzled.

'It is absolutely vital for me to find out anything I can about this man.' His eyes were pleading now.

She made up her mind. 'I will trust you to keep this a secret. One evening at our home, I watched Lord Percival encouraging James to drink until he was fuddled before they began to play cards. James was losing. But when the housekeeper and I sat by them and watched the play, James began to win. It may have been just a coincidence that evening, but when he plays with Lord Percival he loses constantly. And there is something else,' she added, frowning, 'my brother seems afraid of this man – but I do not know why.'

Greg drew in a deep breath. His face relaxed slightly. 'Thank you for trusting me. You can have no idea how important that information is.'

CHAPTER TWENTY-SEVEN

In silence, Greg and Sarah threaded their way down through the winding roads in the general direction of Milsom Street. They were both so deep in thought that neither of them saw Lord Percival as they walked past him. He stood and watched them until they turned the next corner. The expression on his face was very ugly. He grasped his ebony cane and struck it angrily against the railings of the basement area outside his lodging.

Sarah was walking automatically. She did not notice where they were, her mind was in such turmoil. She still felt as if she was on the edge of a cliff, staring down but unable to move backwards. Her plan to seek employment had come to nothing. Why had she let him persuade her? Why had she let him kiss her? Even worse, why had she kissed him back?

She knew the answer to that, of course, and it brought colour to her cheeks to admit it. She was still dwelling on the matter when she realized that they had stopped walking. She raised her head in surprise to discover that they were outside General Gardiner's house. She turned to Greg. Suddenly she was shy and it took a great effort to meet his gaze. Those glorious eyes were fixed on her face. He gave her a rueful grin.

'We have been on a long journey this morning,' he said finally. 'Will you please promise me not to go near Queen Square for the present?'

'I cannot leave it very long.'

His expression became serious. A muscle clenched in his jaw. 'Be patient for a while. Things may improve.' He beat his usual tattoo on the knocker. 'I shall do myself the honour of calling this afternoon to see how you and Lizzie go on.'

He touched his hat as the door opened. He watched her go inside. When the door closed behind her, Greg drew a deep breath. A lot had changed in the past hour. He strode briskly down to the Pump Room, where his father would be expecting to see him. Then he must find Preston. It was time to put more pressure on James Davenport.

The crowd in the Pump Room was quite dense as it was now the middle of the day. Greg found his father in conversation with several old friends. He made his bow to them all, and seeing that his father was well content to remain where he was, Greg wandered round in search of Richard. It was not long before he came across Lizzie and her friend Lavinia Keating. He greeted them politely and smiled around at the group of friends surrounding them.

Richard was among them. Greg gave him a significant look and shortly afterwards, Richard made his way to his brother's side.

'More fencing?' he asked with a touch of apprehension.

'Not at the moment. Be a good fellow and fetch my curricle into town.'

'What, now?' asked Richard with obvious reluctance. He glanced at the group of young people around Lizzie. 'We are just making arrangements for a theatre visit.'

'It is important,' said Greg, 'and tell Preston to meet me in half an hour. Say it is on business. I shall be at The Swan, down the road from here. Oh, just a minute,' he added, as Richard was turning away, 'here is a little gift for you.' He dug a hand into the pocket of his riding coat and produced a small packet. Richard unwrapped it and gave a nod of appreciation at the fob that Greg had bought the day before.

When Preston entered The Swan, he was dressed like a gentleman in a caped driving coat over a discreet dark suit. He joined Greg at a scuffed wooden table and looked enquiringly at his master.

'Adventure?' he asked. Greg nodded. Preston's eyes lit up. 'Not before time,' he said, 'it was getting very dull, Major, for both of us.'

149

'Speak for yourself,' replied Greg.

Preston took on a knowing look. 'So that's what you were doing . . . as if I didn't know. All them fresh shirts and neckties. . . .' He shook his head.

'Never mind that,' said Greg, just slightly embarrassed at being so transparent to his valet, 'I need you to make the acquaintance of a young gentleman called Davenport. He is very fond of card playing. I need to find out how skilled he is but he is wary of me.'

Preston nodded. 'Just show me who he is, Major.'

Greg nodded. 'Richard will show you. Now you get to the shops and rig yourself out for an evening or two in the card room. You need to play the part of a wealthy businessman with money to burn.' He pulled out his watch and frowned. 'I must go now, I have another errand to deal with. I shall be at the Upper Rooms by ten. You will not know me.'

Preston nodded. He raised his brows. 'How deep shall I play?'

Greg considered. 'Not too deep, but enough to see if he is skilled with the cards or merely a young fool.' He waited until Preston had left the taproom, then stood up himself, ducking his head just in time to avoid hitting it on a beam. He made his way out cautiously. It felt good to be able at last to move upon these two men who were almost certainly hiding vital information from him.

In the doorway of The Swan he almost bumped into Richard, who was rushing in to find him.

'My horses?' Greg frowned in alarm at his panting brother.

Richard grabbed at his arm. 'Horses – are – fine. . . .' he gasped and gestured towards the bar. 'Need – a drink. . . .'

Greg looked at him from under his brows but turned back and called for ale. As soon as it was placed before him, Richard grasped the tankard and tilted the brew down his throat.

Greg tapped his fist on the bar counter. 'Well, man? I am in a hurry!'

Richard wiped his mouth. 'This is serious,' he muttered. 'Jenkins and I went to harness your bays to the curricle. I started to drive off, but as I set the horses to trot, the carriage did not feel right. Almost at the same time, I could hear Jenkins shouting at

150

me to stop.'

Greg leaned forward. 'Were my horses injured?' he asked urgently.

'No, no, told you, they are fine. But the outside wheel was loose and just ready to fall off.' He gave his brother a sharp look. 'Jenkins swears he checked everything after you returned from your visit to Theo.'

Greg's face hardened. Eventually he sighed and gave a shrug.

Richard took another gulp of his ale. 'Things are hotting up,' he remarked. 'First your "accident" in the street and now this. You have annoyed someone.'

'Hmm!' Greg nodded, his frown deepening. 'That was supposed to throw me out under the wheels of any other vehicle in the street.'

Richard shook his head. 'Father is not going to like this.'

'He must not know.' Greg raised a warning finger as Richard seemed about to protest. 'I shall have a word with Jenkins. Father is just starting to look better. I will not have him made anxious.'

'Very well,' said Richard reluctantly, 'but it seems to me that you need to be extra careful yourself.' He finished his drink and pushed the tankard back across the bar. 'Whatever your errand was, I fear you will have to cancel it for the present.'

The brothers went out into the street. Richard glared around as if he expected a gang of hired assassins to be waiting there. Greg had to smile. 'They do not operate like that,' he said. 'No doubt we are being watched but we will act as normal.'

'I shall return to the Pump Room to keep an eye on Father.' Richard announced. His hands clenched into fists.

'If you wish. I doubt if he is in danger: it is me they are after.'

'But why?'

Greg clapped his brother on the arm. 'I can think of two possible reasons. Now I must hurry. I want to see the damage – and check on Jupiter!' he added grimly.

'Good God, do you think they would harm him?' Richard was appalled.

'We must be alert for anything.' Greg gave Richard a grim nod and strode away towards the Pulteney Bridge. This was a worrying development. He had taken great care over his contact with Josiah Whitby, but perhaps the meeting had been reported. A vast amount of money was at stake as well as the reputations of several high-ranking gentlemen.

Greg knew that any day now there could be a message about the arrival of the cargo ships. He needed to get to the agreed place where the signal would be given to say the convoy had been sighted. Then he would have to keep Lord Percival under close observation.

CHAPTER TWENTY-EIGHT

'Why do you keep giving me those considering looks?' Lizzie enquired, without looking up from the trimming she was sewing onto her sprigged muslin gown.

'What looks?' Sarah asked. She put her book down and wrapped her arms around her knees, resting her head on them. A few curls tumbled down but she left them hanging loose.

'As if you are waiting for me to say something surprising.'

Sarah hesitated before replying: 'Perhaps I am.' Her heart beat faster in suspense.

Lizzie adjusted the blue satin ribbon and frowned at her stitches. 'Yes, that will do.' She glanced across at Sarah. 'Are you wondering what news I have for you?'

Inwardly, Sarah quaked at what she might hear. She dreaded the announcement that Greg and Lizzie had agreed to get married, but she preferred to know the truth. Then she could discipline her own wayward thoughts. The memory of that kiss set her lips tingling again. She pulled herself together. 'So what do you want to tell me?' She was proud of herself. Her voice was steady and even casual. She kept her head on her knees and watched Lizzie through a screen of hair.

Lizzie snipped off another length of ribbon. 'Well, maybe you will be excited' – she bent closely over her work as she pinned the trimming against the top edge of the dress – 'as you like music so much.'

Sarah's eyes opened wide. 'Music?' she echoed faintly.

'Yes, there will be a concert next week. Sir Thomas came to tell me. He feels certain you would enjoy it. He will get tickets for us all – except Uncle Charlie.' She laughed. 'He claims his gout is still too painful.'

There was a silence as Sarah considered all this. So Lizzie was not going to say anything just yet. This brought her mind to her own situation. 'Was James in the Pump Room this morning?'

Lizzie was struggling with the ribbon. 'No,' she said eventually. 'I have not seen him since he called here yesterday afternoon.'

Sarah raised her head. 'Yesterday? But I did not see him. . . .'

'It was after you rushed back upstairs.' She glanced round with a gurgle of laughter, 'Actually, it was quite funny. He did ask to see you but Greg and I both snapped "No" at him at exactly the same time. You should have seen his face. He just walked out. And then Greg ran off after him,' she added.

Why would he do that? But of course, it was obvious! A cold shiver ran down Sarah's back. James was afraid of Greg because of the 'accident' that involved Lord Percival. That was why Greg kept asking questions. Her eyes widened in horror. Greg's brother was dead and James was concealing information about the matter, information that Greg desperately wanted to know. And, yet again, she was tainted by association with the wrong-doer.

She pressed a hand to her mouth to stop herself from groaning out loud. How could she ever look Greg in the face again, now she realized what her wicked brother had done. If things had seemed bad earlier, they were a hundred times worse now. Her head drooped and she twisted absently at her hair.

'Sarah! This is the third time I have spoken your name. Wake up!'

Slowly, Lizzie's voice penetrated Sarah's thoughts. She cleared her throat. 'What? I beg your pardon. My mind drifted away. . . .'

'Can you help me? This ribbon just will not lie flat against the curve of my dress. I shall never finish it in time for the assembly this evening.'

Sarah got up and examined Lizzie's handiwork. 'Give it to me.' She seated herself in the window and set to work with tiny, exquisite stitches. Lizzie came to watch. Without looking up,

Sarah said, 'I have not apologized for walking in on your private conversation with Greg yesterday.'

When there was no answer to this, she raised her eyes. Lizzie's cheeks were red and she looked uncomfortable. She was fiddling with a skein of silk. Sarah waited, dreading but wanting the news of her engagement to Greg. She had finished sewing the length of trimming and still Lizzie was silent. Feeling a little hurt, Sarah held out the dress.

'There. But surely you have other evening dresses to choose from.'

'Oh, I particularly wanted to wear this one. I want to look my best and this is such a delicate muslin.' She held it up in front of herself and studied her reflection from all angles in the mirror. 'I do think I look nice in white.'

'Vanity!' said Sarah, wondering if this was for Greg's benefit. Then her smile faded as she wondered which of her few evening dresses she could wear.

Her pink muslin was getting rather shabby, in spite of the new trimmings she had carefully stitched on. She decided it would have to be the jonquil yellow sarsenet with puff sleeves. It was over two years old, but as it was very simply cut, it was still sufficiently fashionable. She had some yellow and white ribbons to make a sash for it and if she dressed her hair carefully with a piece of the same yellow ribbon threaded through her curls, she should look smart enough.

It was drizzling when they set off for that evening's assembly, walking beside General Gardiner's sedan chair. In the entrance hall they changed their shoes for satin dancing slippers and bade farewell to the general as he made for the card room. He inspected both of them before he went off.

'You girls are getting so dashed elegant, my compliments to you both.' He shook his head. 'Who would have thought my little Lizzie would turn into such a pretty young lady.' He smiled at her fondly. She put a hand on his arm.

'Thank you, Uncle Charlie. I knew this dress would suit me. But Sarah sewed on the braid.'

'Well, be good girls now. Who is chaperoning you?'

155

'Greg,' said Lizzie with a giggle. Seeing her uncle frown, she amended: 'Mrs Keating kindly looks after us.'

The general's brow cleared. 'We are indebted to her,' he said. 'Perhaps we could invite her to tea. Naturally, I shall be there to thank her.'

He waved a hand to quell Lizzie's protest and limped off. Sarah smiled. 'He is a very tolerant uncle, let us be a credit to him.'

'We always are.' retorted Lizzie, rushing off along the passage. Her eyes were sparkling in a way Sarah knew well. Lizzie was plotting something – or could it be the idea of seeing Greg that had made her so happy? She quickened her steps to keep pace. A moment later they entered the ballroom. The number of people visiting Bath had been growing steadily these past two weeks. Tonight it seemed they had all come to dance. The huge room was full. It was a seething mass of dancers and groups of people watching them and trying to make polite conversation above the sound of the music.

'Can you see Mrs Keating?' Lizzie was looking from left to right eagerly.

'Let us try this way.' Sarah moved down to the bottom of the room. A smile here, a word of apology there, she worked her way along and sure enough, there was Mrs Keating, fanning herself, seated in a corner. Richard Thatcham and John Keating were standing by her.

'This is how I like to see things,' announced Mrs Keating, smiling at the girls. 'Lavinia is dancing with Mr Wilden.'

'If you can call it dancing in this crush,' remarked Richard. 'However, perhaps you are willing to take the risk?' He raised his brows to Lizzie and she at once she placed a hand most correctly on his arm.

'Well, perhaps we should venture to try as well,' John Keating said to Sarah. She looked a little doubtful. 'I think we should stay and bear Mrs Keating company for now.'

He gave his mother an apologetic glance. 'Of course.'

'Not at all,' protested that lady, 'here comes my friend, Lady Broome. We shall enjoy a coze while you young people dance.'

Her son laughed. 'What you mean, Mama, is that we would be

in the way while you exchange scandalous gossip. Well, enjoy yourselves. We certainly shall,' he announced, smiling warmly at Sarah as he pushed a way through the crowd for her.

CHAPTER TWENTY-NINE

From his seat at the back of the taproom Greg surveyed the other customers in the dark and smoky little alehouse. It was a very mixed company around him, everything from poor labourers to gentlemen. From habit he examined them all. If he was being followed, his arm was now strong enough for him to defend himself. They would not catch him again as they had with the carriage accident in Union Street. But nobody took any special notice of him. For them he was just another gent who liked to mingle with the lower orders.

By now Richard would have pointed out James Davenport to Preston. Greg smiled briefly at the thought of Preston in his disguise. He certainly would be enjoying the adventure. And then he could judge the young man's ability with the cards. If that damned Percival was there, Preston could observe how he treated Davenport and if there was any attempt to doctor the younger man's drink.

He sat frowning into his beer, oblivious of the noise. At last the various strands of this mystery were coming together. Perhaps now he would get the evidence that Lord Percival was a cheat and a trickster. Then he would have the truth from James Davenport about those card games in Hazelwick's library. His jaw clenched. At this point, a female voice interrupted his thoughts.

'All alone, mister?' A painted and scantily clad girl slid on to the seat next to him. She pressed her leg against his from thigh to knee. Greg raised his frowning gaze from the contemplation of his tankard. He inspected her. She was thin and pale under her paint,

her eyes shadowed and fearful. 'Mister.' she said again in a pleading tone.

Greg signed to the boy at the counter. 'Bring her a drink,' he
ordered, 'and something to eat.'

He sat on and watched as the lad slapped down a glass of wine
and a plate of stew. The girl pushed back her hair and looked at
the plate. Her eyes flickered to Greg's.

'It is for you,' he said. He stayed until she had finished the food.
Then he rose. She stood up as well, wiping her mouth on the back
of her hand. 'No,' he said firmly, 'you stay here.' He placed a coin
on the table and it disappeared at once into the front of her dress.
Greg judged that it was well after nine-thirty. He left the tavern
and threaded through small alleys going north and east towards
the Circus.

There was still no news of the convoy arriving but he would
use the opportunity to check on whether Lord Percival was at
home. As soon as news did come that the boats were approaching,
the man would be off to supervise his share of the booty. Greg
would then have to follow discreetly.

At intervals, lamps lit the wide expanse of the Circus. Even so,
Greg was all but invisible as he passed along the street in his dark
evening cloak. In spite of the darkness, he knew exactly where to
look to see Lord Percival's house. There were lights showing in
the windows. There was another shadow walking along the pavement at that point so Greg paused.

A moment later he heard a sharp rap on the knocker. The door
of Lord Percival's lodging opened. Against the light from the hallway, Greg saw one figure on the pavement and another one come
out of the house. He stayed where he was until they set off. He did
not want to come close enough to be recognized, but as they saun-
tered along in front of him, he could hear every word spoken.

'. . . certain to get her.' It was the unmistakable drawl of Lord
Percival. He sounded very pleased. 'Gad, but I enjoy taming a
spirited filly.'

There was a snigger at this point. 'Spices the game, hey?' From
the lisp, Greg recognized Lord Montallan.

'Quite so! Teaching 'em to obey is half the pleasure.'

They paced on in silence for a moment. Then Montallan's voice came again. 'You are taking more time and trouble than usual, George.'

'She is worth it. But I warn you, Monty, she is mine. *I* want her – no sharing.'

'Dash it, George,' spluttered the other man. 'Have I not helped you with the brother?'

There was a cold laugh. 'What a fool. And now that pigeon is well and truly plucked. But if he should win money from anyone, I will have it from him. He must be kept in a state of fear. It makes him – how shall I put it? – more eager to help me catch the sister.'

Greg was wrestling with a tide of anger. He wanted to punch and stamp them both into pulp. It was only the years of diplomatic work that made him keep his self-discipline. Later, he told himself, later, they will pay. Now you need information. He was so intent on discovering all their evil plan that he did not notice they had stopped walking. He was almost upon them when he checked himself. He turned his back so they would see only the dark shadow of his cloak. But they were still talking and did not see him.

'So, will I not have my turn with her?'

Greg's fists clenched and his jaw set hard. What kind of depraved gang was operating here? That callous remark made him want to throttle both of them. The blood was pounding in his ears and by the time he was calm enough to listen again, the voices were fading. They had walked on. Drawing a deep breath he turned round and continued to follow. But now there were lights ahead at the entrance to the Assembly Hall. Greg stood in the shadows for a while longer.

His rage made him all the more determined to expose Lord Percival in all his illegal and immoral pursuits. Greg swore to himself that he would bring the swine to justice. Meanwhile, he now had a clear idea of why Sarah was so often uneasy. He would keep a stricter watch on her – and on Lizzie. Greg remembered that Lizzie seemed to like Lord Percival. He sighed. Looking after young ladies was hard work. Perhaps he should give General Gardiner a hint. He had not intended to go into the ballroom but after what he had just heard, he had to see that the girls were safe and well. He drew a calming breath and strode in.

The evening seemed to be passing slowly. Sarah had danced most of the dances, as had Lizzie, and she had also enjoyed a pleasant conversation with Mrs Keating. She had been introduced to Mrs Keating's newly arrived friend, another matron with a pretty young daughter. Sarah sensed that Lady Broome knew all about the Davenport misfortunes from the way she had looked when Mrs Keating presented her. But, after all, Sarah could do nothing about it. She kept her head high and pretended not to notice that Lady Broome was examining her two-year-old dress and her lack of jewels.

Lizzie was dancing again but Sarah was sitting sipping a glass of lemonade and wishing she did not feel so tired. The constant stress was having a bad effect on her. The crowd seemed to fill the entire ballroom and the buzz of conversation over the music was getting uncomfortable. She stifled a yawn. It was one blessing that there was no sign of Lord Percival or his peculiar friend. James also seemed to have vanished.

But she would be glad to go home now. Then she turned her head and everything changed as she saw a tall, broad-shouldered figure advancing towards her. He looked so elegant in his dark evening clothes and snowy cravat. To her annoyance, she knew she was blushing. Her heart raced and she tingled all over in anticipation. But it would not do. Had she not seen Lizzie and Greg seated so cosily together only yesterday? And now she knew what James was concealing from him she felt ashamed. It was time to put a distance between herself and him.

Scarcely had the thought gone through her mind when Greg reached her side. The smile he gave her turned her bones to water. She feasted her eyes on his amber eyes, his tanned skin, his wonderful mouth. His coppery hair gleamed as he bowed and took her hand to kiss it. A thrill of pleasure ran right down to her toes at the touch of his long fingers.

Suddenly she was refreshed and ready to dance all night. But another look at Greg's face told her that something was wrong.

161

There was a tension in him and a crease between his brows. Was he worrying about that kiss they had shared? Was she showing too much pleasure in his company? But try as she would to be indifferent, when he turned to make his bow to Mrs Keating and her friend, Sarah had to admire his broad shoulders and his muscled legs. Amazing how such a big man could be so graceful. He turned back to her.

'Are you enjoying the ball?'

'Tolerably! It is quite a crush, as you see.'

'Indeed. But I do hope you will be kind enough to stand up with me for the next dance?'

She should refuse! But when he was close by, her will power vanished. Sarah smiled and watched the worry lines disappear as he smiled back.

'Come on, then,' he said, and led her on to the floor and fifteen minutes of heaven.

When he led her back to Mrs Keating, his preoccupied mood had returned. 'What has become of Lizzie?' he asked. 'I have not managed to see her yet.'

'She is here, I assure you.' Sarah's elation faded.

Now he was looking around with an air of anxiety. He spotted someone in the doorway and said, 'Ah! Pray excuse me. I will return shortly.'

She sat down with a sense of being cast adrift. She saw that Lady Broome was watching her keenly. Recollecting that she must show an indifferent front, Sarah unfurled her fan and cooled her heated cheeks.

'I can see another gentleman looking very particularly at you. Oh, I do believe he is coming over,' remarked Lady Broome. Her voice was breathless with scandalized excitement. She gave Sarah a catlike smile and nodded towards the doorway. The ostrich plumes in her magnificent purple turban swayed gently.

Horror of horrors, Lord Percival was making his way towards her.

Lady Broome's sharp little eyes were alight with curiosity. It was obvious she knew all about Lord Percival's bad reputation. No doubt his attentions would provide her with rich material for gossip in the Pump Room. Sarah cast a frantic glance around. None of the other young people had returned to this corner.

After the pleasure of dancing with Greg, she did not feel able to endure a dance and conversation with this man. Before he reached her, however, Richard Thatcham pushed his way out of the crowd, slightly breathless. He gave her a grin and a bow.

'Beg you will grant me the honour of the next dance,' he gasped, offering his arm. Sarah jumped up thankfully. He led her into the line that was forming. Still panting, he gave her a half comical look but she was too grateful for her escape to question anything. During the turn in the dance, she caught sight of Lord Percival watching her. The expression on his face was so unpleasant that she knew he would want revenge of some kind.

CHAPTER THIRTY

On the Sunday, two days after the ball, Sarah and Lizzie attended morning service at the abbey. When they came out of the church they found that the crowd had vanished. It was a bitterly cold day with a keen wind blowing. Most people hurried into the Pump Room, or disappeared into their carriages. Very few lingered in the open square. However, in spite of the straw and dust whipping up around them, Lizzie insisted on walking right round the abbey as far as the Parade Gardens, where she stood examining any person still lingering outside.

Sarah looked at her suspiciously. 'Now what are you up to?' When Lizzie gave her a stare of wide-eyed innocence, Sarah frowned. 'I know these tricks of old. Surely you have not made an assignation with some young man?'

Lizzie tucked a gloved hand under Sarah's arm. 'Nothing so vulgar. I was merely expecting to see Richard. We had agreed to take a walk if the day was dry enough.'

'But what about his brother?' The question came out before she could stop herself. She cursed inwardly. It showed she was always thinking about him. 'Come,' she added hastily, 'You cannot go for a walk in this chill wind. I am shivering already and my bonnet is threatening to blow away. Let us go into the Pump Room for shelter. Very likely you will find one or other of the Thatcham family in there.'

They did indeed find Sir Thomas in the entrance hall. It seemed he had been looking for them. After making his usual courteous and formal enquiries after their health, he announced, 'My son has gone into the Pump Room. I believe he is looking for you, Miss Gardiner.'

'Richard?' asked Lizzie eagerly.

A shadow crossed Sir Thomas's face. 'No. He has remained at home. Gregory is in the Pump Room.'

'Oh, but. . . .' Lizzie sounded put out. Her muff fell to the floor. When she rose from picking it up, her face was red. With a word of excuse, she curtsied to Sir Thomas and hurried away. Sarah watched in growing suspicion. Whatever Lizzie had planned with Richard, she was very upset at having her plans dashed.

Sir Thomas sighed as he watched her trip away. Sarah looked more closely. As always, she warmed to his old-fashioned charm and courtesy. In addition, he was so like his son in appearance. She knew that Greg would still make a handsome gentleman when he was older.

Sir Thomas was still frowning into space. The lines on his face seemed more deeply carved this morning. His mouth was set in a grim line. Sarah wondered what could be troubling him. He seemed to have forgotten her presence so she cleared her throat. He started and turned his head towards her. She gave him a friendly smile. 'I believe I heard that the gentlemen were going to a sparring match yesterday? Perhaps Richard is . . . indisposed after the event, sir?'

He gave her a long look from under his brows. Then he sighed again and his face relaxed slightly. 'You must not be thinking that Richard drank too much at the event.' He shook his head. The frown returned and he looked old and shaken. 'Richard accepted a challenge to take part in the sparring. Afterwards, he was offered a drink of cider and it was very shortly after that that he became violently unwell.'

'Do you mean he drank something contaminated?'

'That is what he and his brother tried to make me believe.' Sir Thomas looked at her almost in appeal. 'But he has been so ill that I fear it was a deliberate attempt to poison him.'

Sarah was horrified. 'But why would anyone do that? I cannot imagine that someone would want to harm him.' Even as she spoke, a vision of Lord Percival's angry face at the ball came to mind. She swallowed. Doubt shook her. Surely, even he would not go to such lengths as this? Sir Thomas was eyeing her narrowly.

'It seems you have thought of something?'

Sarah schooled her face into a politely neutral expression. 'I am simply shocked at the very idea. Pray tell me, sir, how is Richard now?'

His mouth twisted. 'He is exhausted and in a great deal of pain.'

'Let us hope he has purged himself of the poison. I will make a special tisane for him to drink if I can find the necessary plant. It is an old recipe my mother taught me, most effective at calming an irritated stomach.' She smiled at him.

This time Sir Thomas managed to smile back. 'Young lady, you have a sweet way with you. I am sure your remedy would help him. Thank you.' He cleared his throat. 'And now, let us find the others.'

'I had to bring him out,' Greg confided to Sarah and Lizzie a short while later. They were all watching Sir Thomas as he strolled round the Pump Room in conversation with a couple of his friends. 'He was so distressed to think that anyone would make an attempt to harm Richard, he could not settle to anything. A turn or two around the Pump Room will divert his mind.'

Sarah gave him a very direct look. 'One is tempted to suppose that someone in Bath is not well disposed towards your family.'

Greg rolled his eyes. 'Our family and many others. But I do not care to see my father so worried.'

'So you went to the fair' – Lizzie frowned – 'and Richard had a bout of fisticuffs with one of the men there—'

'Yes,' nodded Greg, 'He likes sparring. He fought several bouts. Afterwards, of course, he was thirsty. There was a man there offering cider from a leather jar. A rough fellow, in a green frieze jacket—' He stopped and looked as Sarah gave an exclamation of surprise.

'Oh! Good heavens!' She clapped a hand to her mouth. 'How many times I meant to tell you. It was a man in a green jacket who push—'

Greg stopped her with a raised hand. His eyes flickered to Lizzie and back. Sarah bit her lip and nodded. 'And when Lizzie and Richard went out driving in your curricle, they twice nearly ran into a man in a cart. He was wearing a green jacket.'

'Yes, indeed,' cried Lizzie. 'He was very coarse and rude to us but he was the one driving badly.'

Greg was looking very thoughtful. 'I will see what I can discover,' he said, 'but meanwhile I want you young ladies to be careful as well.'

Lizzie's eyes grew as round as saucers. 'But why? We have done nothing.'

Greg smiled at her. 'Ah, but you are friendly with us. And whoever is trying to hurt us might consider that you are therefore also his enemy.'

CHAPTER THIRTY-ONE

General Gardiner hobbled up the steps of the Thatchams' home in Sydney Place. The coach driver had already knocked and a discreet servant was waiting to admit the visitors. When Sarah and Lizzie also got down from the carriage, the general noted a slight widening of the servant's eyes.

'No way to prevent them,' he said by way of apology. 'They insist they can be of help.'

The manservant looked even more aghast when Lizzie's maid, Prue, also appeared and marched up the steps with the girls.

Sir Thomas rose from his armchair as the visitors entered his sitting-room. He also looked in some surprise at the girls. He spotted Prue, hovering in the doorway and his brow cleared. 'I understand. You have come to prepare your medicines. You have wasted no time.'

Sarah nodded. 'We have been successful in finding some blackberry leaves. Now I will brew them into a tisane.' She smiled reassuringly at Sir Thomas. 'You will find that it works very quickly to calm an irritated stomach.'

Lizzie laid down her bonnet on the nearest chair. 'How is he now, sir?'

'Sleeping, I believe.' Sir Thomas was looking at Sarah. 'But he refuses to swallow anything, even water.'

'I assure you, he will like my mother's tisane. And Prue here will make her special gruel. That will undo some of the damage that the poison has done.'

General Gardiner gave a chuckle. 'Just let 'em get on with it,

Tom. I assure you, once the females have made up their minds, there is no way to stop 'em. You and I will stay here while they do their good works in the kitchen.'

Sir Thomas threw up his hands in a helpless gesture. The manservant, wooden-faced, escorted the ladies out. As the door was closing, Sarah heard the general say, 'Shocking business, what do you think is going on. . . ?'

When they reached their own home again, Lizzie was in brighter spirits. Richard had drunk some of the tisane and Sir Thomas had promised that he would make sure his son swallowed Prue's gruel later that day.

'So we have helped, have we not, Uncle Charlie,' she coaxed, seeing his frown. 'And Sir Thomas has promised to send Greg to bring us news this evening.'

Sarah was thinking how much she liked the Thatcham household. Everything was neat and comfortable. There was a well-defined air of order and harmony. The servants evidently took pride in their work. A number of them came from the Chesneys estate, she had learned while they were in the kitchen preparing the potions for Richard. The butler had kept a close eye on the three intruders, but soon accepted that they were competent and their brews would be of benefit to the poor invalid.

The cook was a local woman, but she too was fond of the Thatcham family. She had whispered to Sarah that Mr Richard had been 'mortal bad' for many hours, shouting with pain. Sir Thomas had been beside himself.

General Gardiner looked more serious now than he had before his talk with Sir Thomas. 'It seems there are as many rascals here as in London,' he rumbled. ' 'Pon my soul, Lizzie, you were safer in Lisbon.' He rested his chin on his hands, which were clutching the top of his walking stick. He stared at both of them for a while. They stopped what they were doing and waited, surprised at his solemn air.

At length he raised his chin and sat up very straight. 'I want you girls to promise me you will keep to the main streets of the town.'

169

'Do you really think we are a target?' asked Sarah.

He raised his grey brows and shook his head slowly. 'I will not take any risks. I have given you both your freedom – yes, yes, I know you are sensible,' he added as Lizzie opened her mouth to protest, 'but whatever is going on, it is very serious. I cannot allow anything to happen to either of you.' He gave Sarah a fatherly smile as well. It made her eyes smart with sudden tears. James had shown not the slightest interest in caring for her welfare.

'If you are really worried, Uncle Charlie, we could take Prue with us when we go out alone.'

Her uncle chuckled at that. 'Well, Prue might at least prevent you from buying so many hats and shawls and I know not what. That would be one thing less to worry about.' His face became serious again. 'What I am really thinking of is to hire a manservant to accompany you.'

'But if you hire someone from an agency here, he could be in league with the plotters as well,' pointed out Sarah.

The general looked unhappy at that. Then his face cleared. 'I shall ask young Thatcham. And now, Lizzie, do you know where I left my spectacles? Time for a quiet sit down with the paper.'

When Greg was shown into the sitting-room that evening, three heads swivelled to look at him. He smiled at them all. 'Better news,' he announced. 'Richard has eaten the gruel and is sitting up, looking much more like himself.' He came to take the seat General Gardiner indicated. 'My father especially requested me to thank you all for your kindness today.'

'So Richard really is getting better?' Lizzie still seemed worried. Greg nodded and she gave a little sigh of relief. The conversation became more light-hearted and General Gardiner regained his usual cheerful appearance.

Sarah was concentrating on her sewing while Greg and the general discussed measures to protect the girls. Lizzie perched on a stool by her uncle's side and argued hotly that she could manage very well, particularly with Prue as an escort around the town. They had still not agreed when the tea tray was brought in.

While Lizzie arranged the tea things and fussed over her uncle,

Sarah found that Greg had changed his seat for one nearer to hers. His back was half turned to the other two. 'You mentioned a man in a green frieze jacket. . . .' He cast her an enquiring look.

She dropped the needle into her lap. She fished for it, her fingers suddenly clumsy. 'Oh, yes. How could I forget for so long? I told you how I saw him run up and push you into that tilbury. I tried to follow him up Cheap Street but could not see him anywhere.'

'That could have been dangerous for you,' he interrupted, his brows meeting over his nose in a deep frown.

Sarah shrugged. 'At the time it seemed important to catch him, if I could.' She found the needle and pinned it into the corner of her work. 'Then Lizzie mentioned seeing a bad-tempered man in a green jacket several times when she and Richard went for a drive in your curricle . . . and now you say it was a rough man in a green jacket who was at the fair.'

'Hmm,' Greg was frowning at the floor. 'He does seem to appear a lot. I must ask Jenkins if he saw a man in a green coat when the curricle was tampered with.'

Sarah stared at him. 'Do you mean there was yet another incident?'

Greg jerked his head up. 'Oh, damn, I did not mean to tell you about that.' He laid a hand lightly on her arm. 'You will please keep that to yourself.'

There was a crease between her brows as she examined his face. At length, she nodded reluctantly. 'But if this goes on, sooner or later something terrible will happen to you. It sends a chill down my spine to think of all these attempts to harm you. Do you think the poison was meant for you?'

He rubbed his chin. 'I cannot tell. I would rather it had been me.'

Sarah thought again of Lord Percival's outraged glare when Richard had cut him out at the dance. But she decided she was making too much of the incident. She gave a sigh and folded up her needlework.

'I do not like to see you look so worried,' came his voice.

Sarah looked up quickly. 'It is a deeply unpleasant situation.

When I think first of how badly you were hurt and now your brother's condition, I cannot help being alarmed at what might happen next. And you mentioned yet another attempt.'

'Well, we have survived so far. In fact I suspect that they are growing desperate to be rid of us – and that means we are frightening them.' His eyes gleamed fiercely.

'But why? What is the reason for such wicked behaviour?'

'Yes,' chimed in Lizzie, 'Whatever can you have done, Greg?'

He turned and took the cup of tea she was offering. 'Gentlemen's business, Miss Lizzie. Pray do not try to understand.'

CHAPTER THIRTY-TWO

Two days later, Sarah and Lizzie were putting on their bonnets before setting off for the Pump Room when they heard someone beat a loud tattoo on the front door. They had just time to set the bonnets down again before Richard walked into the sitting-room, his arms full of flowers. Behind him came Greg, looking splendid as usual, Sarah noticed, in buckskins, glossy boots and a claret-coloured jacket.

'Oh, how wonderful,' exclaimed Lizzie, clasping her hands, a delighted smile spreading over her vivid little face. 'Now we know you are getting better.'

Richard was, in fact, still very pale and hollow-eyed but he gave her his usual lopsided grin as he handed her a beautiful bouquet of pink and white flowers. 'Thanks for the help you gave me – both of you.' He turned to Sarah, with the second bouquet. 'Your brew certainly quelled that awful burning sensation.'

Lizzie buried her nose in the blooms and sniffed delicately. 'Heavenly,' she exclaimed. 'How pretty they are.' She examined Richard's face intently. 'Are you sure you are well enough to attend the concert this evening?'

He smiled at her warmly, 'Of course I am. I do not want to miss another of our agreed outings.'

Sarah pricked up her ears. So they *had* planned something for last Sunday. Lizzie darted her a swift glance and had the grace to blush. But she carried on talking to Richard, drawing him towards the window and making him sit down. Sarah watched them for a moment. They seemed to have plenty to tell each other. It seemed that Lizzie was keeping some secrets from her. But after all, she was doing the same, with her plans to become a teacher. And then there was the matter of that kiss. . . .

She turned her head and found that Greg was gazing at her face – or, more precisely, at her mouth. But even as she felt the colour steal into her cheeks, she realized that he seemed to be deep in thought. Her cheeks grew hot but she kept her eyes steadily on him. Still he did not stir. Any moment now, the others were going to notice.

She lifted the bouquet to smell the scent and, as she moved, he gave a start, blinked at her, then raised his eyebrows in a quizzical look.

'I beg your pardon, I was wool-gathering.' He smiled such a warm smile that Sarah's heart thudded against her ribs. She was sure he could hear it pounding. She cleared her throat to ease the sudden breathlessness. 'It must be a great relief for Sir Thomas to see that Richard has recovered so quickly.'

A shadow passed over his face. 'My father has found these last few days very difficult to endure, but yes, he is more cheerful today. And we all owe you a debt of gratitude for your prompt help.'

She shook her head. 'It was the least I could do.' She glanced at Richard again. 'If I am not mistaken he is putting on a brave front. The effects are not over yet.'

Greg's lips thinned. 'It was a vicious and cowardly attack.' His eyes flashed and for an instant she glimpsed the soldier, grim and hard in his desire to avenge this crime. Then he recollected himself and assumed a polite expression. 'But what about you ladies? Is all well here?'

Sarah nodded. 'General Gardiner has become very strict.' She smiled as Greg raised his brows at that. 'Indeed he has,' she insisted. 'He fears we may be at risk as well. Prue goes everywhere with us now.'

He laughed. 'And she is a dragon! But I am glad to hear it. We must all be careful until I – we – catch the villain behind these attacks.' He hesitated. His eyes were probing now. 'I am sorry to raise the matter but I have to ask, you have not returned to Queen Square?'

Her chin came up. 'Not yet. However—'

His large hand covered hers. 'Please do not,' he interrupted her. 'Even if you do what you intended, it seems to me that you would still be at risk. By association with me,' he explained. 'Until we can solve the mystery, you really should not go out alone.'

Sarah thrilled at the feel of his hand clasping hers. It sent such a warmth and comfort through her. She inspected the long fingers and felt the calluses, no doubt from handling weapons. It took all her will power not to move her own hand, turn it to clasp his. Such a gentle hand for all it was so large and strong. She still remembered the feel as his hands had pulled her to him for that precious if guilty kiss. She gulped and repressed the longing for him to do it again.

At the same moment he frowned and loosened his hold. He took a step back. She felt bereft. Blinking up at him she was dismayed to see that he looked angry. There was a remoteness in his eyes and his mouth was firmly compressed. A muscle moved in his tightly clenched jaw.

'Have you seen your brother recently?'

Sarah flashed him a puzzled glance. What relevance did that have to their present conversation? 'No,' she replied eventually, 'he has not called for some time.'

He did not explain his sudden interest in James, but, she knew what was in his mind. James was withholding vital information to do with the older brother's death. She had come to know Greg well enough now to know that he would eventually make James reveal the truth. Greg had a will of steel for all it was hidden under a pleasant, amiable exterior. He wanted justice.

Sarah clasped her hands tightly in her lap. It was wicked of James to deny his help. It also meant that she, as a Davenport, was tainted by association in this. She had seen Greg's deep sorrow over the loss of his brother. This business drove a permanent wedge between them. The idea came to her that he maintained his friendly attitude to her in the hope that she would somehow get her brother to reveal the truth. That was more devastating than all the rest of her problems.

She took a shaky breath and looked up. Greg was speaking to

the others. Then he stood up. 'Richard, we shall be late for our appointment if we do not hurry.'

'Do you not think Richard should stay and rest?' asked Lizzie. 'He is not his usual self yet.'

Richard protested. 'I assure you, I am fine. Brother, I am at your service.'

They took their leave. The girls watched them drive away. Sarah was reassured to see that Jenkins, Greg's groom, was with them. Nobody could have tampered with the curricle this morning!

As soon as they left Milsom Street Greg dropped his hands and let his horses canter down the main street in spite of the number of other vehicles in the road. Richard shot a glance at Jenkins, standing up behind and clinging on for dear life. The groom raised his brows and pulled the corners of his mouth down. Richard settled his hat more firmly on his head and folded his arms. He braced his feet against the inevitable sideways jolts as Greg swerved through the morning traffic.

'Are we really late for an appointment?' asked Richard, as they whirled round the corner towards the bridge, nearly running down an elderly farmer. 'On second thoughts,' he added, after a glance at his older brother's set face, 'forget I asked.'

The only reply was a grunt. Greg was furious with himself. He had seen how Sarah looked at him. She was embarrassed and no wonder! He should never have given in to the impulse to kiss her. But the truth was that she was so damnably lovely. When he was with her he lost the ability to remain rational. But now he felt like a cad.

She was struggling with the unwanted attentions of that evil Lord Percival and could not be expected to trust any man. Especially, he thought savagely, whisking his curricle past a slow coach in Laura Place and getting shouted at by its driver, when her own brother was so dismally lacking in a proper sense of his duty.

Greg felt it was his responsibility to keep an eye on both girls, but it was not really a task for which he was well suited. To start with, they were far too independent, unlike the demure young ladies of London Society. Lizzie knew how to get her own way, easily twisting her uncle round her little finger. Her brothers, too, usually allowed her to do as she pleased. It was a good job she was such a sweet-natured and intelligent young lady.

And then, as for Sarah, she was used to running a country estate and she had learned the hard way that she must look after herself. But he felt a fierce urge to protect her. Lord Percival's scheme was nothing short of criminal abduction and rape. Greg's eyes darted fire. This was yet another score he must settle with that man.

He glanced at Richard, so valiant and still so ill. If the worst had happened, Greg knew his father would not have survived it. He swore that he would bring that rogue, Percival, to justice. If they could not prove that he was involved in the smuggling scandal, he would fight him in a duel. He was debating on swords or pistols when Richard's voice penetrated his thoughts.

'Are we going on past our house?'

Greg came back to the present. They had reached Sydney Place. He pulled up the sweating bays. 'Sorry, old fellow,' he said, 'I was busy thinking.'

Richard cast him a bemused glance. 'Well, I suppose you could call it that,' he said, preparing to climb down. 'Perhaps I will have a rest after all before we go to the concert.' He winked at Jenkins, 'I think we must have completed that journey in record time.'

CHAPTER THIRTY-THREE

'So let us go through all the facts.' Greg leaned his chin on his hand as he sat at the dressing-table in his bedchamber. His valet, now restored to his usual appearance, gave the russet jacket a shake and laid it carefully on the bed. Only the twinkle in his grey eyes betrayed his enjoyment of the task he had undertaken.

'Yes, Major. As you instructed me, I played whist at the Assembly Rooms and got into conversation with Lord Davenport. He was reasonably sober. It was a table with two elderly gentlemen – from what they said they must have been friends of his father. We partnered each other. The luck went both ways but in the end he was the winner. He took a matter of fifty guineas from me that first night.'

'And did any of his friends join you?'

Preston shook his head. 'One or two men watched the game, but . . . you know how they stand there for a few minutes and then go away again. They were mostly older gentlemen. Now, the second evening I went there, he was quite sober and willing to play with me again. This time he suggested piquet. We spent a while discovering each other's game, then I must say, he played well. I could not get the better of him. He did not drink more than a bottle of claret. I lost a couple of hundred guineas to him.' He gave his master an apologetic look.

Greg waved a hand dismissively. 'All part of our work, Preston. And then. . . ?'

'And then, sir, I noticed that overdressed fop nosing around.'

'Lord Montallan?'

Preston nodded. 'That's the one, sir. Most curious he was. When I withdrew from the table, he was joshing Lord Davenport about the luck changing for the better and saying as how he must give him the pleasure of a game . . . but first, he took him away for a drink.'

'Aha!' Greg's eyes narrowed. 'So very likely they are dosing him with drink to fuddle him. This is serious.'

'Maybe they give him more than drink, Major. If they're the same men as poisoned Mr Richard.'

'And what happened on the third occasion?'

Preston frowned and shook his head. 'Last night, he looked bad, as if he had drunk a load of bad spirits and not slept. Not willing to play. I reckon he'd lost all his guineas. And them two other fine lords, they were playing and taking no notice of him.'

There was a silence. Then Greg's fist crashed down on to the table. 'That damned villain has a deal to pay for!' he growled through clenched teeth. With an effort he made himself speak calmly. 'Thank you, Preston. This is very useful information.'

'Anything else, sir?' asked his valet hopefully.

Greg shook his head. 'Not at present. Just find me my pistols.'

Preston was startled into dropping the clothes brush. 'You're never going after 'em now?'

'No – not that I do not wish it.' His voice was harsher than he intended and Preston looked at him consideringly. Greg stood up. 'No,' he said again, 'we need more proof yet, Preston. But I may need your help shortly.'

He held out his hand for the wooden box with his silver-mounted pistols and kit in it. 'I am going to the shooting gallery for some practice.' He held up his right arm and turned his wrist this way and that. 'I must be certain my aim is as good as it was before.'

It was just an evil chance that Lord Percival should be at the shooting gallery at the same time as Greg. He watched while Greg carefully shot wafer after wafer, hitting the target each time. Greg, who normally put the bullet dead centre, was dissatisfied when he only marked the edge on two out of five tiny targets. He had managed to hit three through the centre but that was not good enough. His wrist still needed more exercise to restore it completely.

But his shooting was applauded by the other gentlemen in the room and, to his surprise, it moved Lord Percival to utter a few words of praise.

'Demned fine shooting, sir!' he drawled. 'You have a very steady aim. I declare I have not seen such fine shooting in months.'

Greg gave a curt nod. He reloaded his gun and wiped his fingers, blackened by the gunpowder. The task kept him too busy to make any reply.

'I shall hope to challenge you to a match on another occasion,' persisted Lord Percival. 'Perhaps you know Theodore Weston? He is one of our finest shots, but I venture to say I am a match for him, eh Monty?' He turned to his faithful friend who nodded in agreement.

Greg set his teeth and took aim for the sixth time. His shot pipped the wafer dead centre. He drew a relieved breath. That was more like it. There was another murmur of approval from the watching gentlemen. He moved away to clean his pistol before placing it in the polished wooden case. He ignored Lord Percival's comments, but apparently the idea of a match was causing some discussion.

'So what do you say, Thatcham?' one of the men hailed him. 'I would put my money on you.'

Greg finished pulling on his coat before answering. 'I cannot take up such a challenge.' He gave a slight smile at the chorus of protest, 'You will have to excuse me, gentlemen, until my arm has fully recovered.'

There was an outcry at this. 'But with such shooting as we have just seen, what can you have to fear?'

Greg shook his head. 'It was merely my first practice. I do not consider it satisfactory.'

When they still protested, he told them, 'Ask again in a week. I need more time to improve.' His eyes were on Lord Percival, who had taken off his coat and was preparing to shoot. Greg waited to see the result of that first shot. It hit the wafer dead centre. Lord Percival looked round and acknowledged the applause with a satisfied smirk. Greg waited for the second shot. That also hit the target close to the centre. So the man was indeed an excellent shot.

Could he have caused Henry's death by frightening the horse as he jumped that fence? Greg felt he would never know the answer, but his heart ached for the loss of his brother. Suddenly he felt stifled in the gallery. He had to get out into the fresh air, away from the sight of this man. However, if he left now, it would cause some comment among the others, still watching him as they debated the suggested match.

Lord Percival shot again and clipped the edge of the wafer. His faithful shadow raised his hands admiringly. ' 'Pon my soul, it would be a very evenly fought match, eh?' He nodded at the intent faces then slanted a disdainful glance at Greg. One or two of the onlookers murmured agreement. A few gave Greg a cold stare.

By now, Greg had donned his riding coat and his hat. He picked up the pistol case. 'On second thoughts,' he drawled to the room at large in a very clear, carrying voice, 'it would be a better test of skill to shoot at a moving target. Do you agree, Percival?'

Lord Percival, who had already raised his arm to fire at the next wafer, gave a noticeable start just as he squeezed the trigger. There was a loud curse. He had missed the target completely. Greg raised his brows and stared blandly as Lord Percival swivelled round to glare at him, his face purple with rage.

So that caught him on the raw! But it did not constitute proof. Greg maintained the bland expression until Lord Percival looked away and went back to reloading his pistol. Then, with a nod to the other onlookers, Greg walked out. Now his face was grim. He gave an impatient sigh. He should have held his tongue. That comment had roused the man's suspicions. And if he thought Greg was hunting him, James Davenport was going to need protection as well.

CHAPTER THIRTY-FOUR

Judging by the number of people arriving at the Assembly Hall that evening, the concert was going to be very well attended. The soprano, Madame Elvira, was internationally renowned for the sweetness and range of her voice. Everyone who enjoyed music was eager to listen to her singing. Sarah knew that Sir Thomas had taken seats for them at the front of the hall. She thought that his great pleasure in music would be a welcome tonic for him after all the fears of the previous weekend.

It took a little time to make their way into the large room, following the crowd of people, many of whom were elderly and some of them walking very slowly with the aid of canes and servants to support them. At last the girls, escorted by Greg, reached the front of the hall, where Sir Thomas was watching for them. Richard was already seated. He looked very smart in his evening clothes, but he was pale and lacked his usual vigorous energy.

'Welcome.' Sir Thomas bowed with his exquisite courtesy to the girls. He looked from Lizzie to Sarah approvingly. 'What a charming picture you present.'

Lizzie was wearing her white dress with the blue trimming that Sarah had sewn on for her and she wore a matching blue scarf draped elegantly over her elbows. Prue had styled her dark hair into ringlets from the top of her head. She was attracting admiring glances but seemed unaware of the attention.

Sarah had refreshed one of her simple white muslin gowns with some bands of pink satin ribbon making a pattern on the bodice. The effect was charming, enhancing her creamy skin and the shining gold of her hair. She had dressed it in a knot, bound with a pink ribbon. Little tendrils curled around her ears and a few strands escaped from the gold clip holding the knot in place.

'Do you not agree?' Sir Thomas turned smilingly to his son.

Greg, standing by his father and looking very elegant himself, seemed to have lost his tongue. He gave a noticeable start and managed to stammer, 'Oh . . . er . . . yes, sir. Absolutely charming.' He gazed from Lizzie to Sarah as if seeing them for the first time. His eyes glowed as he handed Lizzie to a seat next to Richard. He then sat between her and Sarah. When Sir Thomas was satisfied that everyone was comfortable, he took his seat at the end of the row, next to Sarah.

He handed her the programme. 'What do you think of the choice of music, Miss Davenport?' They examined it together. Sarah's face lit up. 'A wonderful choice of songs. And I am delighted to see that Madame Elvira will perform this Mozart aria. It is one of my favourites. I feel sure we are going to enjoy the evening thoroughly.' She looked at him keenly. 'It is a most welcome change after the events of the last few days.'

Sir Thomas did not pretend to misunderstand her. He nodded, his amber eyes growing fierce. 'I am just thankful that we are all here together and safe!' He leaned forward and glanced at Richard. Sarah followed his gaze. But her heart began to thump as she sensed Greg's large presence so close by.

She fanned herself and discreetly looked his way again. He was gazing into space, apparently lost in his own thoughts. She took a stealthy survey of his appearance. His clothes were impeccable and set off his athletic figure to perfection. She caught the scent of clean linen and cologne and she could see the fine cloth of his jacket and the gleaming white of his shirt cuffs. It was too alluring. She ached to feel his arms round her shoulders, to enjoy the sensations he had aroused in her by his kiss. Her lips parted and her eyes half closed.

But this would not do! She must remember James's stubborn refusal to shed light on the oldest brother's fatal accident and how it meant that, as a Davenport, she could never become close to

Greg. She turned her head away, just as he became aware of her and seemed about to speak. The orchestra had finished tuning up and the conductor tapped his baton ready to begin. Silence fell in the hall, the orchestra struck up an overture and then they sat and enjoyed the enchantment of a very fine performance.

During the interval Greg offered to fetch lemonade for the girls. He was glad of a chance to move around. Since Sarah apparently did not wish to talk to him, he was better off keeping his distance. She was so tantalizing, especially when he was right by her side. The scent of lavender drifted to him and enticed him to get closer. It was devilish hard to keep from sliding a hand into that silky hair. He clenched his teeth and concentrated on working his way through the crowd without spilling the lemonade from the glasses.

The people were shifting to and fro in the passage down the centre of the hall. A cheerful buzz of conversation filled the air. Greg sidestepped an elderly dowager shuffling her way across the aisle. He found himself blocked by an expensively dressed dandy and a smartly dressed lady. She was a rather ripe beauty with improbable blonde curls, but she had a very fashionable air. They both seemed to be trying to look at something at the very front of the hall.

Greg was about to go past them when she said, quite clearly, 'Very well, George, but I need to see her first. Do you mean the blonde one or the dark one?'

'The blonde.'

Greg could not mistake that voice. It set his teeth on edge, as always. His face hardened. What was the villain up to now? And surely they were referring to Lizzie and Sarah. Were they next on Percival's list for revenge? He tried to follow the pair discreetly as they moved up towards the front of the concert hall, but another dowager got in his way. Greg continued through the knots of gossiping spectators and eventually reached his own party.

Mr Keating and his pretty little sister were talking to the girls. Greg felt a flash of irritation. He smiled politely, however and handed the girls their drinks. He stood watching as the Keatings chatted and realized that John Keating was looking very admiringly at Sarah.

So that is how the land lies, thought Greg, glancing to see how Sarah was responding. She was her usual calm self. Greg took his seat by her side and gave John Keating a cool nod. Lizzie tugged his sleeve and made a comment about the music. He nodded, smiled and looked up again. His eyes narrowed. Close by was the woman who had been talking to Lord Percival. She was walking past, seemingly to inspect the stage. Greg noticed how she took a long look at Sarah as she went by and then again as she went back down the room.

He glanced quickly at Sarah. She was translating an Italian song for Sir Thomas and had seen nothing. Greg frowned, he must warn the girls to be even more careful. Percival was obsessed with Sarah and a man of his unpleasant temper was no doubt smarting at her refusal to have anything to do with him. He watched her talking to his father in her quiet way and saw Sir Thomas smile. His father obviously found her entertaining. Greg, who knew the signs, could see that he was taking her under his wing.

As if aware of his gaze, Sarah turned her head abruptly. 'Is anything wrong?' she asked in a low voice. He shook his head slightly. Unable to resist, he took another survey of that lovely face, his eyes lingering on her mouth. Those pretty pink lips were soft and inviting. He twisted the ring he wore on his little finger and repressed a violent urge to kiss her senseless.

Sarah frowned. She drew back a little. 'You look as if there is a problem,' she insisted.

Greg noted the withdrawal. His face darkened. Why was she treating him like the enemy?

At that precise moment, the conductor appeared and applause broke out. He would have to wait to discover why she seemed determined to keep her distance from him. When the music washed over him and everyone was looking at Madame Elvira as she sang again, Greg drew a deep breath and squeezed his eyes tightly shut.

He was not sure which was the harder problem: keeping his

family and the girls safe, or protecting himself from the irresistible fascination that Sarah exerted over him. At this moment, he was not even certain that she welcomed his company. Perhaps Richard was right to call her an ice maiden. Damn that infernal racket they called singing! But he remembered how she had kissed him, so willingly, so sweetly. His lips twitched. That had been fire and passion, not ice. He would persevere in the chase. He opened his eyes. The song was not so bad, after all.

Later that evening, as she sat brushing her hair, Sarah reflected that this was what life in Bath was supposed to be like. An evening of fine music in the company of kind friends. Nothing to worry about, just a pleasant society event. Part of a normal life for most girls, such as Lavinia. But Sarah was not like most girls. This evening would be one of her happiest memories. However, in spite of Greg's advice, Sarah knew the day was coming close when she had to go back to her old school and beg for a job. She had scarcely any money left and no prospect of obtaining any more except by finding employment.

She gave herself a keen look in the mirror. 'You fool!' she whispered to the delicately flushed face with the shining eyes that looked back at her. 'Just remember he is not for you.' She closed her eyes briefly. Impossible to deny that she was glowing. For a couple of hours she had sat side by side with the man she found irresistible and that was enough to send her into a state of rapture. That was why this evening would be a happy memory, to be cherished when she was a sober teacher.

'Fool,' she whispered again, fiercely. She thumped her clenched fist against her heart. How hard it had been to cut him off and turn away. It was not the least of Greg's charms that he seemed unaware of how attractive he was. Sarah was not too besotted to notice how other women's heads turned to look at him. She yanked the brush viciously through her hair and scowled at herself. Why was fate so perverse, that the one man she wanted – and who liked her – was out of bounds?

CHAPTER THIRTY-FIVE

'Sarah, I need a word with you – in private.'

Sarah turned from her conversation with Lavinia Keating to see her brother, his face pale and anxious, hovering just behind her. She gave him an exasperated look. Surely he could see that this was not a good time or place for her to desert her friends. And how could they be private in the middle of Milsom Street? She hesitated and he made an impatient gesture.

'Oh, very well.' With a word of excuse to Lavinia and Lizzie, she left the shop window where they had been admiring bonnets and scarves and followed James up the pavement to a quiet spot. She looked around suspiciously. 'I am not going any further, James. If you are trying to arrange a meeting with your friend—'

'No, no!' he interrupted, looking from left to right with the air of a hunted animal, 'nothing like that. Have not seen him for several days. Think he is out of town. Thing is, Sarah' – he swallowed and glanced over his shoulder – 'someone is dashed well following me.'

She raised her brows in astonishment. 'What? Are you certain? Why would anyone do that?'

He shook his head. 'Dashed if I know. But I keep seeing this fellow in a drab coat. If I look round, he disappears into a doorway or some such. It is getting deuced uncomfortable.'

Sarah felt a shiver down her back. She remembered the man in the green coat. Everyone she knew seemed to be caught up in sinister events and mishaps Would James be the next person to be injured? She wished she could discuss the matter with Greg but he had disappeared as well. The last time they had seen him had been at the concert and that was nearly a week ago.

She took James's hand in hers. 'It is all rather alarming. Perhaps it would be a good idea for you to go home to Russeldene for a few days. Surely nobody would follow you there.'

He seemed to consider the idea but his habitual frown showed her that he was not going to agree. 'Not at the moment,' he said. His head turned towards the other two girls waiting for Sarah outside the milliner's shop. She saw him smile at Lizzie. Lizzie inclined her head in acknowledgment. After all, thought Sarah, they had known each other for many years. But the look on James's face made her uneasy.

She was now familiar enough with feeling the pangs of love to understand that her brother was nursing a real affection for her best friend. But Sarah had never seen any sign that Lizzie thought of James as anything more than an older brother. In any case, in view of his lifestyle and the way he had wasted his fortune, it was certain that General Gardiner would never consent to such a match.

She tried again to persuade him. 'James, even if you leave town for a couple of days, that would surely be enough to get rid of this ... this person. It could be a thief, or perhaps someone with a grudge against you.'

'No,' he said decisively, 'the only people I owe money to are George and Monty. They would never have me followed. But if they did and I ran away, they would suspect the worst, d'you see?' His face went grim. 'Lord, then I would be afraid. . . .'

Sarah's brow wrinkled. 'Oh dear, what a pickle you are in. It is most worrying.' She thought of something else. 'Do be careful where you eat and drink.'

He gave a crack of laughter. 'You have been reading too many Gothic romances.'

'No, indeed I have not. I mean it. Please take care.' She was walking back to her friends as she spoke. James raised his hat to them and wandered away down the street.

'We have decided not to buy that hat with the feathers after all,' said Lizzie. 'Prue thinks my blue hat could be trimmed in a similar style.' She sighed and walked on towards the next shop, leaving Sarah to exchange a smile with Prue.

'Shall we call in at the lending library?' said Lavinia, 'I have finished the last of my novels and if this cold weather continues, I shall want something to occupy me indoors.'

'When do you leave for London?' asked Sarah.

'Not for a week yet.' Lavinia looked at her earnestly. 'I do feel apprehensive. It will be more difficult than Bath. So many more people. . . .'

'Nonsense,' said Sarah in a reassuring tone. 'The time you have spent here has accustomed you to being in Society. You are ready now to enjoy your season in Town. There will be parties and entertainments every day. And as well as the busy social life, think what a vast range of other things there are – art galleries, museums, the theatre . . . Hatchards,' she added, as they turned in at the door of Bath's biggest lending library. 'You will certainly find all the latest books there. Maybe even Lord Byron's poems.'

Lavinia gave a gasp of scandalized pleasure. 'Do you really think so? He is so much talked about. And his poems are beautiful, do you not think so?'

Sarah laughed. 'Indeed, I could not put the book down. My sister was very angry with me for reading so late, especially when she discovered what I was reading.'

She stopped what she was saying because a smartly dressed woman came up to them and looked very closely at Sarah. This woman was perhaps a little over forty but slim and elegant, with blonde hair in an elaborate style. She was dressed in the very latest fashion and her manner was poised and gracious.

'Do pray excuse me for addressing you without an introduction,' she said in a pleasant, musical voice. 'But I feel so certain that you are the daughter of my schoolfriend, Mary Wilton, who married Hugo Davenport. My sister and I were at Miss Johnson's Seminary here in Bath for several years with her.'

Sarah opened her eyes wide in surprise. 'It is true that my

189

mother was at Miss Johnson's Seminary. But. . . .' She looked enquiringly at the elegant woman, who smiled understandingly.

'Forgive me. I am Caroline Bourne and my sister is Henrietta Avery. Of course, when we were at school our name was Langwell. Has your mother never spoken of us?'

'I cannot recall,' said Sarah. 'She was in poor health for some time before her death three years ago.'

Mrs Bourne looked shocked. 'How tragic for you. I am so sorry. And my sister will be devastated. She was Mary's special friend, you understand. I was several years younger than the pair of them.' She shook her head and gazed at Sarah. 'You have a great look of your mama, my dear. May I know your name?'

After a moment's hesitation, Sarah told her.

'And are you her only child?'

'Oh no, ma'am. I have an older sister, who is married and a brother, who now holds the title.'

Mrs Bourne nodded. 'Well, I am so pleased to have met you. I shall tell my sister all about it. She is an invalid, you know. She only leaves the house to go to the hot bath.' She picked up the pile of books she had laid down on the table while she talked. 'These are for her,' she added with another smile. 'The days pass slowly when one is confined to a chair.'

Sarah watched Mrs Bourne as that lady left the library. She tried to recall if her mother had ever mentioned the name but gave it up and went to find Lavinia and Lizzie. They were looking in vain for a copy of Lord Byron's epic poem.

'It is not likely that they would have it in such an old-fashioned place as Bath,' grumbled Lizzie, growing tired of the search. 'When you get to London, Lavinia, be sure to send me a copy. I want to read about his travels in exotic lands.'

Sarah followed them back out into the street, where it was beginning to rain. She took no part in their conversation. Between Mrs Bourne and James's revelation about being followed, she had enough to occupy her thoughts. She wished Greg would return. Somehow, troubles of this kind seemed less daunting when he was around. He was so large and dependable. She smiled to herself.

'Sarah,' exclaimed Lizzie, 'whatever are you thinking about? You have had that smile on your face all the way home.'

CHAPTER THIRTY-SIX

'Are you sure my bonnet looks nice?' Lizzie almost tripped up as she twisted round towards Sarah too quickly. Sarah put out a hand to steady her friend.

'That is the third time you have asked!' She could not keep the exasperation out of her voice. 'Why is it so important? You look absolutely charming.' She turned her head to give Prue a smile. The sturdy maid nodded a little grimly.

'Give over, Miss Lizzie. There's no more fashionable hat in town. Not even that lady who spoke to you yesterday in the library, Miss Sarah, has anything so smart – and she was fine as fivepence, I must say.'

Lizzie did indeed look elegant in her fur-trimmed blue pelisse, and the blue bonnet with its new ribbons and three ostrich feathers. Prue and Sarah had worked all the previous evening to get it ready.

In the sharp wind Sarah was thankful that her own pelisse of dark-green velvet was edged with fur and that she had an enormous matching fur muff to keep her hands warm. She wore a neat little hat with a turned up brim and green ribbons to match her pelisse. This outfit had been bought in preparation for her come-out two years before but due to her father's ill health, she had spent only a few weeks in London. At least now she had these good quality clothes for the winter weather. As she always preferred very simple styles, they were easy to bring up to date with fresh trimming according to the latest edition of *La Belle Assemblée* that Lizzie purchased each month.

They reached the Pump Room and began their daily promenade round the large room, exchanging greetings with a number of other visitors. It suddenly occurred to Sarah that there was an air of excitement about Lizzie. She had definitely become more insistent about going to the Pump Room over the last few days. Perhaps she was hoping that Greg would be there. Maybe they planned to announce their engagement soon.

The idea made her heart sink like lead. She wondered how she could face the future without any further contact with either of them. Lizzie was more of a sister to her than Alice had ever been. But it would be impossible to stay close to Lizzie when she became Greg's wife. The attraction between herself and Greg was too strong for her to fight. She grew hot at the memory of how easily she had kissed him . . . and he had been quite unrepentant. Yet he did not seem to be a rake, so he could not resist the attraction either! So, to avoid further temptation and scandal, she would have to disappear from their lives.

The prospect made her feel desolate – even more so than becoming a teacher – but she was sick of always rebuffing him, of fighting herself to hide her attraction to him. And even if there were no Lizzie in the equation, how could she honourably accept any proposal from him or hope for acceptance from his family, when her brother had done them such wrong? They would never forgive James for hiding the truth about the accident to Greg's brother. Sarah sighed, remembering how much they were still grieving.

It was difficult to attend to Lizzie's chatter as they paced the Pump Room in search of their friends. There was no sign of Greg again today. He had not said anything about going away on business but he had been absent for six days now. As usual, they walked around until they met up with Richard. The first question was always where his brother had gone. Richard did not know. Each time they asked he grinned at them and demanded to know if he was not an acceptable substitute.

'We have to remember that someone is very ill-disposed towards us,' he reminded them when they protested. 'I cannot let anything happen to you on my watch.'

'Well, I suppose that at the same time, we are keeping a check on you,' teased Lizzie, smiling back at him. He was now looking like his old self and was once again a lively member of their group of friends. This morning they all collected in a corner and discussed plans for activities to mark Lavinia's last few days in Bath. Sarah was still preoccupied with her melancholy thoughts and scarcely heard the lively chatter.

She jumped when someone laid a gloved hand on her arm. It was John Keating. 'Come, Miss Davenport,' he said in mock reproach, 'surely you are not too busy to join in our schemes for the next few days? We want to take away fond memories of our time in Bath.' His face grew serious. 'Although I fear I shall have some regrets ... unless. . . .' He gave her a speaking look and seized her hand. 'Excuse me, but there is nowhere else where I can ask you this—'

Sarah withdrew her hand. 'Pray do not, Mr Keating,' she said breathlessly. 'I am deeply honoured but . . . I cannot return your regard.'

He drew in a deep breath. After a pause, he said: 'Well, I have always known that I am not first with you, but if ever—'

'Oh, this is wretched,' she exclaimed, looking at his white face. 'You are most obliging, sir and I am truly sorry I cannot do other than say no. We shall all miss you and your sister a great deal.'

His mouth twisted into a wry smile. 'Damned with faint praise.'

She shook her head, swallowed and turned away. Before she could examine her feelings at this declaration, she found herself face to face with Mrs Bourne, who stopped and greeted her smilingly. Sarah was struck by the extreme elegance of the lady's clothes and her look of such decided fashion. She wondered if Mrs Bourne had a very wealthy husband.

'I am so glad to have found you again, Miss Davenport,' said the lady, extending one languid hand in its expensive kid glove. 'My sister was delighted by the tale I told her yesterday. She longs to meet you, the daughter of her dear schoolfriend.' Mrs Bourne sighed. 'But she is unable to walk, although the hot bath is providing much relief from the rheumatic pains she suffers.'

Sarah made a polite reply. Mrs Bourne waited for a moment,

then gave Sarah a hesitant look. 'I do not suppose—' She broke off, glanced away then nodded resolutely and began again. 'Would it be too much to ask— My dear Miss Davenport, it would give Henrietta so much pleasure to make your acquaintance. Is there a day when you could take tea with us?'

This was a little sudden. However, Sarah understood the lady's anxiety to keep her sister in good spirits. She had nursed her own sick father and knew how much a visitor meant to someone unable to get out into society. Moreover, it was a way of avoiding a further conversation with Mr Keating. So she smiled politely at the elegant Mrs Bourne.

'I believe my friends have made plans for every day this week. But I can excuse myself from their schemes for this afternoon, if that is acceptable?'

A gleam showed in Mrs Bourne's eyes. 'I knew I could depend on you. Thank you, indeed we will be most happy to see you this afternoon.' She gave Sarah her direction. It was at a house in the Circus. When Sarah heard that, she felt her heart thump uncomfortably. But James had said Lord Percival was out of town, so there could be no risk of running into him.

There was an assembly that evening and when she returned to her friends, Sarah found that they had all firmly agreed to be there. Lavinia was to dance every dance.

'That way, she will be perfectly ready to take her place at any London ball,' said Mr Lucas Wilden cheerfully.

'I shall be returning to London soon,' said Richard, 'and if we meet at any balls, we may stand up together if you wish.'

'Oh, thank you,' breathed Lavinia. 'It is so much more comfortable to know I shall have some friends in Town, especially at the beginning.'

'But no waltzing!' said her brother, poker-faced. 'You should keep practising the steps but never dare to dance it until a dowager gives you permission.'

Lavinia's eyes opened very wide as she looked round the circle of faces, all frowning sternly at her. She went pale then she saw Richard's mouth twitch. Her expression changed to one of indignation.

'You are being horrid,' she laughed, 'you will drive me to distraction with all this advice.'

Sarah happened to be looking at Lizzie when Richard made the comment about returning to London. She saw a change come over Lizzie's face, as though she had been struck a physical blow. Her eyes darted to Richard. Now he was looking at Lizzie with a question in his eyes. Sarah put up a hand to twist her curls as she began to make sense of Lizzie's recent behaviour.

She thought of the jokes and the dancing they had shared, how they often had their heads together; Lizzie's pleasure in riding round town with him; all things she had assumed were just agreeable novelties after Lizzie's strictly chaperoned years in Lisbon. Then there had been the panic when he was so ill. The scales fell from her eyes. She drew in a deep breath. Her heart beat so fast that she was dizzy. There was a buzzing noise in her ears.

Like a bucket of cold water came the realization. Even if Lizzie now understood that she loved Richard, it changed nothing in her own situation. James had made it impossible for the Thatcham family to want a link with the Davenports. Lizzie's voice broke in on her whirling thoughts.

'Oh, Sarah! You have quite spoiled your hairstyle by making all those ringlets. Let me put it right.'

At that very moment, Greg was descending the stairs in the house in Sydney Place. He was freshly shaved and immaculately dressed but his eyes were heavy and his face bore the signs of fatigue from several nights of watching and riding. The smell of fresh coffee tempted him into the parlour. He found his father there, reading the paper and with the coffee pot on the table in front of him.

'Ah!' said Greg with satisfaction. He poured himself a cup and downed it in two gulps. Sir Thomas raised his brows but made no comment. He continued to watch as Greg poured out a second cup. The brew had an immediate effect. Greg looked up, met his father's eyes and smiled.

'Everything well here, sir?'

Sir Thomas nodded. 'I am pleased to say that Richard seems

fully recovered. And we have been spared any further incidents.' He looked under his brows, his face impassive.

Greg swallowed some more coffee. 'Which would indicate that I am the prime target.' He saw the flash of alarm in his father's eyes. 'Be easy, sir. I think we are reaching the end of this story.'

They looked at each other. Eventually Sir Thomas nodded. He sighed. 'I know you cannot speak of your work. We agreed on that long ago. But I mislike the situation. These attempts to dispose of you – or by default, your brother – are becoming tedious.'

Greg's hand clenched into a fist. 'They will pay for that,' he muttered. He stared moodily out of the window, reliving the past few nights of hard riding and surveillance. Together with Preston, he had joined Josiah Whitby and his Riding Officers as they observed the theft of supplies from the cargo ship. The evidence was there now to incriminate the whole gang, including Lord Percival.

Greg's lips thinned. There were witnesses to the man's involvement in the planning and execution of the crime – and therefore, it was certain that he was the person passing on information from his friends in the government. He would not escape being arrested as soon as Josiah Whitby could obtain a warrant. But in Greg's opinion, this was still a risky business. He wanted swifter justice on this murdering villain.

For one thing, he did not want to wait for a lengthy trial, and for another, he feared that with such powerful friends, Lord Percival might simply be allowed to slip away to start his criminal activities elsewhere. Greg was not prepared to risk that. His eyes narrowed as he checked through the steps of his scheme. It should work. He would have justice for all his family and for Sarah as well.

He brought himself back to the present and glanced at the clock on the mantelpiece. 'Almost noon. Where is Richard?'

'At the Pump Room I assume, together with his friends. I have insisted that Jenkins goes with him everywhere.' Sir Thomas made a little gesture, which showed more than words how much it mattered to him. 'I could not bear another crisis like the last one.'

'No indeed,' agreed Greg. 'But he should be safe enough at present.'

Sir Thomas gazed at him fiercely. 'He *has* to be safe enough at all times.'

There was a pause. Greg sat waiting, aware that there was some important news to come. His father kept turning his quizzing glass over and over in his hand. Finally he raised his brows, grimaced and looked directly at Greg.

'Obviously, over these last few days, I have made it my business to – ah – be present when Richard went to any social event.' He dropped the quizzing glass and fumbled as he tried to pick it up again. Keeping his eyes on his son's face, he continued, 'From what I have observed, it seems to me that Richard has become very fond of Charlie Gardiner's little niece.'

Greg noticed the underlying question in his father's steady gaze. He raised his own brows and smiled. 'I rather thought that was the way the wind was blowing.'

Sir Thomas sat up straight. 'You do not mind?'

'Not at all. Why should I? She is a delightful young lady.'

'You did not ... er ... ah. ...' Sir Thomas cleared his throat. 'You did not rather like her yourself?'

Greg threw back his head and laughed. 'Oh, I *like* Lizzie, very much. She is a pearl. And she is the sister of a good friend of mine. In fact, I see her as a sister already. So. ...' He raised both hands in a fatalistic gesture.

'Egad, that makes things seem more hopeful,' said Sir Thomas, brightening. 'Well, well, I seem to have been somewhat behind events there.' He looked at Greg through narrowed eyes. 'It seems to me that both you boys should be thinking of settling down and the sooner the better.'

Greg could scarcely hide his astonishment. 'Father, what in the world has provoked this notion? I go away for a few days and you are suddenly full of matrimonial plans for us. Has Grandmama been writing to you again?'

Sir Thomas was watching him closely. Under that unwavering gaze, Greg became slightly self-conscious. He turned away to pour more coffee.

'Thought you preferred tea,' chuckled his father.

Greg was tired and flustered by his father's insight and he was not going to discuss this matter any further yet. He took a sip of his drink but suddenly, he just wanted to be alone. He stood up. 'Excuse me, sir, I think an hour's sleep will do me more good than this.' He pushed his cup away.

'Very well. You certainly look as if you have not slept for a week.' Sir Thomas reached for his newspaper. A thought struck him. 'Ah, before you do go, I recall that there is an assembly tonight. I would be much obliged to you if you would attend it with Richard.'

Greg mumbled something and closed the door softly. He found a yawning Preston in his bedchamber, tidying away the discarded travelling clothes.

'Wake me by five o'clock,' said Greg, pulling off his jacket and cravat and casting them down carelessly, to his valet's displeasure. 'No need to look so pained, man. Go and get some sleep yourself. God knows we both need it. And I shall require you to undertake some more gambling again this evening.' He yawned. 'Let us see if we can catch Lord Percival cheating.'

When Preston had gone, Greg threw himself on the bed and laced his hands behind his head. He frowned up at the ceiling. Now he must plan every detail if he was to succeed in his schemes. But he kept seeing a pair of green eyes and a lovely face framed by golden curls, her features pale and strained due to problems she could not resolve. Greg heaved a sigh. If his plan worked – no, not if, *when* his plan worked – he would be free to do something about that.

CHAPTER THIRTY-SEVEN

'Pray send your maid away, Miss Davenport. My manservant will escort you home after your visit.' Mrs Bourne stood in the elegant hallway of her Circus home, smiling at Sarah.

'If you are sure it is no trouble, ma'am. Very well, then, thank you.' Sarah nodded at Prue, who curtsied and went out through the door that the manservant was holding open for her. Sarah knew that there was plenty to do at home with preparations for the assembly that evening.

She followed Mrs Bourne into the sitting-room, which overlooked the huge open space in the middle of the Circus. There were sedan chairs crossing it as invalids were brought back after their treatment in the hot bath. Mrs Bourne sat down in a rustle of expensive silken skirts. She smiled again at her visitor.

'It is very good of you to come – and at such short notice. We will take our tea first, then I will bring you upstairs to my sister's room.'

'I had thought she would be able to sit with you in here,' commented Sarah. 'It must be more pleasant for her to have company through the day.'

The servant came in just then with the tea tray. While Mrs Bourne busied herself with the cups, Sarah glanced round the large and elegantly furnished room. Everything spoke of wealth and good taste. Everything except, in Sarah's opinion, the sickly scent from the large arrangement of white lilies on a low table by the window.

Mrs Bourne rose to bring a cup of tea to her guest. 'Yes, as you were saying,' she said, 'Henrietta does remain here when she is able, but some days, unfortunately, she suffers a lot of rheumatic pain and prefers to keep her room.' She smiled, 'Is this how you like your tea, Miss Davenport, or would you care for more cream?'

Sarah accepted her cup and made polite conversation. She wished again that she had not accepted this invitation. Since she had noticed Lizzie's warm feelings for Richard, which seemed to be reciprocated, her mind was preoccupied with wild hopes alternating with the cold voice of reason warning her that she had no choice. She did not regret refusing to listen to John Keating's offer. He was an excellent person, but she did not love him and without love, she would never marry.

With the knowledge of the bleak and empty future that awaited her, she found it hard to take her part in the polite nothings of Mrs Bourne's chat. She was relieved when that lady stood up and said, as she smoothed her skirts down, 'Well, Henrietta is probably getting impatient to see you. Let us go up to her chamber.'

She led the way up the wide staircase and along the landing. Everything was simply but tastefully furnished. The house was very quiet, Sarah noticed. Mrs Bourne went to the last door on the left and tapped on it.

'Sister, may we come in?' She did not wait for an answer but pushed the door open and stood back for Sarah to go in first. Summoning up a smile, Sarah walked into the bedchamber and stopped short in surprise.

'But there is nobody here—' she was saying, when she heard the door close softly behind her. She heard the click of the key in the lock. Immediately she ran to the door and seized the handle. She turned it but with no success. She tugged and pushed but the door did not move. Her heart was beating so fast she nearly choked.

'Mrs Bourne,' she called breathlessly, 'the door has stuck. Pray let me out.'

There was no reply. Sarah swallowed down the fear. This must be a mistake. 'Mrs Bourne,' she called again, 'what can you thinking of? Pray let me out.'

Silence. Sarah thumped on the door with both fists. 'Let – me –

out!' she shouted. When she stopped pounding on the door, Mrs Bourne's voice said coldly, 'It is of no use to do that. There you are and there you stay.'

'How dare you!' choked Sarah. 'What is the meaning of this? You cannot keep me here. Where is your sister?'

'There is no sister,' came the cold reply. 'And do not think you will be missed. I shall send the servant to say you were persuaded to dine here.'

'But ... they will not believe you.' Her clenched fists still pressed against the door, Sarah felt a cold chill run through her. This had been carefully planned. She must think. It was only on the first floor – perhaps she could escape through the window. She rushed over and flung up the sash. But the land behind the house fell away down the slope. It was by far too long a drop. She looked for a convenient drainpipe, but there was none within reach.

Could she call for help from someone in a neighbouring house? The buildings nearby were all closed and silent. She looked frantically for an open window or for any person in the gardens below. There was no sign of life anywhere. With a little sob she gave it up and drew her head back into the room to inspect her prison. It was a small, square chamber with no closets or any connecting doors. For furniture, there was a bed, a clothes chest and a rather fragile looking chair.

Still scarcely able to believe what was happening, she ran back to the door and tried the handle. It did not budge. She paced across the room and back, panting with the effort to keep calm. What could she do to help herself? Another examination of the room showed that it was quite bare. She ran her hand round the walls, feeling in vain for a concealed door. Even the bed was not made up. There was just a Holland sheet spread across it.

She turned swiftly to the clothes chest, pulling open the drawers and the cupboard section. All completely bare! Sarah gave a sigh of disappointment. She glanced at the spindle legged chair and turned back to look out of the window again.

No, it was really much too far above the ground. There was no hope of escaping that way. What a fool she was! This was Lord Percival's house. The lilies should have been warning enough. So

Mrs Bourne was in league with him. He was obviously prepared to go to any lengths to get her in his power. But there was no way she would submit to his evil plans without putting up a fight.

And even if in Milsom Street they believed she had stayed with Mrs Bourne for dinner, they would certainly come looking for her before too long. She glanced over her shoulder at the chair. How rickety was it? She crossed the room again and gave the chair a shake. It was not at all solid. She knelt down and set to work to loosen one of the legs.

Greg strolled into the Assembly Rooms in company with Richard. His lean face was stern, causing Richard to glance at him once or twice and finally to ask him outright what was wrong.

'Nothing is wrong,' said Greg, schooling his features into a bland look, 'allow me to feel a mite fatigued still.' He raised an eyebrow at Richard's look of incredulity. 'If I do appear somewhat preoccupied, it is with the prospect of dancing the night through. Really, Brother, you have been zealous in promising Miss Keating that you would find her a partner for every dance.'

Richard grinned his lopsided grin. 'Always ready to help the ladies,' he said. 'Besides, when I realized I was getting better, I swore I would take every opportunity to enjoy life.'

Greg shot him a piercing look. Richard stopped abruptly. 'Gad, you look just like our father. But, seriously, old fellow, I made a few decisions during those days when I was lying there with my insides on fire.'

Greg gave him a brotherly pat on the shoulders. 'Does one of those decisions involve Lizzie?'

Richard's mouth dropped open. 'How could you guess that?'

'I *am* your brother and I was not born yesterday. And I can see that Lizzie likes you a lot.'

Richard heaved a huge sigh and gave his brother a shy smile. 'I certainly hope she does. I mean to talk to her before I leave for London.'

Greg raised his brows. 'You are not wasting any time then.'

'That is what I mean, old man. If you want something, what is the point in waiting?'

'Precisely,' said Greg. His eyes glinted as he gave Richard an assessing look. 'It seems my little brother is growing up fast.'

Richard looked as if he would like to retaliate but Greg was distracted by the sight of a pair of dandies on their languid way to the card room. Richard followed his gaze.

'Gad! Is that the infamous Lord Percival? He and his friend make a showy pair.'

Greg silenced him with a movement of his hand. 'Brother, I regret that I cannot join you in the ballroom at present. Perhaps later.' He moved towards the card room but remembered something and came back. 'Will you check that James Davenport is safely in the ballroom and try to keep him there?'

Richard frowned. 'I do not care for him above half.'

'No matter. He is definitely in danger. He must not go anywhere alone.'

'You mean he is the next one on the list for—?'

Greg's brows snapped down and Richard turned his comment into a cough.

'How Lord Liverpool thinks you will make a diplomat, I cannot guess.' Greg softened his reproof with a slight lift of one brow and strolled away. In the card room he wandered around, inspecting the play at different tables. He stopped just out of sight when he heard the drawling voice of his enemy. The man was seated facing Lord Montallan at a small table a little apart. They appeared to be playing piquet.

Greg could not see where Preston was but he had given him precise orders about engaging Lord Percival in play during the course of the evening. It should be easy enough to needle him by winning, then see what tricks he would employ to win his money back.

'. . . Davenport is in the sullens. Knows that with no fortune any more he has no chance of getting her,' Lord Montallan was saying in a low voice, 'so I told him I would get her, even marry her if need be, what!' He gave a snort of laughter and refilled his glass from the bottle of port on the table between the two of them. 'After all, she is a considerable heiress.'

Greg dug his fists into his pockets but he remained still and silent, unnoticed by the two men as they kept their eyes on their cards.

Lord Montallan set his empty glass down, selected another card and added, 'He looked very cast down at that. Pretty little filly, ain't she? Lively, what!' He waited for his friend to agree, then went on, 'Told him we could share her, though – as usual. Gad, George, you should have seen his face.' He gave a coarse laugh. 'I swear he had never thought of such a thing. Looked ready to call me out.'

'You were a fool, Monty,' came the reply. 'We have never initiated him into that side of our affairs. We must keep him sweet, while he can still be of use.'

There was the sound of more wine being poured. 'And then. . . ?'

'And then,' said Lord Percival in a voice of venom, 'he has to . . . er, disappear. Herring has his orders.' He set out his cards. 'My trick, I believe.'

Lord Montallan grunted assent. Picking up another card, he remarked, 'That fellow is a clumsy brute, but he will do anything you tell him. Er . . . how much longer is Davenport going to be useful?'

Lord Percival's voice sank. 'Tonight. Maybe tomorrow.'

Greg listened, tight jawed. As he suspected, now they had their share of the money from the transport ship, they were going to finish their business in Bath. Before Josiah Whitby arrived to arrest them, Greg wanted his chance to solve the mystery of his brother's debt and his fatal accident. It was time for Preston to engage Lord Percival in a game of cards to provoke the villain into cheating. Then Greg could force a quarrel on him.

Taking care to keep out of the candlelight as much as possible, Greg moved away looking for Preston. He found him at last, engaged in a game of whist. The players were so absorbed that they were not aware of his presence. Greg could only stand and wait.

Someone came and stood beside him. It was Lord Montallan, who seemed to be looking for a chance to join the game. With an inward curse, Greg turned away and glanced back at the table in the corner. Lord Percival had gone. Keeping his pace leisurely, Greg left the room and headed for the ballroom. He would check on his brother and the girls. His quarry would not get far. The Riding Officers must have reached the town by now.

As soon as he entered the ballroom, Mrs Keating and her son came up to him.

'Oh, Mr Thatcham, how delightful that you have returned to Bath,' beamed the kind little lady. 'We were afraid we would miss seeing you to say goodbye. We leave for London in a very few days.'

Greg bowed over her hand. 'I shall be in Town again soon, ma'am, never fear.' He gave her his charming smile. 'And I hope to have the pleasure of meeting you all again at another ball.'

'It has been a very pleasant six weeks here,' she said. 'Such a delightful group of young people. Lavinia has become quite accustomed to being in Society. But what a pity that Miss Davenport is not able to be here this evening.'

Greg felt a tingle of alarm. Instinct warned him that something was wrong. 'Is she indisposed?' he enquired smoothly.

'Oh no! She very kindly went to see a sick friend of her mama's and has stayed longer than was planned. Miss Gardiner is expecting to see her at any moment.'

Greg inclined his head. 'Excuse me, ma'am.' He hastened to where Lizzie was dancing with Lucas Wilden and unceremoniously hauled her out of the set.

'Where is Sarah?'

'Really, Greg, could you not have waited until the end of the dance?'

'Not one second!' His voice was urgent. 'Where has she gone?'

Lizzie gave him a cross look. 'She met an old schoolfriend of her mother's, whose sister is an invalid. She went for tea and they sent a message that she would stay to dine.'

Unconsciously, Greg tightened his grip on her arm. She gasped. 'You are hurting me. Let go.'

He relaxed his hold slightly but shook her arm. 'Can you describe this friend?'

As Lizzie did so, he groaned. It was certainly the woman he had seen talking to Lord Percival at the concert. Sarah was in danger. 'The address?' he snapped, but he knew already. It was Lord Percival's house. Leaving Lizzie bewildered and alarmed he whirled away towards the door. But before he reached it, James Davenport appeared in front of him.

'Must speak with you,' he said.

'Not now,' snapped Greg, 'I have not a moment to lose.'

'Come with you, then,' said James, striding alongside him as Greg rushed through the entrance hall and out into the street, coatless and hatless.

'Time to tell you the full story about that week at Hazelwick's hunting lodge. . . .'

CHAPTER THIRTY-EIGHT

It was completely dark and Sarah was tired and cold. She rubbed her arms but it did nothing to warm her. How long had she been shut up in this room? The house was still completely silent. Surely Lizzie or Prue would come looking for her soon, before anything dreadful could take place. She smothered the apprehension at what might happen to her shortly if nobody did come. She tried to swallow. Her mouth was dry and her head was aching.

It would not do to let herself get paralysed by fear. She got up from her seat on the edge of the bed, facing the door. She picked up her weapon, the chair leg that she had managed to work free. It was better than no weapon and she was determined to inflict as much damage as possible with it.

She went towards the window, which showed as a lighter rectangle against the dark of the room. She peered out. There were lights in a small number of windows in the nearest buildings, but who would hear her if she called? On such a cold, wintry night, anyone at home would be sitting close by their fire. They would certainly not have their windows open.

Sarah shivered. Surely her friends must be getting anxious by this time. Mrs Bourne could not claim she was staying there overnight. She realized now how foolishly she had walked into this trap. And Greg was out of town. He would have been suspicious. Probably, it was because he was out of town that Mrs Bourne had dared to carry out her kidnap. And now what was going to happen? Sarah had a horrid fear that it involved Lord Percival.

Did he plan to compromise her into marrying him? But if he already had possession of all James's estate, why should he bother to marry her? *No*, a little voice in her head told her, *he just wants revenge because you thwarted him and Lord Percival will not tolerate that. This is to punish you!*

Her blood froze at the idea. She clutched the chair leg and paced to and fro, ten steps each way, from the bed to the window and back. It kept her from freezing and it helped her to keep alert. And then she stopped, straining her ears. She could make out faint voices. Her heart began to pound. Quickly she pushed the window open, then hastened on tiptoe across the room to stand in front of the door.

She watched and listened. She heard a stair creak. Then she saw a line of light appear in the gap at the bottom of the door. A hand fumbled against the lock. As the key clicked, Sarah darted behind the door. The next moment, Lord Percival strode into the room, holding aloft a branch of candles. He looked around.

'What the devil. . . ? She is not here! Blood and thunder, the window!' He set the candlestick down on the chest. As he did so, Sarah tiptoed forward, raising the chair leg. She swiped inexpertly at his head, hoping to knock him out. The stick caught him a blow but he whirled round and grabbed the chair leg, pulling Sarah towards him as he pulled at it. She stumbled, panting from her effort. She found her arms held in an iron grip. She looked up to see his lips drawn back in a snarl.

'You will pay for that,' he growled. He kicked the door shut. She struggled but could not shake free. His fingers were cutting uncomfortably into her arm. She kicked at his ankle but her boot had no effect against his tougher boots.

'Gad, you little vixen,' he panted. 'You have even more spirit than I hoped.' The snarl had gone now. Sarah watched in alarm as his face took on an altogether different look. A predatory light gleamed in his brown eyes. Then they narrowed as they surveyed her from head to foot. His gaze was insolent, possessive as it lingered on her curves. She was unable to do more than stare at him, refusing to look away. She felt like a mouse in the clutches of a hungry cat.

'So, Miss Davenport,' he drawled, a cruel twist to his mouth, 'at last I have you where I want you. And as I told you once before, we are going to do everything together from now on.' His eyes flashed an evil spark at her. 'Everything!'

She eyed him with contempt. 'Never.'

He threw back his head and gave his braying laugh. 'Oh, but we will. It will not take long to train you into obedience.' He checked slightly at her exclamation of disgust. Then he bared his teeth. 'The more spirit you show, the more I shall enjoy breaking it. You are a more worthy opponent than your brother.'

'Surely, sir,' she said through gritted teeth, 'you have done enough harm to our family. And do you think no one will hold you to account for it? You scoundrel!'

The scorn in her voice was like a whiplash. Angry sparks showed in his eyes, his nostrils flared and he brought his free hand down sharply across her cheek. She gasped and turned her head away, blinking back the sudden tears of pain. Her ears were ringing.

'That silenced you,' he purred. 'Lesson one. Never presume to criticize me.'

She kept her head turned away, trying to overcome the dizziness. Even through the pain her brain was working out how to slip out of his grasp. If she could find the chair leg, which he had thrown down after he pulled it from her, she could hold him off. The candles on the chest flickered in the draught from the open window. In their light, Lord Percival's face looked flat and mask-like except for the large shadow cast by his high nose. His eyes were blazing at her.

'Look at me.' he ordered. He shook her roughly by the arm until she did lift her face up. 'Lesson two. You will obey all my whims,' His voice was husky. She darted a glance at him. He grabbed her hair and twisted his hand into it, yanking her head back. She opened her mouth to protest and quick as a flash, his own mouth came down on hers. She struggled to keep her lips firmly closed but he would not release her. He kept her in a vice-like grip and forced her jaw open, driving his tongue into her mouth. She uttered a moan of protest but could not stop him. He smelled of spirits and something else, sweet and sickly, that made her want to choke.

Eventually, he raised his head. He was breathing heavily. His eyes were half closed. 'Let's have a look at you. God knows, I have waited long enough.' She shrank back as he put a large hand to the delicate muslin at her bosom and pulled hard. The fabric gave easily and he ripped the whole front of her dress away. Sarah gaped in alarm as he plunged his hand inside her chemise and seized hold of her breast.

He squeezed hard, watching her face as he did so. She bit her lip, unwilling to give him the satisfaction of knowing how horribly he was hurting her. Sarah closed her eyes, willing herself not to scream at the touch of his hands on her soft flesh. Beneath the horror and the humiliation, she still tried to find a way to escape. Otherwise, this could only end one way and she could not endure for him to defile her.

In her desperation, an idea came to her. She put out her free hand towards his face. He was so surprised that he slackened his grip on her breast. Sarah took a step towards him and ran her hand down his cheek. He shifted backwards, looking at her warily. She moved forward another step and again smoothed her hand down his cheek.

'Well, I'll be damned,' he croaked, 'the wench likes a bit of rough treatment.' He let her go and tugged at his cravat as if it was suddenly too tight.

Seizing her chance, Sarah pushed at his chest with all her force, sending him backwards on to the burning candles. He gave a roar of rage and alarm but she was out of his reach and rushing for the door. Her one instinct was to escape from this horror. She had her hand on the door handle when she was grabbed from behind.

'Oh no, you don't!' He wound his hand into her hair again, causing her to give a cry of pain.

There was the sound of footsteps racing up the stairs and along the passage. A second later, Greg dived into the room. He looked so fierce she did not recognize him for a moment. Behind her, Lord Percival tightened his grip on her.

'Stand back, Thatcham,' he snarled. 'In any case you are too late to save her. She is mine now. And a willing bitch she is, I assure you.' He held her pinioned by her hair and with his free hand, he clutched her exposed breast again, giving a shrill laugh.

There was murder in Greg's face. He advanced a step further into the room, teeth bared. Unable to move, her face contorted with anguish, Sarah stared at him desperately. How long the three of them stood there, she could not tell. The tension was unbearable. The pain from her various injuries throbbed through her body. She could hear Lord Percival's hoarse breathing and feel his body pressed against her back.

'Greg,' she mouthed, looking at him in helpless appeal.

He tensed, his eyes going from her to her captor. 'Let her go, Percival. You are finished.'

'You mistake,' growled the other. 'Get out of my way or the girl will suffer even more.' He twisted her head as he spoke. Sarah clenched her teeth and kept silent.

'There is no escape,' Greg repeated. 'Your anti-government activities have been exposed as well as your involvement in stealing the nation's goods.'

'You have been very busy,' sneered Lord Percival. 'I knew you were trouble. But I do not fear you. I have powerful friends. You will soon discover that you have been wasting your time. Now, stand aside.'

Greg stood there like a rock. In spite of the pain that seemed to be invading all parts of her body, Sarah felt a tiny hope grow. Somehow, he would free her from this revolting creature. She could feel from the rapid rise and fall of Lord Percival's chest that he was afraid, in spite of his boast. She tried to pull away but at once he clutched her even more tightly to him with his left arm. He pulled something out of his pocket.

'Thatcham,' he grated, 'you have five seconds to get out of my way or I will use my knife on this bitch. When you hear her scream, it will be your fault.'

'Do not mind me,' gasped poor Sarah, looking at Greg, 'just stop him.'

Greg looked even more fierce, but when he spoke, his voice was calm, persuasive. 'Percival, do one decent thing and let her go now!' He paused but the only reply was a wild burst of laughter.

'Very well,' Greg went on in a cold tone. 'There is a government agent waiting downstairs with a warrant for your arrest. And there is another matter.' His face darkened and now his voice was raw with anguish. 'Davenport has told me what happened when you lost money to my brother and tried to hide it by shooting to startle his horse as he jumped a fence. It was murder, Percival.' Greg stepped closer. 'And I will personally see you hang for it.'

Lord Percival gave a wild cry. 'Never, never.' He dragged Sarah with him as he plunged towards the window. 'I should have killed Davenport.' he muttered. 'Too late, all over now. Keep back,' he screamed at Greg.

Sarah was horrified when Lord Percival swung one leg out over the window sill. Any second now he would fall and drag her out with him. She could hear his frenzied breathing and mutterings. She clawed at the hand holding her against him but he would not let her go. She grasped at the window ledge, panting and desperate not to overbalance.

'She goes with me. Tell Davenport what he did to his sister. . . .' screamed Lord Percival hysterically, as he tugged at Sarah. He had both legs over the sill now and was trying to heave Sarah out with him. Greg lunged towards the window and grabbed hold of her arm. Lord Percival, his face contorted with panic, stabbed at Greg's hands but Greg held on to Sarah. Lord Percival raised his arm to stab harder, but he leaned too far back, his grip gave way and he fell. There was a blood-curdling scream and then a sickening thud as his skull hit the paving stones a long way below them.

Only then did Sarah give way to tears. She clutched convulsively at Greg and buried her face on his chest. He wrapped his arms around her and rested his head against her hair.

'Thank God,' he whispered. 'Oh, Sarah, *Sarah*, I was never so afraid in my life.'

'*You* were afraid,' she sniffed against his wet shirt, 'what about m-me? He was going to rape me . . . then he tried to kill me!'

He rubbed a hand across her shoulders. 'It's all over now. You are safe.'

She looked up and Greg drew in a sharp breath. 'Your poor

213

face.' He pulled out a large white handkerchief and offered it to her. Sarah took it and dabbed at her wet cheeks. She then became aware of the state of her clothes. Urgently she tried to gather the torn dress together but the material had been ripped away and her bosom was completely exposed. She had a lot of red marks and bruises there and winced as she touched them.

Greg stripped off his jacket. 'Here.' He kept his face averted until she had slipped it on. It was much too big and the front was rather low but it was an improvement on her previous appearance. But now there was something sticky on her hand. She frowned and looked more closely – it was blood. Then she saw Greg's hands, slashed and covered in blood.

'He has hurt you as much as me. . . .' She wrapped the handkerchief round the worst cut.

He smiled. 'Once again you are mopping up my injuries.'

'Just let us get out of this room,' she said with a shudder, 'and then there are some things I wish to ask you.'

'You are too done up to walk,' said Greg, as she tottered to the door, leaning heavily on his arm. 'Come, I will carry you down the stairs.'

She submitted to being lifted into his arms and slid one arm round his neck to hold on. She rested her spinning head against his sturdy shoulder and felt that she was drawing strength from him.

'What a pair of rogues we look,' he commented, as he went slowly down to the ground floor. 'Bruised and battered, blood-stained and our clothes in total disarray.'

'But alive and safe – thanks to you,' she murmured against his neck. She swallowed the lump in her throat. 'Is it true that a government official is here to arrest . . . him?'

'It is. And your brother is downstairs, guarding the woman who tricked you into coming here.'

Sarah hesitated before she admitted, 'I was certain that James knew something bad and that he was being threatened. And recently he discovered that someone was following him.'

Greg gave a grunt of amusement. 'I organized that for his protection. Once I started asking questions about my brother's death, I was certain that your brother would be in danger. He knew too much about that event.' He sighed. 'It is no pleasure to have my suspicions confirmed. Poor Henry.'

He set her down gently on a chair in the entrance hall. She propped her head on her hand, trying to think. There was something that still troubled her. 'Your other accidents . . . and Richard's poisoning . . . oh yes! Do not forget the man in the green coat.'

'Herring! He has probably been arrested by now. Sarah, all this can wait. You are injured and I must get you home, my poor darling.'

They looked at each other. It was difficult to decide which one was more dishevelled. Greg's usually neat hair was standing out in tufts, his shirt was torn and bloodstained and his hands were a mass of cuts. Sarah was glad there was no mirror for her to see her own appearance. Suddenly exhausted, she buried her face in her hands, just longing to be safe in her own room.

CHAPTER THIRTY-NINE

'Sarah, it is barely a week since your ordeal. The bruising around your eye is still visible. I do think you should stay here another few days.'

Sarah hugged Lizzie tightly. 'You are so kind. But I am anxious to see how things are going on at Russeldene.'

'You will be working all day every day and you are still not well,' scolded Lizzie, folding a shawl and placing it in Sarah's trunk.

'I am used to the work I do there. And now that James wishes to manage his estates properly, I want to encourage him. There is such a lot to do.' She clasped her hands at her bosom. 'How thankful I am that his debts to that madman have been cancelled and we can keep our home.'

'Yes, I am also very glad of *that*, if only for your sake.' Lizzie dropped Sarah's slippers into the trunk. 'James is quite different now. I think after that conversation he had with Greg and Uncle Charlie, he realized that—'

'When was this?' interrupted Sarah, with a frown, 'I knew nothing of that.'

'It was while you were still poorly. They were in the sitting-room for hours. Whatever they said to James, he was very shame-faced when he left. All Uncle Charlie would say was that James has been very lucky to escape as lightly as he did.'

Sarah bit her lip. She would have to find out what had been decided. She checked the room. 'That seems to be everything. Shall we go down?'

They perched on the sitting-room window seat as usual. Sarah gave Lizzie's arm a squeeze. 'I would beg you to come with me, but I know you will not leave your uncle here alone. And now that you have accepted Richard's offer of marriage, Sir Thomas is anxious to improve his acquaintance with you before you leave Bath.'

Lizzie's cheeks went a becoming shade of pink. Sarah smiled. 'How happy everyone is for you. And how easily you and Richard fell into love. But you kept it a secret for a while.'

'Ye-es, until I was sure he felt the same way about me. You remember the day he was poisoned? We were going to discuss everything then. So you can understand how desperate I felt.'

'Of course. He was very ill. And after he recovered I can understand why he wanted to fix his future happiness so quickly.' She said nothing about her own future, happy or otherwise. With each passing day it seemed more likely that Greg had gone for good. He had been very tender and loving on the night of her ordeal, but she knew that people acted differently in moments of high tension. Maybe after seeing her virtually naked and being mauled by Lord Percival, he no longer felt attracted to her. Perhaps he was pining for Lizzie, now that he had lost her.

She knew Lizzie was watching her, so she summoned up a bright smile. 'Well, we have to separate . . . but not for too long.' She leaned over the little table with its usual clutter of books and sewing things. Having taken three novels from the pile, she held them out. 'These are mine, but if you wish I can leave them for you to read. You can return them when you come to stay at Russeldene.'

Lizzie took the books with a nod. 'It will be something to do.'

Sarah turned to the window. She could see the chaise pulling up outside. 'Lizzie. . . .' she began, but was unable to say another word. As she again hugged her friend, a sob from Lizzie made her own tears spill over.

'What a pair of watering pots we are – and we should both be happy. You will call and stay a while with me as you return to London . . . and soon you will see Richard again.'

'Yes, I know,' sobbed Lizzie forlornly, 'but he has gone back to his work and n-now you are leaving and I shall be all alone here.'

At this moment, General Gardiner walked into the room. 'What is this?' he demanded in his cheerful way, 'Now stop it, both of you. Can't abide females weeping! Come, Lizzie, Sarah, have you not noticed?'

They mopped their eyes and stared at him. He moved his hands impatiently.

'Oh, Uncle Charlie,' screamed Lizzie in delight, 'you are walking without your stick.'

He beamed. 'Aye. Indeed, I think the waters have done their work. We shall be able to go back to London in a very short time. And I am sure that will please you mightily.'

She flew to put her arms round his neck. 'I am so glad you are well again. I do not like to see you suffering with that horrid gout.'

Sarah leant back in the chaise as it rumbled out of Bath. She kept her eyes closed and tried to banish a number of unhappy memories. It was only by great good luck and the help of such a steady, courageous man as Greg that she was now able to return to her home.

In her despair she had so nearly gone to beg a post as a teacher from her former headmistress. There again, it was Greg who had saved her from that fate. She gave a bitter little smile as she thought of how very few coins still remained in her purse. Perhaps now there was a chance to set the family finances back on a sound footing.

She opened her eyes and turned to look at James, seated in the opposite corner. He was leaning his head on his hand, staring moodily out of the window. Becoming aware that she was watching him, he darted a glance at Sarah.

'Thank you at least for not reminding me that it is all my own fault.' He shifted his long legs and sighed irritably. 'Well, now I can see how bad it all looks. Thatcham was mighty unpleasant—' He broke off, shrugged and twisted his mouth petulantly. 'But I had no choice. George was so' – he hesitated for a while – 'so *dazzling*. It seemed a glorious triumph to be admitted to his circle.' He stopped again. 'I have lost so much money ... have to see what I can do for you, Sis.'

Her eyes widened. 'Greg really did spell everything out in detail for you.'

James gave that irritable shrug. 'I hope I can see for myself – never realized until last week just what kind of things George and Monty were getting up to. And don't ask me to explain because I shall never say. But I knew then I had to break with them.' He gnawed at his fingernails. 'I nearly lost you.' He shook his head and sighed again. 'And I've damned well lost Lizzie.'

Perhaps it was the cold short December days that made her feel so unsettled. Throughout her stay in Bath, Sarah had longed to be at home in Russeldene, carrying out her familiar tasks and living in the dear surroundings of her childhood home. So she decided she must be very perverse to wish now that she were back in Bath. She found that she sorely missed the cheerful company of Lizzie and General Gardiner.

But more than anything, she missed Greg. There had been no news of him since that terrible night when he had saved her from being dragged to her death by the half-crazed Lord Percival. Even now, Sarah woke up several times a night struggling and clutching at the headboard in panic. Then she would remember Greg's strong arms holding her close and his voice murmuring soothing words to her.

He had called her his darling and cared for her as if she were very precious to him. But that was nearly two weeks ago now. However many times she reminded herself that there were too many barriers for her ever to be anything to him, she could not suppress that wild longing to see him, touch him, hear his voice. Oh, she wanted him! It would take a lifetime to forget him.

Even if she never did see him again, she knew that nobody else would ever take the place he held in her heart. With a fleeting smile, she thought of kind John Keating. But she preferred this loneliness to marriage without love.

So, back to work, she told herself, drifting into the study. It was time to go through the accounts again. For some time she stared at the page, but the numbers would not add up. She put her pen down, propped her head on her hand and listlessly watched the rain through the window.

There was one thing that everyone agreed had improved: James looked much better than for a long time. He was making a genuine effort to learn the business of running his estate properly and had developed an interest in the farming and the plantations on which Russeldene depended for its income. With a few years of strict economy, he would restore their fortunes and improve the lot of the labourers on his land.

She should be glad to feel secure again in her home. Sarah shuddered as she thought of the times she had walked around Bath, trying to find a way to earn her own living. But that brought her thoughts back to Greg and the kiss they had shared in the Gravel Walk. With an irritable exclamation, she jumped up. It was no good to dawdle here. The accounts would have to wait for tomorrow.

Meanwhile, she would go and check that Lizzie's room had been prepared. In just a couple of days her friend would arrive and stay for a few weeks. Lizzie would be full of schemes ready for her wedding to Richard in the New Year. Sarah now knew that Lizzie and Greg were fond of each other as brother and sister but that still did not remove the barriers she saw to any closer relationship between herself and the man of her dreams.

She satisfied herself that everything was ready for her friend in the room next to her own, where Lizzie had always stayed since her first visit some five or six years earlier. She cast a glance at herself in the oval mirror. The bruises had gone now, but it was true that she looked a little pale and her eyes seemed larger than before. There were hollows in her cheeks. Mrs Wiggins kept trying to bully her into eating but Sarah had no appetite. She tried to conceal the fact by slipping bits of food to Misty under the table.

Sarah pinched her cheeks and rearranged a couple of curls that had tumbled down. She pulled a face at herself and left the room to go back downstairs. As she reached the housekeeper's room, Mrs Wiggins appeared.

'Ah, there you are, Miss Sarah. There's a visitor asking to see you.'

'If it is old Mrs Witherspoon, I do not feel I could endure—'

'Oh, no,' said Mrs Wiggins with a chuckle, 'not but what it's highly disrespectful of you towards an old friend of your parents! But this is a gentleman – a young gentleman,' she added, taking a critical look at Sarah. 'Good job you're wearing that nice gown today. I always did like that check, the pink and white is so cheerful.'

'Mrs Wiggins, what does it matter? Do you mean someone local? Has he come to see James?'

'Mister James is out and cannot be found at present. But I know a proper gentleman when I see one. As there's a nice fire in the study I put him in there. Do you go in, Miss Sarah, and I'll bring refreshments shortly.'

Hoping that it was not some young man who had come down from London to spend time in the country with James, Sarah made her way into the newer part of the house and turned down the passage to the study. She pushed open the door and stood transfixed on the threshold by the back view of a tall, well-proportioned man. She knew those broad shoulders! Her heart turned a somersault.

He was standing by the fireplace, one arm leaning against the mantelpiece and one booted foot on the fender. His head was bent forward so that she could only see the copper gleam of his hair. When she shut the door, he straightened up and turned. Sarah was frozen to the spot. Her heart seemed to swell in her chest so that drawing a breath was impossible.

There was a question in his eyes as he examined her face. Sarah gazed at him hungrily, at his finely chiselled features, at his firm mouth and most of all at those glowing amber eyes, fixed on her. Neither of them moved nor spoke. Sarah was trying to control the beating of her heart. She knew her voice would tremble.

He seemed to be trying to read her face. At last he inclined his head. 'I trust I find you well?'

She nodded.

After waiting for a moment, he went on, 'I returned to Bath as soon as I could, but you had already left. Lizzie was certain that you would see me, however, and indeed, I have some documents

221

for your brother—' He broke off, his lips tightened and there was a bleak look on his face.

'Oh!' It was one syllable but it contained a wealth of disappointment. He had not come to see her, or only as a courtesy. Sarah stiffened her shoulders. She had an apology to make.

'Since returning here, James has told me the whole story.' She twisted her hands together. 'It has caused you and your family so much unnecessary pain. I am very s-sorry. . . .' She tailed off miserably and risked a quick glance at his face. What she saw there made her even more desolate. He was looking very grave.

'There is no way we can make amends,' she continued in a low voice. 'I have learnt how much money that villain claimed your brother owed him, whereas the opposite was true and he was the one owing money . . . and James kept silent about it. I am so ashamed.' She bit her lip and put a hand up to her hair, pulling on a strand and twisting it violently.

Greg was looking very stern but at that, a gleam came into his eyes. The corner of his mouth twitched. Self-consciously, she forced her hand down to her side.

'We have now dealt with that problem, thanks to your brother's testimony,' he said briefly, 'but what about you? Are you remaining here?'

She gave him a speaking look. 'It is entirely due to you that we still have a home to come back to. It was my worst nightmare to think that not only had James lost Russeldene, but that he had done so to that . . . that. . . .' She choked and shook her head, unable to continue.

Greg came a step nearer. 'There is no need to think about him any more,' he said softly. 'We cannot undo all the harm he did, but a number of wrongs can be put right.'

She tilted her head up to look him in the eyes as he came closer. His linen was so white and crisp, his blue jacket moulded his noble contours. She caught the scent of his tangy cologne together with clean linen and soap. This interview was harder than she had ever imagined. To be so close to him, and know that it was undoubtedly the last time she would see him. She wanted to sob with misery, but she must act the part of a polite hostess.

'Do you wish to see my brother?'

His face was like marble. 'I think we have already said all that is necessary. I have decided to spare my father any more anguish. Davenport is not certain that the shot was fired at Henry's horse.' He made an impatient gesture, 'It could never be proved.'

Sarah twisted her curls frantically as she considered this. 'But—'

Greg stepped right up to her and pulled her hand away from her hair.

'Sarah, my darling, much as I love that habit of yours, I cannot let you continue. You are looking so delightful as you are – and I have something much more important to ask of you.'

Her heart began to pound. He was looking so serious. Then his hand clasped hers firmly. He raised it to his lips.

'Sarah, I have waited a long time to ask you this – I had to find out about my brother first – but now, please tell me that I am not mistaken.' He examined her face keenly. 'You have always kept me at a distance, but I am as certain as a man can be that you are not indifferent to me.'

She stared at him, willing him to continue. Without realizing it, her free hand crept up to clutch at his lapel.

His eyes crinkled in a smile. 'I love you Sarah, I want to spend my life with you. What do you say?'

She slipped her hand round his neck and pulled his face down to hers. They kissed in a frantic hurry, broke free, stared at each other, then Greg's strong arms clasped her tightly and he kissed her again. This time it was a long, slow kiss, tender then passionate, stealing the very heart out of her body. Some time later, Sarah was clinging on to him because her legs were shaking. Greg held her close.

'Mmm, you smell of lavender,' he murmured, rubbing his chin against her hair, 'and your skin is so soft.' He ran his fingers over the back of her neck. She gasped with pleasure and clung even closer. He grasped her by the upper arms and held her away to look at her delicately flushed face, her half-closed eyes. He smiled and put a hand into his pocket.

'So will you marry me?'

She swallowed. 'Greg, it is obvious what my feelings are . . . but James . . . your brother – in all honour, how can I say yes?'

His eyes glowed at her. 'What James did does not concern you, my honourable love. My father assured me that you would accept me. How can I go back and tell him he was wrong about you?' He went down on one knee. 'Sarah, pray do me the honour of becoming my wife?'

She could not help the tears that suddenly ran down her face. And before she could dash them away, Greg slid an emerald ring onto her finger. He jumped up and pulled out a handkerchief to wipe her eyes.

'Here we go again,' he said, 'we are always mopping each other up.'